Myluv

&

Myluv

Kevin Jackson

Myluv & Myluv

©Kevin Jackson 2025

All rights reserved. No part of this publication may be reproduced, stored in any retrieval system or transmitted in any form or by any means, electronic, mechanical, photocopying, recording or otherwise, without the prior written permission of the copyright holder, for which application should be addressed in the first instance to the publishers. The views expressed herein are those of the author and do not necessarily reflect the opinion or policy of Tricorn Books or the employing organisation, unless specifically stated. This publication is a story of fiction. No liability shall be attached to the author, the copyright holder, or the publishers for loss or damage of any nature suffered as a result of the reliance on, or the reproduction of, any of the contents of this publication or any errors or omissions in the contents.

ISBN 9781917109536
A CIP catalogue record for this book
is available from the British Library.

Published 2025
Tricorn Books
Treadgolds
Bishop Street
Portsmouth
PO1 3DA
www.tricornbooks.co.uk

Myluv

&

Myluv

CONTENTS

FOREWORD		VII
CHAPTER 1	DARKNESS	7
CHAPTER 2	DAWN	16
CHAPTER 3	THE DOGS FIND PETRA	44
CHAPTER 4	THE DOOR KNOCKERS	82
CHAPTER 5	HEAR NO EVIL, SEE NO EVIL	101
CHAPTER 6	THE SEARCH WARRANT	114
CHAPTER 7	BACK AT THE RANCH	125
CHAPTER 8	THE AUTOPSY	135
CHAPTER 9	YOU SHOULD BE DANCING	144
CHAPTER 10	ST IVES	183
CHAPTER 11	PAIDWICK CASTLE	207
CHAPTER 12	THE FARMERS	221
CHAPTER 13	IT'S DAWN AGAIN	247
CHAPTER 14	RIP PETRA?	273

FOREWORD

Myluv & Myluv is my second novel and, as with Humanhai, complex human relationships are explored. It is a story of fiction with descriptions of compassion and love from some, but shocking behaviour displayed by others. You'll leave with unanswered questions about righteousness, betrayal, love and loss, but with hope that things can get better.

I write from my heart and vivid imagination. I enjoy the graphic descriptions where small details can paint a picture in one's mind.

Some choose not to see, or we just don't see. Personal beliefs and values shape our views that could be selfish and not in the wider interests of those around us. The strongest control us, those more powerful survive, often without interest in us, the lesser people. Individuals strive to become pack leaders within their environments, they who must be obeyed. Some still behave like the wild animals they are in this so-often cruel world.

I drafted this story for the lesser peoples of the world, those deemed weaker through no fault of their own but for being who they are, and where they are. We are all human, we are all sisters and brothers ... we could be equals ... but we are not, as we live in a world where power is all.

AI is the next big powerful thing when it is able to have consciousness, feelings, beliefs and values ... but humans developed it, both good ... *and bad*.

I'd like to thank Jenny, plus Sarah, Vincent, Dan and his Tricorn team plus Liz Bourne for her fabulous editing skills.

For you, the reader, enjoy this thought-provoking story of fiction with a huge touch of reality. Best wishes, Kevin.

CHAPTER I
DARKNESS

It was in the early hours of that stormy morning, darkness was all around on the lonely remote Cornish beach. Betty took her time whilst trying to carefully cross the wet and slippery stones that were normally covered by the sea; the tide was out. Her head-torch beam facing down to her feet and just ahead, so she could follow her older dog Lucy, who diligently led the way. The intensity of the storm's rainfall limited the beam's forward view. The bad weather hadn't yet raced through and was causing havoc along the coast; the red weather warning said it could cause damage with a threat to life. As Betty struggled, she thought, *I really don't want to be here! Bloody nuisance it is! It better not be those flipping daft sheep me dog is after! ... I don't want any deadens.*

Betty was continually buffeted and being pushed to and fro from the gusts as they swirled around her. Her middle-aged balancing skills were continually tested from the seaweed clusters around the larger stones; she often slipped whilst on them. The rain was torrential and mostly horizontal. She couldn't see more than several metres ahead, it was rain fog. She didn't want to be here; her younger dog, Daisy, had run off and hadn't returned, she needed to find her. Betty's sodden eyes squinted as she finally saw Daisy jumping excitedly, barking as she did around an object. As the woman neared she shouted loudly, "DOWN!" Both dogs instantly lay either side of the item that had caught Daisy's interest. There was sudden shock within Betty.

"What the fuck is going on here!"

Her torch beam lit a younger woman wearing a very familiar red jacket. Betty gasped and held both hands over her mouth with the shock. She shouted, "PETRA ... PETRA!" There wasn't a reply. Petra's eyes were wide open and motionless. They stared at Betty as though they were crying for help. Blood oozed from her nose and neck. Her twisted and contorted body looked painfully out of shape.

Petra, a young talented artist, had gone alone for a late-night walk in the stormy weather last evening, but hadn't returned. She frequently walked at odd hours and last night was no exception; it was her way of winding down from work. The freedom to walk was both relaxing and energising as it helped with her creativity. Alex, her husband, had gone to bed just after she left, a short time after 10pm. He soon fell asleep and woke that morning at 5:30 without Petra by his side. This wasn't unusual as Petra's night-time walks could last for hours, but it was suddenly concerning now as he awoke to the sounds of the storm. Heavy rain was splattering against the bedroom window along with the noises of their wooden frames rattling with the windy gusts. He quickly got up, realising the storm had intensified and that she was still out in the terrible weather; it had worsened considerably since last night. He went outside to look for Petra and for the past hour he searched without success, he came home with anticipation that Petra may have been in their warm and cosy cottage.

Alex stood in the garden and looked into the darkness of early morning for one last time; he was terribly upset as he hadn't found Petra or seen her torch light. It was very wet, windy and cold on that Friday morning in October. Alex needed to concentrate on the horrid weather but couldn't stand still in the garden; he was being blown and continually rocked to and fro with the strong gusts. He had become soaked by the torrential rain. For Alex there were now two storms, the one blowing him violently around outside, and the other inside his head; the latter was now starting to ache with worry. He and Petra could have missed each other whilst he looked for her; she may have returned on a different route than the one he'd taken. Alex had heard the day before that bad weather was coming. The storm had raced its way across the Atlantic from the remnants of hurricane Milton that had left a trail of death and destruction across the USA. The tail end of the hurricane had just arrived in the UK with the red warnings issued. The storm here would be vicious and could cause loss of life with structural damage to property. As Alex made his way towards the back door of their home, without warning a sudden gust of wind pushed him off balance. He fell onto the door and swore loudly as he just caught his fall. "Fuck it!" He struggled with the wind behind him as regained his balance to try and open the door carefully. As he did, he was suddenly blown inside but struggled to close the door against the gusts whilst shouting into the cottage, "PETRA, ARE YOU THERE?" He managed to forcibly close the door against the wind and looked quizzically into the kitchen. There wasn't a reply. He shouted louder, "P E T R A?" Again, there wasn't an answer. He removed his soaking wet jacket; the falling water drops made a puddle below. He slid his boots off and placed his coat next to where Petra's bright red jacket and torch would have normally hung. They weren't there. His dripping wet face was fraught with concern and the hope faded. He quickly turned and inadvertently walked through the puddle. He spoke angrily, "Bollocks," as his socks quickly soaked up the cold water. He pulled the wet socks off whilst thinking *Petra just may be home, but you just haven't removed your jacket, boots and head torch.* There were no wet footprints ahead, but he still needed to satisfy his desperate mind. He rushed barefoot through to the kitchen and on into the hall as he shouted whilst looking around and up the stairwell, "PETRA! Where are you, PETRA, are you there?" The storm noise was intensifying and there wasn't a reply. He glanced into the living room and quickly ran upstairs. He grabbed a pair of socks and put them on his carpet-dried feet, then checked the two other bedrooms and the bathroom, *just in case* she was there.

Alex looked even more desperate as he spoke aloud in a concerned tone, "Where the hell are you, Petra, where are you?" He became more distraught as he ran down the stairs, nearly falling, to pick up the cordless landline phone from its dock in the hall. He rushed into the kitchen where he picked up Petra's mobile phone from the worktop. It was in its usual place below the photo calendar that he had proudly made. He glanced at the October images and gulped. The photos displayed two women, one of Petra, where he had handwritten ***Myluv*** in bright red ink below her face. The other photo was their best friend Suze. His eyes welled with tears that fell and merged with his already rain-wet face. Guilt, fear and angst filled his mind with the missing love that he so desperately wanted; here and right now.

Alex turned and sat at the kitchen table with both phones, one in each hand. He was thinking, *Petra would frequently leave without taking her phone, she saw it as a work tool rather than a leisure gadget and had never taken it anywhere other than when she was working.* Alex placed the landline phone on the table. He then momentarily gazed through the window, hoping to see the beam of light from Petra's headlight torch, or the light of daybreak. He saw nothing apart from darkness and his sad appearance in the reflection. The wind was howling and rain continually spattered on the window. This was the darkest and most horrible time Alex had ever experienced without Petra. They had recently married and had dated each other for the past ten years. He was nervous, extremely worried and now very fidgety. He took his phone from his damp trouser pocket and held it next to Petra's, one in each hand. He thought, *I have both our mobiles, I'll be ready for a call, any call.*

He waited a few moments for any of the three phones to ring. To him it seemed like hours, but neither rang. He was nervously bouncing his left knee up and down quickly with the ball of his foot, unaware he was doing so. Over a short time, the speed of his knee bounce increased. He thought, *Petra could be in someone's house, or at one of the nearby farms. There are frequent areas without signals, and if Petra were in trouble she may have called her own number or sent a text. She could never remember phone numbers, apart from her own.*

After a very short time, Alex looked at Petra's phone; he knew the numeric code to unlock it and keyed in the numbers. He scrolled through the apps to see if there were missed calls or texts. There were none, although he did notice a strange email from an unfamiliar name yesterday. This, he thought, was sent by a work client as he read the sender's name out loud, "Nilrem." He couldn't understand the body of the text message but saw what he thought were other names within the CC field, "Ruhtra Gink, Yaf el Anagrom and Eumin." He thought they were strange foreign names. Petra had been commissioned by foreign clients frequently; such was her reputation as a rising star within the art world. Petra and Alex often shared each other's phones for web browsing when their own wasn't to hand. However, they would never check each other's emails or texts, as they were always work-related, plus they respected each other's privacy. He thought, *These strange names must just be clients from abroad, Petra had many.* He closed the phone and put it onto the table thinking nothing more about the names. He sat perplexed and festered with Petra's whereabouts whilst he looked through the window into the darkness. His knee continued to move up and down, a repetitive 'tic' action he didn't notice.

Anxiety and frustration had eaten into Alex. He now needed support. He called his best friend Suze. There wasn't an immediate answer, it was too early at 7:10 in the morning. He let the phone ring and ring. It was answered just as he was about to hang up. Suze answered with a sleepish tone. She had a soft quizzical voice, and she didn't look at her phone as she answered. "Hello?"

Alex's face lit up as he felt a sense of relief. He optimistically spoke, "Suze, hi. I'm so glad you've answered. Look, sorry to bother you so early, I'm worried sick … is Petra there?"

She wiped her tired eyes as she recognised Alex's voice calling at this early time. Suze replied with slight concern, "Alex, what's the matter?"

Alex spoke with panicky desperation. "Petra's … Petra's been out all night, I've been out and can't find her, I'm worried sick! Is she there … is she with you?"

Suze, now anxious, swapped her phone to the other hand as she switched the light on and pushed herself up into a sitting position against the pillows and headboard. She could hear the stormy weather against her window along with the desperation in Alex's voice. She replied with concern, "Alex, no, Petra isn't here. Why, what's the problem?"

Alex's voice became distraught. "Petra went for a late-night walk last evening at ten, she hasn't yet come home, I'm worried! I've been out in darkness for the past hour, out since six o'clock, looking for her and the weather is crap. I'm worried sick about her, could you come over, could you *please* come here, right now, rather than later?"

Suze sat up straight. She frowned with her reply, "Crikey! Should you be calling the police on 101 or 999?"

Alex hesitated with his answer. After a while he said, "No, not yet. She's done this before, as you know. But this time the weather is rotten and evil. I'm really worried, previous times the weather hasn't been so bad. We've got the tail end of hurricane Milton that caused mayhem in the US."

Suze thought as she replied reassuringly, "She's most probably just holed up somewhere. Somewhere safe, like the beach cave where you found her once before. She may even be at Paidwick Castle?"

The cave and castle were familiar to Alex, Petra and Suze, The Trio as they called themselves. In the past they'd picnic, sleep over and swim from the beach near the cave. The cave was a secluded hideaway down a steep hidden path known only to The Trio along with the few timid wild Cornish goats found wandering in the area.

Alex continued, "I didn't go there as it's raining. It'll be slippery and dangerous to get down to the cave. It'll be impossible to get back up and I'm not sure about the tide as it could be high. I tried the castle ruin, but she isn't there." His face was blank as he stared out through the window to see his face in reflection.

Suze replied, "OK, I'll call a taxi and come right away but I'll be at least an hour at best. Call me straight back if you hear anything, OK?"

Alex felt reassured. "Thank you, I'd really appreciate it. I'll wait here for you."

Suze spoke, trying to alleviate Alex's state of mind and obvious concern. "Don't worry, I'm sure it'll be OK. Petra often walks alone and maybe she's just sheltering somewhere safe. Maybe not the cave but somewhere safer, like the other ruins. I'll be as quick as I can. If anything changes call me, and vice versa. OK?"

Alex replied, "OK, love you. See you soon, come as quickly as you can ... please. I'm desperate!"

She replied, "Love you too, try not to worry, see you soon! Bye." The call ended.

Suze was due to see both Petra and Alex for lunch that day and then stay over with them for the weekend. They were each other's best friends. It was a pre-planned visit, and she had arrived at Petra's apartment above their art gallery in St Ives in the very early hours of that stormy day. St Ives was on the north coast of Cornwall. Suze had arrived there earlier that morning, just after midnight from travelling on the last train out of London. The Trio had previously agreed to this plan to save the awkwardness of Suze arriving very early that morning in darkness to Petra and Alex's cottage.

Alex sat staring out into the darkness through the window. The three phones were charged and ready to take calls; he regularly checked they were charged whilst being unaware of his nervous tic. He festered whilst he waited for Suze's arrival, and more importantly hoped that Petra would at least call, if not appear home before Suze. Time passed as Alex sat there with huge apprehension, listening to the ever-increasing wind noise and the rain continuously hitting the window. When his focus shifted away from *that* noise, he heard the clock which now became quite annoying. *Tick-tock, tick-tock, tick-tock, tick-tock, tick-tock.* It was a cherished gift from his grandparents and hung on the wall to his left, next to the beautiful photo calendar.

Alex looked at his wife's photo with an expression that showed his anxiety; she was out there in this horrible weather, she could have had an accident, she may even be unconscious ... or worse. He now became very frightened and even more upset as every second came and went. *Tick-tock, tick-tock, tick-tock, tick-tock* from that damn annoying but also valued clock. Alex thought, *Time passed away; it could never return.* He hoped Petra hadn't *passed away* and that she'd *soon* return. Tears again welled in his eyes as he gulped at that thought.

CHAPTER 2
DAWN

Petra had been out all night without her phone; alone as far as Alex knew. The weather was rotten and worsening, daylight was only just appearing. Whilst Alex focused on the hope of a phone call along with the unrelenting wind noise, he heard *that* annoying ticking clock, it was 7.45am. He didn't hear the doorbell, but he did hear the loud banging coming from the front door. He dashed out of the kitchen full of hope that it was Petra. He ran into the hall to answer the door. It wasn't Petra or Suze; it was a female stranger.

The sudden rise in expectation suddenly disappeared as he saw the unfamiliar visitor; his heart immediately sunk again. There stood a youngish casually dressed female. A woman with a long coat slung over her head and shoulders, to protect herself from the rotten weather. She stood with a very slight inquisitive smile as she struggled to stay dry with the brisk wind continually blowing her hair and coat about wildly. She held onto the coat with either hand, like a parachutist holding the steering lines of their chute, continually moving them to guide them safely down. The woman moved her hands whilst trying to hold the unfastened coat over her head as the gusts suddenly changed direction.

The visitor asked, "Hello, are you Alex Munro?" She then changed her smile to a more serious appearance. At the same time, she tried to catch something flapping wildly in the wind that was attached around her neck. When she had caught the object she held it out towards Alex's quizzical face. It was her police identity card attached to its lanyard. It showed the official 'Devon and Cornwall Police Constabulary' banner with her photo along with some other statutory text that was far too small for Alex to read from a distance. As she let go of the ID, she then tried to catch the other side of her coat that had blown away from the hand that had previously held it. She grabbed the coat and again pulled it over her head. Alex's optimism continued to deflate as he fidgeted; he was now even more concerned and apprehensive. He now realised something horrible must have happened to Petra. His face showed anxiety as it painfully contorted whilst he looked the woman.

He answered her question with a stutter, "Yes ... yes, I'm Alex."

The woman replied, "I'm Police Liaison Officer Dawn Tew, do you know a woman called Petra?"

Alex quickly blurted out, "Yes I do ... why?"

The shock of this uninvited official visitor was racing into Alex's mind. He could feel pressure building within himself when he heard Petra's name mentioned. He began to feel heat in his face as it blushed red, his pulse quickened as he felt his heart was pounding, and his mouth dried. He swallowed nothing other than gulps of air that swept over his dry throat. It strangely felt as though Dawn had spoken in slow motion but at the same time it happened *so* fast. Alex went blind to the here and nows; the feeling of pressure built within him. He began to feel sick and nauseous, his head ached like nothing before.

Dawn, a fully-fledged and seasoned police professional, had seen this type of reaction before. She quickly intervened, drawing on her experience. She knew her introduction along with the shock of information she was about to deliver could cause huge upset; it nearly always did. Some recipients could faint, or worse, become extremely aggressive. Aggression was a sad reflection of today's behaviour thrust upon frontline emergency workers who were just trying to do their job. Some 'clients' would hit out in angst at those trying their best to help them in times of crisis. Obscene verbal threats, physical assault with related injuries were all too common. Alex, she thought, was a fainter, and he could collapse and fall before even hearing the news she was about to deliver.

She quickly held her wet hand out and grabbed Alex's as she spoke. "Alex, please may I come in? We need to sit and talk." She didn't rush because of the horrendous weather that was continuously battering against her, she was too professional to rush. She just needed to get inside with Alex seated, just in case he did faint and injure himself. She didn't want any more client accidents on her visits, nor did she want to become a statistic from injury by a client.

The intervention, spoken politely but with an assertive tone, awoke Alex's senses into some rational state that gave him slight focus. He was naturally a gentle man, not normally aggressive or easily angered. His thought processes recovered enough to stabilise the pressure build-up within himself along with the craziness that had lodged within his mind.

Alex spoke. "Er … um, yes. Please come in." He spoke with indecision as he was clouded in a fog, his senses were blurred as he wobbled like he was intoxicated with alcohol, or some other substance that had been spiked into his system. But in this instance, the toxic feeling was caused by the unannounced visit of Dawn, and she was a police officer here to deliver bad news. As the seconds ticked by, Alex slowly composed himself, although he now really felt sick. He could vomit at any time. He gulped again. As Alex moved away, and without thinking, his body went onto autopilot fight-or-flight whilst still being guided by Dawn's hand as she entered.

Dawn quickly closed the door to shut out the raw wind and rain. The news she was about to deliver would leave a shockingly cold feeling. Dawn wanted to keep the environment as warm as possible. Warmth could help her delivery ... she hoped.

To keep the momentum going, as they walked, Dawn repeated, "May we sit down somewhere?"

Alex turned to face her and then froze to the spot as he asked, "What's going on, please tell me, is ... is it about Petra?"

Dawn continued to move and gently guided Alex's hand as she replied, thinking *third time lucky* and with more emphasis in her voice, "Alex, I have some important news, *please* may we sit?" She quickly followed up with, "Is there anyone else at home with you?"

He shook his head with a 'no'.

She spoke gently, but now more assertively as she steered Alex into the kitchen where she saw the sofa. She kept hold of Alex's hand and guided him to the sofa where they both sat. Alex was now tearful and started to wipe his eyes as he looked away through the window. He didn't want to hear what Dawn had to say. Daylight had delivered dawn, but for Alex the passing of darkness had brought a Dawn he didn't want. He then turned to her.

She spoke softly with a serious expression. "Alex, do you know Petra Kline?"

He nodded and said, "Yes ... she's my wife. We've just got married, several weeks ago." Alex burst out crying, he was in agony as he wiped his eyes. He looked at Dawn and blurted out, "She *was* Petra Kline but now her name is Petra Munro."

Dawn momentarily thought about this, but given two

witnesses had stated they knew Petra Kline, she knew that Petra had to be the same person; maybe they weren't aware of the recent marriage. She continued, "Alex, it is with deep regret that I have to inform you we've found a body. We think it may be Petra."

Alex couldn't believe what he heard. He went into shock and started shaking in denial and disbelief, but the realisation gradually soaked in as Dawn *was* a police officer telling him very tragic news. News that no one *ever* wants to hear. This time a thunderbolt hit Alex between his eyes. It was like being hit by a bullet from a sniper, an explosive bullet, unexpected and excruciatingly painful. His headache intensified as he felt his brain was exploding with Dawn's shocking revelation. Alex forcibly pushed Dawn's hand off his and staggered up to his feet. Dawn suddenly became apprehensive; experience had taught her this could be the moment for aggression, uncalled for and aimed at her. She was just the messenger, but as so was guilty of the delivery of the unwanted news. She readied herself and quickly stood up, stepped backwards and far enough away from any impending thrown fist or foot. Alex looked enraged and awfully upset. Fortunately, he turned and moved away to sit at the table with his back towards her. As he sat, leaning forward with elbows on the surface, his head sank into both hands. His hard-skinned palms cupped around his unshaven face. They then got wet with the tears that were streaming down his face, like the rain outside relentlessly sliding down the window.

He sobbed and said, "Why, why Petra … why?"

Dawn moved forward, she gently touched Alex on the shoulder as a precursor to ask, "Alex, shall I make us some tea?" Experience had taught Dawn this diversion to make a hot drink often helped, particularly as Alex was alone; he clearly wasn't able to do anything other than be in shock with the intense upset right now. Alex replied with a 'yes' nod. Dawn spoke softly. "OK Alex, you sit there, I'll make us some tea and then I can explain the situation."

Dawn stood and started to make tea. She asked, "Alex, do you have anyone you could call to be here with you, a relative, neighbour or good friend?"

Alex sat numbed with the shocking news that his newlywed wife, and best friend Petra, was dead. She, like time, had passed away never to return, there would be no going back. He then cried aloud in agony, although at the same time hoped this was a horrid nightmare that would end upon his waking. He'd wake up and Petra would be there next to him in bed … but it wasn't going to be like that, not now, not ever. His mind shifted back to the harsh reality and then back to Dawn's question, he sobbed as he answered, "We have a best friend, Suze. She's coming here now. I called her just after seven as I was getting very worried about Petra being out all night, unexpectedly, and in this rotten weather. Suze will be here anytime now. She's coming from St Ives. She said she'd be an hour so that'll be 8ish." Alex looked through his sodden eyes to the window. His vision was blurred from the flowing tears. Although it was now daylight he could see the weather was once again worsening as the room had quickly dimmed. He noticed the fast-moving clouds had darkened, like the space within his head. Outside the clouds raced across the sky with ever increasing haste; blown by the cold wind. It was as though in this moment, and coincidently, a greater unearthly power had summoned the weather to worsen with Dawn's sad revelation. The cold weather could bring frosts, and they would arrive soon. It would get a lot colder, just like it was in Alex's heart. He heard the 'click' from the room temperature thermostat; an indication that signalled the heating was to come on. His heart needed warmth right now, and a lot of it. Alex was so upset his brain was fogged with murkiness and indecision. His thoughts were miserable and unbearable. He was preoccupied with horrible questions, 'what if, if only, I could have, I should have!' He was consumed with guilt that he could have done more to prevent Petra's unexpected death. The grief was stopping his normal awareness and coherent thought. Angst, pain and unanswered questions inhibited his usually clear mind.

Dawn made the tea and whilst doing so she saw, and admired, the very smart calendar hanging on the wall next to the clock that was ticking loudly. She noticed the photograph of two beautiful woman with **Myluv** written on the top image. Alex looked at Dawn and nodded 'thank you' as she placed his tea on the table. He then quietly spoke. "That's Petra on the top, she is **Myluv**." He wiped a tear away and continued, "It's my pet name for her. I loved her dearly. Some people have pet names for their lovers, like 'Babe' or 'Darling'. Petra was **Myluv**." Alex groaned and began to cry; Dawn comforted him as best she could. He blurted, "I loved Petra. She was part of my world, a very special place where we shared unimaginable love."

Dawn didn't think it right to ask who the other image was of, although she did think it strange there were two women. Dawn sat down on the chair next to Alex. He looked at her and couldn't not notice how attractive she appeared. She explained, "Alex, we had a report this morning at 6:15 from a dog walker. They had found a person on the beach who appeared to be unresponsive. She knew the person was Petra, she'd seen her many times before and knew her well. The woman called us to report the incident. We and the paramedics arrived very soon after. Sadly, the person found on the beach was pronounced dead, we believe she was Petra …"

Before Dawn had finished Alex gasped and loudly cried out. Dawn quickly grabbed his hand and put her other on his shoulder. After a while she continued. "We believe it was Petra as the person that reported to us is a local farmer, and she knew Petra very well. She said they had often chatted to each other as Petra regularly walked the area past her farm. Petra was wearing a bright red rain jacket, and the woman told us that Petra lived here with you."

Alex was in denial that Petra had died, that is until he heard 'Petra was wearing her bright red rain jacket'. Suddenly it became real. Petra's favourite 'to walk in' was her bright red rain-proof jacket, the one that wasn't hung in its usual place within the utility room. Again, Alex cried aloud and sobbed as he asked, "How did Petra die?"

Dawn spoke quietly. "We think Petra fell from a cliff. But we're not sure just yet, we need to continue our investigations. As soon as we know more we'll let you know."

Alex gasped; disbelief was in his mind. *No! … No! … This can't be true!* he kept thinking. He asked, "Can I go and see Petra?"

Dawn replied, "You can, but not right now. We'd like you to identify Petra, but only after we've established the cause of her death. As I said, we think she fell from the cliff, we've arranged for a pathologist to confirm this. As soon as he does, and he's completed an investigation, we'll let you know. After that time, we'll ask you to come and formerly identify Petra."

Alex was crying and hadn't realised he was squeezing Dawn's warm hand to the extent she felt pain. She was unable to continue with the unintentional grip and forcibly pushed his hand away from hers. She then gently placed hers on top of his to continue with the compassion she was trying to give at this extremely sad and emotional time.

After a while, when Alex seemed slightly less upset, Dawn asked, "Alex, have you a photo that I could take to help us identify Petra, like her driving licence, passport or some other recent picture? We need it to satisfy ourselves it is actually Petra. We don't disbelieve the person who reported Petra to us, but we need to be sure ourselves." She maintained contact with Alex's hand throughout and said, "As Petra is on the beach, we may have to move her body before the tide comes in. We'd take extremely good care of her as we move her to the coroners to establish what actually happened. She'll be in a safe environment and a warmer place rather than the cold wet beach."

Alex was numb. He sat motionless as tears rolled down his face whilst he looked at the calendar. He didn't make eye contact with Dawn as she continued. "Alex, please could I also have your full name, address, phone number and those of Petra?"

Alex listened and thought it stupid to ask for Petra's address, it was here with him.

Dawn continued, "I'd also like to see your marriage certificate, as her surname would have recently changed. We have to be correct with identification until you formerly attend just in case it isn't actually Petra."

Alex reluctantly obliged and gave Petra's details as his own, also her work and gallery address in St Ives. She would sometimes stay over there if she were working late on a project. It was her home before she moved in with Alex several years ago. He mentioned the St Ives address was also the address that Suze was staying at after her arrival from London. He began to wish that he could have talked Petra out of going for a walk in the atrocious weather. His guilt levels rose as he started to blame himself for the tragedy.

Whilst Dawn was collating the information Alex felt his mind wandering with memories of Petra and how they had met some years earlier. Petra lived with Alex in the small hamlet of Dartin. The area was very rural and predominantly farmland. It was steeped in ancient mythology. Rumours and folklore lingered. Paidwick Castle was nearby, an ancient ruin supposedly linked with King Arthur. Paidwick Castle had not weathered at all well; it didn't have the myths or history as Arthur's Tintagel had, although Petra loved the ruin. She imagined what it could have been like when it was in its glory. She had always felt a strong connection there, it was 'her place with the space'. It allowed her creative thoughts to flow. She was introduced to the ruins by Alex years earlier. Paidwick Castle was a perfect place for privacy if you went there at the right time during the summer, and most times during the other seasons. Petra loved the mystic and mythological aspects that this ancient ruin gave her. She often walked alone and stayed there, sometimes for hours, either to let her thoughts travel, or to *feel* the connection she had. Often, in all weathers and throughout the year, she would wild-camp and sleep over alone. Even her best friend Suze never went there, it was Petra's special place. During daylight she'd sketch ideas for her artistic work, either there, at home or at her St Ives gallery. Her favourite time to visit the castle ruin was during the night so she could *intensely feel* the gothic myths come alive under the cover of darkness. She would always visit the ruins alone as Alex had grown tired with the site; to him it was 'just another place' that he had outgrown from his childhood days. This suited Petra fine. Alex had gone there first thing this morning with his search, but Petra wasn't there.

Alex Munro was 42, about 5ft 10in tall with a good head

of neatly cut hair. He was clean-shaven and relatively fit given the nature of his active work and outdoor pursuits. He wasn't overweight and was always well groomed; he dressed casually but smartly. Typically, he would wear checkered shirts with clothing that matched the farming fraternities. He drove a dark green 4x4 double-cab pick-up utility vehicle that was provided by his employer with the logo 'Farmers Combined' prominently displayed across its side. He wasn't particularly wealthy and earned a reasonable salary that was just about comfortable for his needs. Home was a small three-bedroom cottage that he shared with Petra and Suze when she travelled from London. Living in Dartin suited both Petra and Alex as they loved the ruralness of the area, the privacy and the wide-open space around their home. The coast was within easy walking distance across farmland and along the many quiet footpaths and lanes. When Alex wasn't working he enjoyed the isolation where he could relax and pursue his hobby of photography. The immediate neighbours were friendly, but they never intruded into each other's personal lives. They got on well but tended not to socialise with one another; they each had their own families and friends. The local farmers would wave as they passed by in their tractors, they were familiar with the residents and in particular with Alex and Petra, sometimes referred to as 'The Duo'. They also knew Suze. When she was around they were called 'The Trio'. They'd often go for walks around and through the farmland.

Alex was seen as an affable good-looking young man. His clean-cut looks had attracted the young and older women. He had dated female farmers, and some of their daughters. Naively, at one time, he had several romances going on at the same time. He never quite got the magical connection that he had found with Petra, who he had met by chance. Their relationship was now seen as rock solid by their friends, family and colleagues. As Alex matured, his artistic ability shone through. His hobby of taking photographs around Cornwall meant he had often been published in national farming magazines and travel guides.

Unexpectedly, Alex came back to the here and now and reinvolved himself with the process that Dawn had instigated. He turned his mind back to Dawn's tortuous visit and left his thoughts about the past focusing again on Dawn. But, whilst he was dreaming, he hadn't been aware of the front door being opened, or it being closed. *Someone* had let themself in and they had now entered the kitchen. Alex was still unaware of the visitor as he sat sobbing, uncontrollably at times, whilst facing the window. His mind was full of memories as well as the sudden sorrow that Dawn had given him. He didn't feel the hand that gently touched his back. He wasn't at first conscious of the hand's gentle movement, smoothing up and down in a comforting way, like the hand that soothes a baby's back at a time of distress. The hand softly slid across his back and made several slow passes to and fro as it gradually made its way up to Alex's neck. His numbness had shut out any feeling apart from the pain he now felt inside with the loss of Petra. But, as the warm hand smoothed his neck, he gradually became aware of the caring touch. Dawn *had* noticed the person; she was looking at her with a baffled smile. Alex's thoughts and numbness had lessened with the comforting touch. His wandering mind came back to why Dawn was here and the touch of a warm hand on his neck. He woke from the ramblings in his mind, like an awakening from sleep; he had imagined the gentle touch on his neck *was* from Dawn. At first he felt it odd that Dawn would be soothing him, but it did feel nice and needed. He slowly turned his head to look at Dawn. It wasn't her soothing him; his mind began to race with expectation that *it was* his beloved gently touching him in that familiar loving way. This was how she would touch him. Maybe the news he'd been given from Dawn was wrong. But this wasn't Petra, it was Suze, his next best friend.

Suze had entered the cottage quietly with her key. As she gently closed the front door, she removed her muddy walking boots and slid her feet into Petra's slippers without a thought; they shared the same size. Sharing between them was a frequent and acceptable characteristic of their special friendship. This was a very familiar place for Suze as she, Petra and Alex, were the best of friends. They were, after all, The Trio.

As Suze had entered the hall she looked around whilst tears were filling her eyes. She saw beautiful works of art that Petra and she had hung there, along with stunning photographs that Alex had taken. Suze knew something serious was wrong as she didn't recognise the car parked on the driveway. It wasn't a marked police car, but she had noticed the hi-vis jacket on the back seat with the police logo badge not quite hidden from the view. She had thought, *Now the police are here it may mean Alex has called them … or something really serious has happened to Petra.* Suze slowly and quietly entered the kitchen. She saw the very upsetting scene with Alex sobbing whilst he sat at the table alongside a strange female who she assumed was the police officer. She at once knew something very bad had happened. She saw Dawn's lanyard with the police ID; this accelerated her thoughts of tragedy. Tears continued to roll down her face as she touched Alex's back, and then his neck with her gentle touch. She didn't know how traumatic the meeting was about to come. When her eyes finally met Alex's all she could do was bite the side of her lower lip. She then cried out loud with the pain she saw from his facial expression; Petra had gone. Alex tried to stand but staggered as he stood to face Suze, as though he was drunk. But he wasn't drunk, just *so* terribly upset. As he rose, the wooden chair he sat on scrapped across the floor and nearly toppled over.

Alex blurted out, "Petra ... Petra's dead ... she ... she's been found on the beach near our cave ... dead!"

Suze screamed and collapsed into his arms. They held tightly into each other ... the hug was filled with compassion and sadness, along with the agony and hurt they shared with the loss of their best friend, wife and lover, Petra. They cried uncontrollably together as they hugged.

Dawn retrieved tissues from her bag and thickly applied her lip balm whilst she watched the embrace. She gave tissues to both Suze and Alex when the opportunity arose as they lessened their embrace. When they let go of each other Dawn introduced herself. "Hello, I'm assuming you are Suze. I'm Dawn Tew, Police Liaison Officer. I want to offer my sincere condolences to both you and Alex at this awfully sad time."

Suze wiped her reddened damp face with the tissue and tried to smile. "Hello Dawn. Thank you. I'm just *so* shocked. I got here as soon as I could."

Alex again asked Dawn, "Could I see Petra ... could Suze and I see Petra?"

Dawn explained the sad news to Suze and finished by saying, "When appropriate, Alex will be required to formerly identify Petra at the coroners. You may come too; you'll need the support of each other."

Suze replied, "I'm so ... so terribly shocked by this news. I just can't believe it's happened. I don't want to believe that Petra has gone ... *she can't have died*. It's unreal!" She fell into Alex's arms crying again.

Dawn replied sympathetically, "Suze, we are doing all we can to care for Petra. She's in good hands and is not alone. As soon as we can, we'll let you know when you can see her. I realise this is a shock to you both and we'll offer you help and assistance anytime you need it. We'll be here for you both."

Time passed. Dawn offered support and gave out the relevant contact numbers for other agencies that could help, along with her work contact details. After a while, when she felt it was right to do so, she decided it was time for her to leave. Her nightshift had finished. There was never a good time, but sometimes overstaying could prolong the difficult process. When she was satisfied that she wasn't needed she said her goodbyes and left. Dawn appeared sadder than when she had arrived; she had again seen another heartbreak. Dawn put her coat on and saw herself out into the miserable weather. As she walked to her car she had a thought about Alex and Suze with their obvious closeness ... she felt it was a bit strange – best friend, and maybe more. It sat in her mind, although she had seen similar behaviour with others who were really close. She felt pleased that they both knew each other so well but still said a silent prayer in her mind for Petra as she drove away.

Suze and Alex sat on the sofa. Suze spoke with sadness and with faltering speech, "Alex, I'm so ..." She hesitated before regaining composure. "I'm *so* sorry for your loss." She spoke in a soft, wavering, tearful, almost uncontrollable hurt voice as she continued, "I'm *so* sorry for *our* loss."

Alex groaned and sobbed louder as he hugged Suze. Their heads were cheek to cheek and their tears mixed with each other's, like the rain drops on the window converging as they roll down the glass. They kissed each other as they hugged; they could now, *they* were alone. It was now done in a *romantic* way, as well as for comfort ... they chose each other's lips. They were alone to grieve in their joint love for one another. Strange to some, but Petra would have understood and approved. They fell to the floor, crying whilst embracing each other. It was an extremely emotional time. The rain was falling; the wind was blowing rain drops against the window that made more spattering sounds on the glass as the gusts of wind thrashed about. Suze regained some slight composure as she opened her damp closed eyes to watch the inclement weather outside. The weather was similar to how she felt right now: rotten. The raindrops on the window replicated the look of her and Alex's tears, forever appearing and relentlessly sliding down their respective surfaces. Alex slowly released his gentle hug from around Suze, only slightly and momentarily. He moved his head away from Suze's so he could look at her eyes. Suze paused her sobbing and sniffed several times as she too released her arms. Their sorrowed faces, just inches away from each other, met with eye-to-eye contact ... like the lovers they were.

Without warning, Alex gasped again and firmly hugged his best friend and lover, second only to the recently departed first, his lifelong world, Petra. They were taking deep breaths mixed with sniffs and snuffles as their hug persisted. Time didn't matter; the continually annoying ticking clock wasn't heard. No words were spoken; it was just the warm embrace that mattered. Time meant nothing with this sad tragic loss. It was meant to be healing but it was too painful for that. It was far too soon to heal.

After a while, Suze released her hold as she started to speak in a semi-sobbing way. "How," she stalled, "how about we have a cuppa?" She wiped tears away from Alex's eyes with her soft warm fingers as she spoke with a gentle tone.

Alex relaxed as best he could and made a simple smile as he spoke. "Thank you, I'd like that." It was a distraction in gesture only.

Suze, like Alex, was in the deepest shock possible. No words or actions could really help at this moment. Their pain was excruciating and never ending. Alex hadn't drunk the tea that Dawn had made, and it was now cold. He released his arms and took Suze's hands within his. Suze felt the rough skin of industrious hands against her soft skin. "Sit and stay." She spoke softly as she gently moved away from their embrace, wiping her eyes once their hands released. She pulled the chair forward so Alex could be more comfortable. Alex sat and peered through the window at the terrible weather; it was miserable and getting worse. Tears slid down his face. Suze only slightly regained her composure whilst gently wiping her damp eyes and face with a tissue. She used the same tissue as she turned to gently wipe Alex's wet eyes and face whilst trying to smile, just very slightly, like a mother does to her child. This was not a happy time, so her smile was more about the acknowledgement from Alex. He took the gesture with gratitude. As she wiped his eyes and face, there were no words, just immense sorrow; they were both very raw from the tragedy that had beset them.

The relationship between Suze and Alex could have been misunderstood had they been seen by others in this moment of deep personal upset. It may have come across as very odd, even sexual, and therefore wrong. They *do* love each other, dearly. They were extremely good friends who had a special close loving bond. They shared their love with Petra, a bit like loving brothers and sisters, plus more. Petra would have behaved in exactly the same way had the tragedy happened to Alex or Suze. Such was The Trio's special relationship with each other. The Trio *were* lovers.

Suze, still sobbing asked Alex, "What actually happened?"

Alex stuttered as he collected his thoughts. "I don't rightly know. Petra had gone for a late-night walk just after ten last night. I'd gone to bed and awoke early this morning to find she wasn't here. I got up thinking she'd be downstairs, but she wasn't. I could hear and see the weather was atrocious, so I went looking for her. I came back after an hour or so, thinking she may have returned, but she hadn't. I called you and waited here worried sick. As I waited there was a knock at the door." Alex faltered. "It … it was Dawn. She said Petra had been found on the beach … dead. They … they think she may have fallen from the cliff above our cave." As Alex finished, tears were again streaming down his shaking face. Suze moved closer to comfort him as they both cried together. The heartbreak and angst were shared but it didn't lessen the pain between them.

After some time, Suze composed herself as best she could. She walked towards the kettle. She lifted the kettle and turned to the tap; she did this automatically without conscious thought as she was very familiar with this home, she was part of it. She would regularly stay over, the three were best friends and had been lovers for many years. As she prepared the tea her mind was tingling and nagging away at the loss of her dear friend Petra. Unanswered questions were buzzing around in her mind. She and Alex needed answers. Suze spoke. "They say closure is needed when a loved one dies suddenly and unexpectedly. We need to know what happened. People need to have answers as to why someone has died suddenly. If the loved person dies through a sudden accident, as with Petra, then the shock and heartbreak is truly immense. The suddenness of the death is heartbreaking as no one expected or planned for the death to happen … I'm just so shocked and gutted, utterly distraught." Suze burst out crying but continued, "We never got to … we never got to say goodbye to Petra … for the last time!" Suze screamed with horror. Her moment of rational composure had suddenly gone as quickly as it had come. The kettle suddenly fell from her hand and smashed onto the granite worktop. She raised her hands to her head shouting and screaming, "Why! Why! … Why?"

Alex rushed from his chair and ran over to Suze. As he did, she screamed again and collapsed, sitting on the floor crying whilst curling up into a ball shape. Her knees were bent and her heels were tight against her thighs. She held her head in her hands between her knees. Alex shouted, "Suze, Suze!" She was crying inconsolably and terribly upset whilst shaking with hurt. Alex went down on his knees and put his arms around her. She was writhing about in agony with the pain of loss. Alex cried. His head touching Suze's. There was hurt that no one should endure. Their hearts were bleeding tears through their eyes. The pain was excruciating. It was unbearable as Alex knew that Petra and Suze were like sisters as well as lovers. He was also their lover. Their relationship was special, and now that had gone. Suze screamed, "Why her, why now?"

Alex had met Petra whilst visiting her art studio in St Ives, some ten years earlier. After several visits to Petra's studio, they became friends; he was attracted to her persona, beautiful appearance and hippiness as she was to his good looks and gentleness. They often had lunch and thereafter their relationship blossomed. They soon became best friends and over time loving partners. They shared a common interest with their artistic pursuits, and both loved the outdoors. Petra had lived in an apartment above her art gallery. She migrated to St Ives as it was a well-known artistic centre with a Tate art gallery and many smaller independent galleries. The area gave her inspiration as it had for many arty people, with splendid pieces of art shown and sold from their galleries. Petra initially commuted from London by train to St Ives, or Penzance if she flew in via helicopter. She worked as a freelance artist for wealthy clients who were predominantly London based. The commute to London enabled her to see Suze, her best friend. Petra was a hippy-dippy joyous female and fell in love with Alex as he was the opposite, very astute, particular but also handsome and like her, hardworking.

Petra was 36 and born in Germany where her liberal and extremely wealthy parents still lived. Her mother had inherited her father's successful industrial empire some 30 years before. Petra was schooled privately in England and became a UK resident of dual nationality. There was a distant German and English family connection, and it was considered a UK education could be better for Petra. She was the only child and could one day inherit her parents' empire and wealth. She had made it clear she didn't want to work for the family business. This was accepted and there was still a very good relationship between Petra and her parents. They wanted Petra to be happy by achieving her own ambitions to become a successful artist, rather than impose their will on her to become a businessperson to lead the empire.

Petra was a quirky child who liked anything artistic hence studying at an acclaimed art school in London after finishing her early years at an expensive private school. She was very free-spirited, casual and extremely beautiful, with natural russet-coloured hair. She was a sporty person and liked to keep fit, either at a gym, running or walking. She was 5ft 6in tall with a good athletic build and had a gorgeous vibe about her. Her native language was German, but as she schooled in England her accent became more English. Only a few could hear her very slight German accent and some mistook it for a West Country accent. Petra's persona and attractiveness were like magnets as was her art. All sorts of people and clients gravitated to her, including Alex and Suze. Petra had lived in a large swanky house that her parents owned; this was a luxurious house in Kensington Palace Gardens, London. After Petra graduated her parents gifted the house to her as a kind gesture for all her successful hard work whilst studying. Petra met Suze Barnard when they started art college together in their early twenties. They quickly became the best of friends as they shared similar interests and could have been twin sisters.

Suze was 35, bright, artistic and also quirky. She was very attractive with a fun persona and had a level outlook on life. At the same height and build, but with long blonde hair flowing down her back, Suze and Petra hit it off as soon as they met. Suze shared the same classes as Petra and soon moved in with Petra at the posh Kensington house. Their friendship was more important than wealth; their bond was unique and special. They saw themselves as equals.

Suze and Petra were both childlike in many ways and would often share everything, even the same bed for company where they would chat about anything and everything. Their friendship grew in strength and over time they saw each other as sisters when describing their friendship. As time went by their bond increased. They mutually realised they were falling in love with each other, not only as best friends but also romantically with a deep emotional connection. This happened quite naturally without pressure from either side. It had evolved slowly from the day they met with their instant connection. As time passed their friendship love and togetherness became normal and they both felt good and harmonious as one. Love in a romantic way naturally developed thereafter as they gradually shared their heartfelt feelings with each other.

Petra didn't want to become a spoilt child relying on her parents' wealth forever and was determined to create her own income with her art. Petra wanted to be a regular, 'normal' person who progressed with her own ability and efforts. Suze thought the same way, adding to the commonality between them. They both worked very hard to achieve their independent self-sufficient status. When Suze could pay for items she would. She never abused the gifts that Petra made to her and was very thankful and appreciative. If the roles were reversed they both felt the opposite would be true. The relationship grew in strength over the years, and their bond appeared unbreakable. Their love remained solid and special even after Petra met Alex.

Suze graduated and worked for a couple of graphic publishers before getting a substantial wealth opportunity with a national brand, also based in London. She and Petra continued to be lovers. Suze would travel to see Petra at every opportunity, at least fortnightly. They video-called each other two or three times every day. Petra acquired the building next to the Tate in St Ives ten years ago and transformed it into a successful art gallery with the apt name of **Myluv & Myluv**, referring to her and Suze's love for each other. At that time Petra had offered Suze the opportunity to live with her in the apartment above the gallery and to become a partner. The plan was delayed as Suze forged ahead with her career in London but their love for each other remained and got stronger because they were apart.

Petra's relationship with Alex developed unintentionally over time. She had informed Suze about Alex the first day she met him. It could have been awkward, but she and Suze mutually accepted the new dynamic as Petra's relationship developed with Alex. Suze met Alex soon after Petra had feelings for him. If Suze disapproved then Petra would cease the new relationship. It transpired from Suze's introduction to Alex she fully approved and accepted him into the relationship, such was Alex's good personality and his all-round nice persona.

Petra's relationship with Alex grew from friendship to lovers. Suze adapted as best she could now that her best friend wasn't so freely available. There wasn't any animosity or upset with Petra being a shared person. Suze was equally involved with Petra, and she never had the feeling that two's company, three's a crowd. Petra, being very liberal, wanted Suze to join in with Alex and soon the relationship moved from a twosome to a loving threesome. It happened quite naturally and without fuss. As Petra's relationship with Alex blossomed, Suze could have befriended or dated others. She didn't. Her relationship and love were still with Petra. She was 100% faithful to Petra. Frequently Petra would mention that she missed Suze, either by text or call. They had lived together for nearly four years and had bonded into a very special beautiful loving relationship that neither had experienced until that time. Weekends were special, Suze and Petra would take every opportunity to visit each other, with or without Alex. Alex didn't mind and was fully informed by Petra from their initial meetings that she had a loving relationship with Suze. A routine developed that suited The Trio as Petra and Suze would never conceal their special relationship from Alex. In fact, when he understood their bond and didn't feel threatened by it, he welcomed it as an extension of his love for Petra. Whilst at Dartin Suze initially hoped that Petra and she could have some time together, on their own. Just so it was like the good old college days. If it didn't happen, it never really mattered as being there with Petra was ample reward. Over time, unintentionally and by accident, OK … with a little luck and guidance from Petra, the three-way relationship did develop mutually in a natural way and at the same time quite nicely.

Initially, while Suze visited Alex's home she had her own room. Petra's engineering ability and her planning wanted to discreetly build trust between Suze and Alex. As time went by, Petra's plan blossomed. The loving relationship between Suze and Alex grew. The turning point of no return happened quite innocently after Suze had taken a shower. She simply forgot to get dressed before leaving, she never did at home in London, or whenever she was with Petra, why would she, they were lovers. On this particular day she walked out of the shower to go to her room without even having a towel around her. Alex, unaware that Suze had showered, had innocently gone upstairs to his and Petra's room to get a book. He heard Suze singing, he assumed from her bedroom. He was poised *not* to look, being polite … but then he did. More for curiosity than anything else, and to say hello. He assumed she was in her room. As he turned he saw Suze without a shred of clothing looking at him. She had left the bathroom unaware that Alex was there. They both looked at each other with initial scepticism. Suze covered her breasts with her hand and her pubic area with the other. Her eyes and mouth were wide open with a concerned look. Alex blushed and immediately looked down at the floor. But then, very soon after, he lifted his head and they simultaneously smiled. Alex saw Suze in her glory. Suze admired Alex for who he was with her best friend, but now in this delicate moment with her being nude she felt both powerful, but at the same time very vulnerable. She was intrigued with her feelings for Alex and wanted to explore them further. But her rational thought was telling her this could be the wrong time, it may not be right with Petra, and it could be viewed as deceitful without her knowledge and approval. Alex knew Petra was beautiful, but he now saw Suze's full beauty, along with that magnetism that Petra possessed. He was attracted to her damp long golden blonde hair dripping across her naked body. Initially her blue eyes showed the shock of being seen without clothing. Her eyes soon changed to a forgiving peer, like his. Alex blushed more and quickly turned away ... but then looked back. She smiled cheekily towards him.

She spoke softly and sensuously. "Hi Alex, sorry, I didn't know you were there."

Alex sheepishly replied, "I'm sorry ... I ..."

Suze casually walked over to him, as a feline does when it wants something. Her body moved stealthily and carefully towards him, staring at him like a cat does. He thought she was purring as she crept closer. He gulped as thoughts swirled around in his mind. *What shall I do now ... no don't do that!* was the thought from his good side. Whereas from his naughty side, *Yes, go on!* But he tried to ignore that. He stared at her as she came closer towards him. He wasn't looking at her body. If he was, it wasn't recording. He was too nervous and so closed his eyes.

Suze got so close he could feel her soft breaths as she whispered softly into his ear, "Don't be sorry, it's OK, I don't mind, it's normal to peep." She then slowly turned and walked towards her room. She hoped he would be watching her. He was. He was frigid, his feet stuck like ice cubes do to a moist warm surface. As he thawed, slightly shaking with all sorts of thoughts, his vision regained focus on her departing body. He was amazed by her beautiful form, as he was with Petra's. As Suze casually walked into her room, leaving the door open, she went towards the full-length mirror where she could see Alex reflected. He was still facing her and watching. She smiled into the mirror. He still had a blushed red face. As she looked into the mirror at his image she put a finger over her lips and made the 'shush' sound. Alex *was* embarrassed but at the same time excited. His good thoughts had told him to quickly leave his room, looking like a dog with its tail between its legs when it's been berated for being a bad boy. He looked at the floor as he skulked to the stairs with thoughts of *if only*. The powerful Suze had dominated, controlled and felt good with her performance. She didn't feel threatened, she was victorious. Alex didn't pose an obstacle to her relationship with Petra.

As Alex went downstairs, almost head in hand with disbelief about what had just happened – *or didn't happen* – he saw Petra in the kitchen as though she was waiting for him. She was. She was smiling. Alex, now extremely excited, but at the same time embarrassed, walked to Petra.

She spoke softly and sensuously. "Alex darling, what's the matter?" *She knew* what had happened, *she had engineered* the process. She put her arms around his buttocks and cheekily squeezed them as she pulled him close to her body.

He spoke nervously. "I've just come from upstairs and seen Suze in the nude, she came out of the shower, in front of me. I'm sorry, it happened so quick I couldn't turn away, I froze and became frigid! I just couldn't move!"

Petra smiled and pulled him even tighter into her body, both hands around his bottom. "Alex don't worry. I always see Suze like that, and she sees me like it. It really doesn't matter, I'm sure. Suze and I love each other, as we do you. We share everything, and that could include you if you'd like to share us together. I'm sure she'd be OK with that, and maybe you would too?" She then kissed his ear lobe. Alex was dumbfounded but at the same time pleasantly curious. He had heard that some Germans were *really* liberal and open with their relationships, without prejudice. Apparently he had heard more were naturists and would often remove their clothes at the first opportunity immediately after work as soon as they arrived home, or wherever it was OK to do so. It *was* frequent with Petra and Alex; Alex thought there was nothing wrong with it in their home, or at secluded places, but until now Suze *was* a visitor. He knew Petra and Suze had a special relationship with each other and he'd accepted that as it predated his time with Petra. But now there was a new configuration. Alex thought, *Crikey, what do I do now? Where will this go, do I want it to go anywhere? My darling Petra has sanctioned something that had never entered my mind!* The thought had never occurred to him; it was Petra's guidance that instigated the process.

Time passed after the shower incident, nothing untoward developed and the relationships were good. Petra gradually sensed Alex was becoming more confident around Suze and vice versa. There was greater warmth between the two of them, just as there was when Petra and Suze met each other. When the time was right she suggested that he and Suze could take their clothes off … in front of each other whilst she watched and orchestrated the process as a guardian of the norms. It could have been an awkward moment for the three. Petra supervised the experience; she smiled and slow hand-clapped as item by item their clothes came off. It was an enlightening experience that bonded the trio with harmony, togetherness and most importantly, love.

Thereafter they quite naturally became a threesome. They shared the same compassion and love for each other in the same way a couple would. Alex and Suze didn't think it odd or wrong when they too found the beauty of a new dynamic love. It wasn't a sexual fad that would come and go, this was like a marriage and was to be forever. The Trio loved each other equally in a unique and special way that most people wouldn't understand. They didn't care what others thought, it wasn't their business and anyway, The Trio kept their pact a secret.

CHAPTER 3
THE DOGS FIND PETRA

Earlier on that tragic and vile weather morning, Betty Smith, a local farmer, whose farm was immediately next to the sea, had been out walking her two dogs. They were fine-looking border collies and the breed choice for many farmers due to their intelligence, excellent agility and herding abilities. Their need to be ever-active led most of the breed to be on-the-go all of the time, which was great for working farmers, but not so much for some domestic owners.

Betty was an early riser and preferred to go out for a walk first thing every morning, no matter what the weather threw at her, in darkness or daylight. Farmers tend to be strong and resilient; they work in all weathers throughout the year, come rain or shine. Betty was no different, as were her duo of the preferred canines. The early morning walk never differed and she'd usually set off around 5am and always before 6am. There were cattle and sheep that she and her husband, Alan, supposedly cared for on their several hundred-acre farm along the southwest coast.

A few years earlier the cattle stock fence, above the cliffs adjacent to the farm, fell away from an overnight landslide following a period of stormy weather. The cattle, inquisitive as they are, wandered towards the landslip area but some got too close. Several fell to their deaths onto the beach below. It was a tragic accident, and Betty carried the guilt thereafter that she *and* Alan could have been more diligent, if they were, the incident may never have happened. Since then, Betty became obsessive and vowed to walk the farm's perimeter cliff route every day of the year to check it was safe and intact. Alan was slightly lazy and unreliable. The stock fence was renewed further back from the cliff edge, however Betty, being conscientious, *needed* to check the new fence every day without fail. She couldn't trust Alan to do it … she didn't want another sad tragedy with the loss of life.

The secluded beach where the cattle fell couldn't be seen from the clifftop due to a granite rock overhanging it. It was thought the beach could only be accessed from Tamorna Cove, about 300 metres distant, and even then only during the lowest point of the infrequent spring low tides. This happened just twice a month. The beach, however, was the same beach Petra had discovered whilst watching the timid wild goats use a discrete path. As the tide came in the beach was quickly inaccessible, even from Tamorna Cove. The attraction for The Trio was privacy whilst skinny dipping from the hidden beach. The cave above was a perfect place to have a wild camp. This morning Betty set off just after 5am on the very stormy day with her two dogs. It was the morning of the low spring tide.

On this tragic morning, Betty walked her usual route around the clifftop. The two dogs were off-lead and led the way, bad weather didn't affect their walks, the pair knew this was *their* playtime and that work would follow after they'd had their breakfast back at the farm, such was the routine. They joyfully played and romped ahead. Daisy, the younger dog, suddenly darted off across the clifftop path into the hidden goat route that led to the beach below, she was barking non-stop as she'd seen a goat and her instinct to herd meant she had to follow. The path was steep, awkward and quite dangerous to walk, but to a four-legged animal it was OK. Lucy, the older dog followed Daisy. She too started to bark.

Betty, still on the clifftop path, blown by the strong south westerly wind with rain against her face, made her way carefully to the clifftop where she shone her head torch down the cliff. Both dogs could just be heard above the wind noise somewhere below. Her torch beam wasn't quite bright enough to see through the pouring rain down the 40-metre drop to the beach. Her light lit the falling rain like beautiful diamonds cascading down a waterfall. She shouted at the dogs, but they continued to bark and couldn't be seen. She used her dog whistle several times with three short toots, this being their recognised recall. Eventually Lucy, the more experienced dog, clambered back up the hidden path to Betty. She was unsettled and fussing about around Betty's legs. Betty realised something was amiss. Daisy, the younger dog, stayed on the beach where she continued to bark. Betty hadn't wanted to go down the way Lucy appeared from; there didn't appear to be a path, it looked too overgrown and would have been extremely precarious in this wet stormy weather. She didn't go too near the edge as she was well aware of the severe drop. Betty became more anxious as Daisy hadn't returned so she continued along the muddy clifftop path towards Tamorna Cove. This was a short distance, some 300 metres ahead, and she knew the beach could be accessed from there during the spring low tides. Once at the cove Lucy led the way across the beach towards the barking Daisy. The rain, often falling horizontally as the gusts increased, limited Betty's torch beam. She carefully made her way across the stoney beach toward her barking Daisy. The tide was out, and Betty had only once ever been to this section of the beach before, when the cattle tragedy happened. Suddenly, after a fair distance Betty's torch beam lit a shape that was the size of a dolphin. As she approached the object her torch light found the shape wasn't a dolphin, it was a human body. As she got near, she could see a bright red jacket. It was a woman … whose brilliant wet russet-coloured hair was dancing wildly in the wind. Her light shone onto the woman's face; she recognised her immediately … it was Petra.

Betty had known Petra, her neighbour, for as long as Petra and Alex had been together some ten years earlier. Petra was well known in the community for her artistic skills and for being a regular walker and runner in the area. Very firmly, Betty shouted at Daisy, "Stop!" and then followed up with "Down!" She was annoyed with the incessant barking. Daisy laid, followed by Lucy. Both dogs lay, soaking wet and panting. They eagerly looked at Betty as they waited for their next command, tongues held out sideways from their mouths whilst they breathed heavily in the wet air. Betty was further shocked when she saw what she thought was blood on the stones near Petra's head. Betty raised her hand over her mouth and gasped as she said, "Oh my God! What has happened to you, my dear Petra?" There wasn't a reply. All sorts of thoughts shot through her mind, along with shock, panic and upset. She carefully knelt next to Petra and touched her cold wet hand. There were no signs of life. Betty called out, "Petra, Petra … are you alright … Petra?" Lucy and Daisy lay patiently, still panting and watching intensely. There was no reply or movement from Petra. Betty had thought Petra was seriously ill but realised the worst. Betty became more anxious and awfully upset. She quickly stood, got her phone, and dialled 999. It was 6:15.

"Hello, police emergency how can I help?" said the Emergency Medical Dispatcher, the EMD. Betty was shaking and panicking.

"Hello, it's …" she stalled.

The EMD calmly asked, "Caller, are you able to talk?"

He said this as sometimes callers were in a dire situation and could be overheard when they don't want to be. Maybe for their own safety, for example in a domestic abuse situation.

Betty answered, whilst now sobbing, "Yes … I'm able to talk. I've … found Petra, my neighbour … she's … she's seriously injured … or even dead! There's blood coming from her head and neck!" Betty gasped at what she'd just said. Reality was setting in. She started shaking.

The EMD spoke calmly. "OK caller, what is your name?"

"It's Betty … Betty Smith." She stalled again and was crying more intensely.

"Betty, is the person breathing?"

Betty gasped, as she quietly spoke. "No … no, I don't think so."

"OK Betty, you're doing really well. I'm Mike, I just need to know exactly where you are."

Betty, with tears streaming down her already wet face replied, "I'm on the beach, just beyond the slipway at Tamorna Cove, that's off Tamorna Lane. It's about five miles west of Penzance."

Mike replied, "Betty, I can't hear you, there's a lot of wind noise. Can you repeat what you've just said, talk louder."

Betty spoke louder and repeated her previous line.

"OK Betty, I've got that. I'll send an ambulance and the police out right now." Mike had previously dispatched both the police and ambulance before Betty had finished. He kept Betty talking, as was necessary, to check the well-being of both her and the reported person. Mike asked for her phone number but as Betty was giving it her phone suddenly slipped and dropped onto the wet stones.

She shouted, "Bollocks!" As Betty struggled to find her phone she clumsily ended the call. She held the phone to her ear; the line was quiet. Betty phoned her husband Alan.

"Hey, you'd better get here quickly! I'm on the beach, next to Tamorna Cove. I've found … I've found Petra … I think she's dead!"

Betty cried as Alan, steady as he was, said, "What? Petra dead? Are you sure? That can't be right, can it?"

Betty was obviously upset with herself for crying. She snapped back at Alan, "Of course I'm bloody right! … I'm sure … I've rung 999 and they're coming, but *you need to get here* right now, no messing … right now!" Betty immediately ended the call, with angst that Alan hadn't believed her; he never did. She knelt next to Petra, holding her cold hand whilst crying. She stroked Petra's wet face. "Petra, Petra, what has happened to you my dear? I'm so … I'm sorry, I really am."

Alan was both perturbed by the news and his disbelief with Betty. He knew Petra well; he liked her and would chat to her whenever he could. He was already dressed; he had got out of his bed the same time as he heard Betty in her room. He hurriedly set off and drove to the cove.

Alan arrived a short time later and made his way carefully towards Betty. He could occasionally see the distant light from her head torch through the rain. He struggled on his way against the wind and rain as he slowly approached Betty. Daisy barked and broke her stay; she ran aggressively towards him barking ferociously. Her upper lip was lifted showing her sharp teeth in an angry manner. She charged towards him, jumping up at the last minute, mouth wide open in attack mode. Alan carefully timed his kick; he'd had plenty of practice. His right boot hit Daisy's head, fully sideways-on. She yelped and fell. Alan shouted, "Fuck off you stupid bitch!" Daisy cowered for a moment with her eyes glaring at him; she'd been in this situation many times with her hatred for Alan. He again got the better of her.

Her tail went between her hind legs as she stood sheepishly and scampered back to Betty. Betty hadn't seen or heard the commotion as Alan was adept in doing things ... discreetly. He knew secrecy paid dividends.

Alan approached Betty, with both dogs now alongside her. They were viciously barking at him. They stood close to Betty, as though they were protecting their pack leader. Lucy also hated Alan and had learnt that his right boot always hurt. Alan ignored the duo as he could now see the red coat being lit by Betty's torch. His disbelief that Petra was dead now sunk in. He was upset as she had now gone forever and he wouldn't see her again. He was fond of her company. It was utterly gruesome to find his dead cattle and now this very attractive neighbour in a similar place. He shouted at the dogs to sit; they ignored him. He shouted to Betty, "Get your fucking dogs away from me ... or else!" Betty continued to cry as she ordered the dogs to lie. That they did. Alan knelt next to Betty where he placed his arm around her.

She looked at him venomously as her wet face contorted with angst as she snarled, "Get your hands off me, you fucker!"

He nervously smirked at her whilst he disgustingly poked his tongue out, waving it up and down several times with it almost touching her face. She pushed his arm away in anger. He looked over her shoulder and saw Petra. "Wait here, I'm just going to check her."

Instantly Betty responded, "Keep your hands off Petra, you vile man. Don't you dare touch that sweet girl! I wished I hadn't called you to come. I know what you've been up to ... you pervert! I've seen you watching her."

Alan retorted, "Piss off you stupid cow, you know nothing!" Alan, being a farmer, did know *some* things about first aid after watching vets treat his livestock, plus he liked watching medical reality programmes on TV. He stood and carefully walked around Betty avoiding the two dogs. Lucy and Daisy were still snarling and showing their teeth to him in a ready-to-pounce state. He knelt alongside Petra, in front of Betty.

She growled, "Don't you touch her, you sick bastard!"

Alan replied, "Fuck off!"

She responded, "Yeah, you'd like to fuck her ... wouldn't you, you bastard! If truth be known you have fucked her ... you filthy fucker you! Do you want to fuck her now? Go on ... you can now, she can't tell anyone now, can she? You'd like that, wouldn't you? You sick fucking pervert! I've seen you watching her undress when she swims! You filthy bastard you! Take some more pictures of her!"

Alan ignored the barrage of venomous words spewing from Betty's mouth. He checked to see if Petra was breathing by putting his ear near to her mouth and nose. He wanted to feel and smell her warm breath again. There wasn't any breath or warmth. Just a cold stare as Petra's dead open eyes watched him. He wasn't perturbed with her eyes looking at him, he liked them. He saw blood dribbling out from the rear of her neck, and she had a bloodied grazed face. He also saw blood coming from her nose. He tried to find a pulse from her awkwardly twisted wrist, which was bent backwards, but couldn't. He didn't want to touch her neck in case it aggravated the bleed. Petra's other arm was awkwardly behind her back, and one of her legs looked painfully contorted back-to-front. Alan didn't want to move her, as much as he'd like to. She appeared lifeless.

"Petra, Petra," he called out several times whilst conducting his checks with a leering smile that Betty couldn't see, he was blocking her view. There was no reply and no sign of life. He then unzipped her red jacket that exposed her naked torso. She had no clothes on beneath the jacket.

Betty immediately shouted, "What the fuck are you doing?"

Alan turned and sneered at Betty, "I'm going to do CPR!" He still had that leering smile as he cupped his sodden wet hands ready to place over Petra's chest.

Betty replied, "You daft fuck! You don't even know what CPR means!"

"Yes I bloody well do!" said he. "CPR means Cup Press Release!" He then moved his body to ensure Betty couldn't see what he was doing. He put his cold wet cupped hands deliberately over Petra's breasts. He caressed and fondled them. He smiled at Petra whilst he played with her breasts, fondling and squeezing her breasts in and out. He discretely whispered to Petra, "Bye my love, I shall miss you … as you will miss me." He turned to look at Betty who couldn't see what he was doing. "See, it's easy when you know how! CPR, it's easy! I've got to do this 15 times and then blow into her mouth."

Betty was dumbfounded, as she again looked at Alan's back. She still couldn't see what he was doing. He discreetly took his phone out and took pictures of Petra's breasts. He then lent forward to her lips and pretended to blow; he was actually kissing her dead lips.

Betty spoke. "When I've watched the TV docs I thought the medics did CPR differently?"

Alan sat up. "Nah you daft bitch!"

Just then they both looked back to Tamorna Cove. Blue lights could be seen flashing.

It was 6:36. There were no sirens as Tamorna Lane was a quiet winding single-track road. Alan quickly stopped his version of CPR and zipped up Petra's red jacket. Betty was busy watching the blue lights and hadn't noticed Alan's abhorrent behaviour. They both stood. He pretended to hold Betty's hand, but she continually pushed it away as the police officer hurriedly made his way across the beach. The torch attached to his stab vest lit the way as he carefully stepped across the beach that was still being lashed by rain. The ambulance crew weren't far behind, both carrying backpacks.

As the police officer arrived he saw Petra's body along with her obvious bloody injuries. He noticed the awkwardness in the way she lay. He spoke. "Hi, I'm PC Paul Landy, what's happened?" He asked that question because at that time, although he'd been given the message from the control room, he came with an open mind. He looked at the scene, at Betty and Alan, and their dogs, who were now really well behaved and just lay there still awaiting the next command from Betty. He looked at Petra and felt her tragedy. He gulped at the shock of seeing her body lying in such a contorted way. The two paramedics soon arrived and at once went to Petra where they conducted checks with their more qualified medical expertise and equipment.

Paul let the experts get on whilst he led Betty and Alan away. He quickly questioned them about the tragedy. He believed their story of the events that had led them to this tragic discovery. Alan remained silent as Betty spoke and answered Paul's questions. As he finished the senior medic came over and asked Paul to talk to her in private. The medic led Paul to Petra.

"Hi Paul," spoke the medic with a straight face. They obviously knew each other as they shared the same patch and had previously worked together.

Paul nodded and replied, "Hi Julie, what's the situation?"

Julie spoke with dignity. "I'm afraid Petra, if that is her

name, is dead. There's nothing more we can do. I think that Petra may have fallen from those cliffs." As Julie spoke she pointed to the cliffs that rose some 40 metres fairly steeply up from where Petra lay. Julie continued, "I think there may be more to her death than just a fall."

"Why do you say that?" asked Paul with a curious frown.

"Well, you don't just fall and die with the injuries Petra has sustained. There's more. I'm concerned that some of the injuries appear not to have been caused by a fall."

Paul spoke. "What, you suspect that some of her injuries may have been caused by something else?"

Julie replied, "Yes. She isn't wearing anything under her coat and there are strange marks around her neck. I'm thinking she may have been attacked in some way, and maybe there's a sexual connotation. Also, her jean fly zip is undone!"

Paul suddenly understood and realised the incident could be something far greater than a tragic fall. There were serious indications that a suspected crime had been committed. He'd have to ramp the incident up to his superiors. He said, "Thank you Julie. I'll move this incident up. Could you please check that Betty and Alan are OK whilst I get the ball rolling?"

"Of course, I'll take them to our van out of this shocking weather. They're like us, cold and soaking wet!"

Paul's bodycam was working as soon as he arrived. It would have recorded the scene and subsequent conversations. Betty and Alan were now witnesses and mandatory statements were required. Paul quickly needed assistance; he spoke on his radio to his sergeant who agreed. The sergeant spoke with his inspector who said he'd pass the incident over to the Criminal Investigation Department, CID. In the meantime, more uniformed officers would arrive to assist and secure the scene.

Julie had carefully led Betty and Alan to the ambulance where she was ensuring their welfare was OK. She noted the continual banter between them and the choice swear words they used at each other in every sentence they spoke. At one point she felt it was too extreme for spouses and rather strange. She didn't challenge either of them with their behaviour or their bad language. She felt threatened and intimidated, particularly by Alan. Her medical colleague was tidying the equipment away next to Petra following the thorough medical checks. He had carefully covered Petra with a blanket that immediately became wet. The wind was continually blowing the blanket off, so he secured the corners with large stones to ensure that dignity prevailed.

Paul now had to secure the scene, as best he could with 'POLICE! Do Not Enter!' tape. He used four bollards from his vehicle that he placed around Petra's body, although he struggled with the wind and subsequent tape securement. He finally managed as best he could with the dreadful weather. He walked back to the ambulance where Betty and Alan sat with blankets around them. Before he entered the vehicle Julie beckoned him to her.

"Paul, these two are a bit odd. I sense there isn't any love between them as they were at each other's throats several times. Alan seems shifty and is quite aggressive to Betty. She is belittling him and almost goading him to be just that. They knew 'Petra' and Betty was perturbed when Alan spoke about her, I'm thinking she was jealous? I know this sounds strange but see what you think when you take their statements."

Paul listened with curiosity. "OK, understood. I'll dig a bit deeper."

Julie and her colleague released Betty and Alan from their

care and passed them over to Paul. He took their statements whilst asking relevant pertinent questions. Although he formed a similar view to Julie, he wasn't unduly concerned although he noted their odd behaviour too. Betty didn't allude to Alan's wrongdoing with his CPR as she wasn't sure he had got it wrong; she didn't want to come across as a fool if he had performed it correctly, and she hadn't seen him abusing Petra's body. Paul, however, did feel it right for CID to interview them separately to try and uncover why they were behaving in a strange way. He spoke to both Betty and Alan who were sat with solemn faces.

"You may well see additional officers as part of this enquiry. They will visit and ask more questions to get a better picture whilst they establish facts and evidence. Thank you for calling in this tragedy to us. Please do not share the incident with anyone just now."

Betty, with sodden eyes, and Alan now appearing upset, nodded in agreement. Betty spoke. "It's just so sad that this has happened. Petra was a lovely woman and part of our neighbourhood community. Alex, her partner, will be devastated by this." She wiped her eyes and sobbed.

Paul responded, "I'm sure he will be, and our thoughts go out to him ... but please do let *our* liaison team contact him first to inform him before you make contact. It's best that you leave it to us, so I emphasise again, please don't share this tragedy with anyone else just now." Paul had said this as he knew the investigation had to confirm whether or not Petra's death was either an accident, suicide ... foul play ... or murder.

Betty and Alan left the scene to drive to their farm. Betty and Alan were in shock and travelled silently as they travelled.

At 7:37 Detective Constable Jackie Smith and Police

Constable Susan Hill arrived to lead the investigation. They were from CID; it was their department that would investigate the incident to establish the cause of Petra's death. Paul saw them arrive and vacated the ambulance to meet them. He briefed DC Smith, who he had never met before, and stood by to secure and preserve the scene until more uniformed officers arrived. His sergeant was coming to attend, along with other officers to maintain a secure boundary and assist CID where and when required. Jackie and Susan had their bright hi-vis jackets on, giving limited rain protection, and they wore their police logo hats.

After the brief introduction niceties, Jackie and Susan carefully walked over to where Petra lay. Jackie led the way. A short distance across the beach, and without warning, Susan slipped on a wet stone. "Fuck it!" she yelled as she toppled towards and into Jackie, whose body fortunately stopped the fall.

"You idiot! You nearly took me over too!" shouted Jackie with surprise.

They steadily regained composure with Susan's demure, "Sorry boss!"

"Well, watch where you are going!" Jackie replied firmly.

They didn't talk much as the wind and rain were not only annoying but also the crashing wave noise didn't allow for conversation to be heard well. Jackie continued to carefully walk ahead, now with a more serious appearance across her face. She'd only just met her new sidekick Susan that morning. She thought, *Shall I call her Miss Lightfoot rather than Susan?* She laughed in her mind thinking, *First day drama, let's hope that is it. She should be good as I've read her college report.* Susan, for her part, carefully maintained a greater distance behind Jackie; she didn't want to mess up her first day with CID, although *this* was a bad start. She thought, *Steady on*

Susan, don't let your over-eagerness let you down, concentrate!

Jackie arrived at the crime scene marked by the police warning tape. She carefully stepped over as it wildly jumped up and down in the vicious wind. Susan followed behind more cautiously but as she stepped over her boot snagged on the tape. The tape broke away its fastening from one of the bollards and flickered wildly about like that seen in a Chinese ribbon dance. Susan thought, *Oh bugger!* She momentarily froze like a statue as she waited for Jackie to notice her second mishap. She didn't.

Susan shouted, "Jackie! Look, the tape has come away!" as she pointed to the dancing tape.

Jackie turned to look. "Well, tie it back then!" She didn't realise it was caused by Susan's clumsiness as Susan hurriedly re-fastened the tape.

As they approached Petra, Jackie, being the mentor for Susan, started to speak loudly. "Well Susan, here we are. We need to be careful to preserve evidence *and* have due respect for Petra's body. Is your bodycam recording?"

Susan looked down and saw the indicator light was flashing. "Yes!" She spoke in a very keen way.

Jackie replied, "Good. Have you ever seen a dead body before as part of a crime scene, or other?" Jackie asked the question as it could be quite shocking and upsetting to see a badly injured dead body for the first time, particularly as the dead person *may* have been murdered. She wanted to prepare Susan for the distressing event. Susan stared at the wet flapping blanket covering Petra. She could see a red patch that appeared to be getting larger.

Jackie and Susan met each other for the first time earlier that morning. Jackie had only been in this constabulary a few months. She too was considered a newbie in the department and was finding her way around. It had been awkward here in her new job, her boss and other work colleagues hadn't yet gelled with her. She felt there was some animosity towards her. Susan had only just finished her two-year police probationary period in another area and wasn't known. This was her first CID attachment and today there should have been a meet-and-greet session where Susan could meet the CID team when they arrived at work, but this was cut short as Jackie was tasked to attend this crime scene.

Jackie had asked the death question to Susan just now as in this role it was becoming more frequent to see dead bodies and seriously injured victims. Jackie knew this was going to be a blood-and-guts case, particularly as there was a fall from height. Jackie had seen many bloody deaths that were now more common with younger adults. She thought, *The advent of smart phones and social media are partly responsible for the increase among kids. Knife crime had become the latest trend with some young adults and teens, even those* not *involved with gangs. I just hope Petra's death is a tragic accident and not a murder.*

Jackie turned to look at Susan waiting for her reply. To answer Jackie's question, Susan raised her voice over the wind and crashing wave noise. "I found my aunty dead, but that was her old age. I've attended some awful fights where blood and guts have been strewn about, but no, I haven't come across a *dead* body at a crime scene. Some bodies were seriously ill, but they died later at hospital."

Jackie replied with a serious tone, "OK. Listen. We don't know what we'll be faced with when I lift this blanket. We do know it's a young female from this area, Petra. We've had an identity given by the neighbours that found her, along with the address of the deceased. We also know there are injuries. Above all, we must be respectful of Petra. We proceed with dignity, and we try not to disturb evidence that may be useful for forensics ... OK?"

Jackie had been given the information from Paul as he handed over the investigation to her. Jackie wanted to portray utmost professionalism so Susan could learn.

Susan replied, "Thank you boss, I understand." She spoke in a solemn tone.

Jackie replied firmly, "Don't call me boss! I've had enough of those in my time, just call me Jackie!"

Susan sheepishly nodded but in her mind she replied, *Yes boss*. Susan was still young and inexperienced, she had a lot to learn.

Jackie asked for a pair of examination gloves. Susan gave her a pair, but they both struggled to pull them on with their hands being so wet.

Jackie spoke. "Not wanting to teach you to suck eggs, this is a criminal investigation. The gloves are to protect ourselves from blood and any other contaminants, like drugs or chemicals that could be on Petra's body or clothing. These could be absorbed through our skin. We don't know Petra, for all we know she could be carrying a disease or be contaminated with something dreadful that could transmit to us. Think back to the Novichok nerve agent used in the Salisbury incident. Importantly, and in addition, we must not contaminate the evidence with our own afflictions or DNA being left on whatever we touch at the scene. This complicates the forensic evidence investigation; it needs to be about the deceased along with any other evidence found nearby."

Susan nodded in acknowledgment.

Jackie struggled whilst carefully lifting away the blanket against the wind and rain. There lay Petra, motionless and bloodied. Her wet russet hair glistened and sparkled like diamonds within the officer's torch light as the rain drops landed. Her wet face and bloodied nose still showed her beauty. Her body was in the same awkward position as found by Betty, Alan and then PC Paul Landy and the medics. Her blue eyes were open and appeared to be staring. They were motionless and now blinded with her death. Her eyes appeared to be looking at Jackie and Susan.

Jackie spoke. "Petra's eyes have a silent death cry for help, for justice to be done. We need to find reason why Petra died so she … she can rest in peace."

Susan silently wished, *Petra, if only we could hear your last thoughts we could find the reason for your death.*

At this moment they were unaware that Petra had been sexually abused by Alan, whilst both alive and dead. Petra wanted peace … she needed Jackie and Susan to uncover why she'd fallen, why she had no clothing on beneath her bright red jacket and to bring justice to those responsible for her death. As Susan looked towards Petra she thought, *The beauty of her face has disappeared as the ugliness of her tragic death shows.* Susan then focused her eyes, *I can see blood clotting around Petra's nose and neck. Now fewer of the fluid remnants are flowing out from either. What is remaining is being diluted with the pouring rain that gives the impression she is still bleeding. Her contorted body looks awkward and painfully out of shape. This was no simple beach fall. This injury happened from a major fall … and maybe something else that we're unaware of.*

Susan's thoughts stopped as Jackie spoke. "The medic had noticed strange marks around Petra's neck, can you see them here?" She pointed to the welts and continued, "There are red bruises at regular intervals that disappeared behind her neck." Jackie looked upwards to the cliff beyond; daylight was coming. "There aren't any obvious indications, like landslides. It appears far too rocky for that and there is no rockfall here on the beach."

Susan deliberately followed Jackie's eyes as they looked around. Jackie spoke her thoughts for Susan's benefit. "I'm wondering why a beautiful woman would be out alone, in the dark, and on a clifftop in this atrocious weather?" She paused and continued. "I'm going to check Petra's pockets." Jackie looked at Susan's face and thought, *I need to know that Susan isn't going to pass out on me as I examine Petra.* She had noticed Susan's flinch as soon as she saw Petra. Susan was thinking, *It looks to me that Petra was horrifically injured and died very soon after, if not immediately. Crikey! I feel a bit nauseous as I'm looking at the horrific injuries. I'm not a blood-shy white coat syndrome person, I'll deep breathe and try to remain calm. Yes, I do get anxious, but not so scared to postpone tests or surgery.*

Jackie spoke aloud, shaking Susan away from her thoughts. "I'm going to look for any ID, purse or wallet, phone, anything that Petra has. Susan, pass me an evidence bag please." Susan retrieved a plastic bag from her bulging pocket and handed it to Jackie, who thanked her and spoke whilst conducting her actions for Susan's learning benefit. "OK, I'm checking Petra's red jacket right-hand pocket." Jackie's gloved hand inserted into the zipped pocket. "Nothing here, I'll try the left-hand pocket." Soon after she said, "Nothing here either. I'll try the external breast pocket … nope, nothing there either."

Susan looked on as Jackie said, "I'll unzip the jacket to see if there are any internal pockets. It's just very strange that Petra has nothing in her pockets, maybe there's more inside." Jackie unzipped the bright red and now very sodden jacket. "OK I'll carefully pull the jacket open whilst trying not to move her body. Remember, we don't want to move evidence that will complicate forensics." As Jackie pulled open the jacket she and Susan saw that Petra wasn't wearing any clothing upwards from her jeans.

Susan spoke. "Crikey! I don't think that's normal given this weather!"

She had no upper body clothing on apart from her red jacket. Her breasts were exposed, and her chest had painful-looking severe bruises that spread across her stomach.

Jackie spoke, with a slightly shocked voice. "These bruises could be the result of a fall from height, hitting the rocks on the way down, maybe. But what has caught my attention are the now more noticeable red marks around her neck. I can't quite see all the way around to the back of her neck, and I don't want to move her body, that'll be for forensics when they arrive. What I can see, I think, are large necklace chain marks, these *could* be commensurate with some form of strangulation, maybe by the said chain?" Jackie quickly checked the front pockets of Petra's blue jeans, and then made a significant discovery. "Susan, note this ... the jeans are unzipped, and Petra doesn't appear to be wearing any pants, unless they are awfully brief and lower than the open zip. We'll let forensics check this out. It could be she doesn't wear pants, some people don't. Or it could be for some other reason, a sexual overtone maybe. Her jean side pockets are empty. I can't see any rings around her fingers. Right, let's cover her up. I'm calling this in as a potential murder with the possibility of a sexual assault!" As Jackie continued she felt a twang in her head, a strange headache that went as soon as it came. She ignored it.

Susan was taking it all in. Very sad as it was, this is what Susan needed to see and hear from an experienced officer like Jackie. She had only just met Jackie but very quickly felt she was with someone diligent and special. She was thinking, *I want to help Petra and by working in this type of environment with Jackie I could better serve the public in the fight against crime. The perpetrator, if there were just the one, for this hideous crime needs to be caught. That is, if it is proven to be a crime. It could still be a regrettable accident. And maybe this is how Petra dressed, or half-dressed. For Petra's sake, we need to find the cause of death. The forensic experts are the best equipped to establish the cause of death. Time is of the essence ... the tide is coming in and coming in fast.*

Jackie stood, nodded at Susan, pulled her phone out and called her station. She spoke to Detective Sergeant Ian Walsh to request the incident be conducted as a murder investigation. A forensics team and pathologist would be required. It was for Ian to make the decision, as was protocol, to call his inspector so the investigation could be authorised and sanctioned for the forensics team to be included. The pace would now ramp up. Jackie moved carefully to cover the front of Petra's body with her red jacket and then the blanket. She didn't want to disturb anything that may help the forensics team when they arrive. Susan looked on, numbed with the experience but also very appreciative of Jackie's methodical expertise and helpful explanations. They left the scene ensuring dignity and respect remained for Petra. It was just too tragic and very sad that a young woman was found in such suspicious and horrible circumstances.

As they walked across the beach to the ambulance they saw uniformed officers arrive. The officers included a sergeant, who was talking to Paul. As Jackie and Susan approached, the sergeant smiled. The sergeant had previously met Jackie not long after she was appointed to the constabulary and had collaborated with her on other cases.

"Hello Jackie, what a crappy day we've chosen for this investigation!"

Jackie smiled back. "Hi Steph. Yes it's absolutely rotten. It couldn't have been much worse and there's another issue now. I think the tide may be turning quicker than we thought so we need to move fast. Petra's body isn't too far away from the crashing waves. I just hope forensics get here as soon as possible. In the meantime, could you secure the scene with officers and shut off access from everywhere?"

Steph replied, "I'm on it, no problem. Paul has taken statements from the witnesses Betty and Alan. He's not 100% sure, something doesn't sit right, he thinks they aren't connected but has told them they'll be seen again. I'm guessing you may want to interview them later when you've finished here?" Jackie nodded and introduced her new sidekick, Susan.

Jackie was intrigued with the 'not 100% sure'. she knew that the coal-face police officers often smelt a rat and their leads were invaluable. She made a mental note and therefore *did* want to see them herself. She needed to prioritise and wanted to continue her investigation by visiting the clifftop where Petra may have fallen from now that daylight had arrived. She guessed that Petra hadn't been dead for too long and if she had fallen there could be evidence along the clifftop.

Jackie said, "My search hasn't found any obvious possessions, phone, rings or any identity documents on Petra. Forensics may find something as we haven't done a full body search so please could you secure the car park, the entrance road, clifftop and anywhere the public or reporters may appear from. Could you also get some sort of screen and cover for Petra's body? There's just the paramedics' blanket covering her. With Petra's location and this stormy weather it may prove difficult, but please do your best. Also, could you check out the tide times, we may have to move the body before forensics get here."

Steph acknowledged Jackie's requests. She was someone Jackie had confidence in, and they got on better than some others that Jackie had to work with since she relocated here from London.

The coast path ran from Tamora Cove around to Porthcurno with its beautiful sandy beach, up and around the well-known Minack Theatre built into the cliff, and then on to Land's End. The section of path was separated from the numerous farms along its route by stock fencing or hedges to one side. The other side being open to the clifftop along its route. Two uniformed officers accompanied Jackie and Susan up and along the very wet and muddy path from Tamorna Cove. As the group made their way along the path it became obvious that it was a popular route for walkers. It had become windier and felt wetter as the rain became horizontal with the wind gusts. The muddy path narrowed and then widened in several places, flanked here and there by gorse bush and bracken. There were occasional grass sections where the cliff edge became accessible; views of the beach couldn't be seen along all of the route. Jackie and Susan walked along, occasionally and carefully looking down at the beach when they could see it, trying to align themselves to where they thought Petra lay. Jackie had walked approximately 300 metres and thought she was near the potential fall point. She asked for one uniformed officer to go forwards about 100 metres and the other to walk back the same distance. They were to stop walkers and others from entering into the search area.

Jackie spoke. "Susan, you go that way, and I'll go this way, we need to try and find the fall location."

The rain had eased to drizzle as Jackie and Susan separated to walk their separate ways. They carefully walked near to the cliff edge with each trying to see the beach where Petra lay. The cliff view didn't always show the beach below so several back and fros along the path and into the gorse and bracken were needed to find accessible viewpoints. After a while Susan saw Petra below. She looked down at the covered body and tutted to herself. *Petra, how on earth did you fall from here?* She stood upset and with sorrow.

At that moment, Jackie couldn't see Petra and Susan wasn't in sight either. She called out, "Susan where are you?" There wasn't a reply. She raised her voice. "SUSAN, WHERE ARE YOU?"

She heard a whispered voice coming from behind a bush to her left. "I'm having a pee! I couldn't wait! I won't be a minute." Susan reappeared red-faced whilst fastening her trouser belt. She approached Jackie with a slight smile. "Sorry, I needed to go! But I've found Petra and more! Follow me!"

Jackie responded, "Gee, great! I hope I'm not going to walk on your pee!"

Susan replied with a poor imitation of a Scottish accent, "We're going somewhere different to that 'wee' spot." She then chuckled cheekily.

Jackie thought, *Well, at least my student has got a sense of humour, that's good! She'll need it in this job!*

Susan led the way into an opening that she had found after having a discreet pee, out of sight of the two male officers. She and Jackie made their way through the bracken toward the cliff edge where Susan turned, smiled and pointed down to the muddy earth that was very near the edge. "Go careful and look, there! There is Petra below! Now look down near your feet, can you see those footprints, four distinct shoe or walking boot prints? Look, the four tread marks are a similar size! *They* appear to have walked towards the clifftop, side by side. But just here, one pair rotates in that direction and then appears to be at the cliff edge, facing away from the edge. The other pair are facing the cliff edge. One pair of prints in front of the other. Oh wow! Look! ... there are slide marks! Slide marks from the pair of tread marks that were facing away from the edge ... they've then slid over the edge! Crikey ... I wonder if it were Petra that could have been pushed by the person with the tread marks facing towards the edge?"

Jackie interrupted, "Strangled and then pushed over?" Jackie was listening and looking carefully throughout. She had analysed every word Susan spoke and followed the narrative. She agreed with the description and plot. "Brilliant Susan! Well spotted and you've formed a very plausible scenario for this scene!"

Susan hadn't finished as she continued eagerly, "Now, be careful as it's slippery. Carefully look down over the edge and you'll see a diagonal ledge sticking out from the vertical drop. It runs down towards where Petra has landed! If I'm right, hitting that and then rolling down the 40 odd metres would cause huge significant injuries."

Susan smiled as she looked at Jackie who began to grin as she replied, "Good work! From what you've said, my initial thought is it looks like there may have been a struggle, maybe Petra was pushed over. And if you look at the prints only one pair appear to walk away!"

Susan nodded and instinctively started to take photos with her phone, specifically the tread patterns, the directions of each tread and the subsequent slide marks. She even placed her boot near to the tread marks to give a size perspective relative to her known size. Even though her pockets were full of useful items, she didn't have a tape measure. She would ensure she had one next time. For now, her boot size was the comparison.

Whilst Susan took photos, Jackie phoned her boss, Ian, and addressed him as 'Sarg'. "Sarg, we've found evidence on the clifftop that suggests foul play or worse. The deceased may have been pushed from the cliff path some 40 metres above where she lay. Can you advise forensics to check it out as I'd like to visit Petra's home address as soon as. Uniformed are here securing the scene."

Detective Sergeant Ian Walsh was old school and was soon to retire. He didn't like taking on too much work as there was computer usage that he didn't understand. He couldn't adapt to the new ways. If he could skive off, he would, but he now knew that this potential murder investigation was moving at pace. Ian replied, "OK Jackie, understood, I've passed it to Peter a while ago. He may well be there now."

Jackie was pleased with the response; she thanked Ian and ended the call. Ian had been awkward to her since she arrived at the department. He didn't think women were capable of senior roles and felt threatened by her being there, even though for now she was junior to him. No sooner had Jackie finished the call her phone rang. She answered it.

"Jackie, where are you?" It was her boss Detective Inspector Peter Drew. He had a curious tone and no opening 'good morning, how are you?'

Jackie quickly replied with enthusiasm, "Morning Guv, I'm on the clifftop overlooking the beach where a witness found the body of the deceased. She's called Petra and it would appear she's a quite well-known local female. We've found some evidence that there may have been foul play, even murder, and it could be a push off the cliff, along with strange neck marks ... that may have been strangulation from a large neck chain."

Peter wasn't pleased that positive things were happening so soon; it meant more work that he could have done without on a Friday. He had arranged to have a weekend away and this incident could prevent that. He shouted, "Don't you know it's POETS day?"

Jackie replied, "Yes I do, but this is a potential murder investigation."

Peter sounded miffed with his reply. "Whatever, just get on with it."

Jackie liked that but strangely felt her boss didn't. If the case could be closed quickly, he'd return to a less stressful routine.

He spoke again although his tone was different. "I'll get the pathologist there and we'll set up a murder enquiry. Bloody nuisance, this is all I need right now! I was going to Spain tonight! You ensure the scene is secured with the bobbies. I'll be there shortly, I'm nearly there. OK?"

Jackie replied optimistically, "Thanks Guv!" Jackie was pleased with the early find that Susan had made; Jackie wanted to have a meaningful dialogue with her new boss Peter. This was the opportunity, sad as it was, to develop a good working relationship with her boss via a murder enquiry. Since her recent arrival he'd been brusque, rude, distant and evasive. She thought he felt threatened with her being a highflyer arriving from London. Jackie also noted that she heard him mention bobbies. She immediately thought, *He's so stuck in the past! Bobbies* was such an old term, like *coppers* or *the old Bill*. *Officers* sounded much more appropriate, and the word was inclusive of everyone.

Jackie looked at Susan with a smile. "Good news, the Gaffer *is* calling in the pathologist! We'll go down and check that uniformed officers are securing the scene on the beach, and now up here. We don't want any of the evidence to be disturbed. There may be more than we've uncovered, forensics will have a good look." She stalled. "And well done you for finding the footprints! Have you got any evidence markers you could put down?"

Susan smiled with both the compliment and the fact

that she'd already put down the brightly coloured evidence markers. "Look!" She pointed to the ground and there they lay, neatly placed around the evidence.

Jackie smiled again. "Excellent! I initially thought you were a larger person than you actually are! It would appear you're not large at all, just rounded by your pockets being so full of equipment! Come on, let's get back down to Tamorna Cove, it's blowing a hooley up here!"

Susan laughed. "Look at me now, I'm as slim as a slimline tonic!" Susan knew she wasn't large; she had loaded her pockets before they left the station with everything and anything that might be required on her first day with the CID, apart from the elusive tape measure.

Jackie led the way down to the car park but not before she asked both the two uniformed officers to maintain their positions until relieved, so the evidence wasn't disturbed. The drizzle had eased a little, but it was still very windy, Jackie and Susan didn't talk as they both concentrated whilst walking to avoid slipping on the muddy route back to the cove. They arrived safely down at the car park. It was being cordoned off along with the beach area where Petra's motionless body lay.

Jackie spoke. "Susan, could you go back across the beach and take photos of Petra's boots ... particularly the tread marks?"

Susan enthusiastically replied, "I was just about to suggest exactly the same thing! And I'll see if Petra's size is on the underside where the tread is, if not I'll put my boot up against her boot as I did on the clifftop." Susan departed across the beach just as Peter was arriving.

DI Peter Drew reluctantly had to put his badged police rain jacket on as soon as he left his car. He disliked wearing it but he needed it because of the weather. He'd moved on from being a bobby a long time ago. He enjoyed the freedom of *not* being identified as a police officer; wearing the uniform in his role wasn't a requirement. Without it he was anonymous in a crowd. This had its perks when he needed to buy cigarettes, vapes and alcohol. Before smartphones, he used to disappear into betting shops to gamble whilst on duty, he didn't care as he looked like a civilian. Over time it became too risky as he could be identified, but with technological advances, and the introduction of smart phones, he found that it became easier to gamble online. He used his personal phone for his illicit activities. He often bragged about his regular winnings that contributed to his flash lifestyle; he owned several rental villas in Spain that also provided him with an income. He'd return from the many weekends away there with suntans that he could explain away by using his wife's sunbed. She now never left their home, apart from shopping, and that was so she could top up her booze supply. She was a woman glued to the television. The phones and other miniature devices became discrete and intimate tools that were useful to join in with the social media boom, to chat on apps, via text or to search the internet, join dating sites and watch porn, as Peter frequently did. Criminal activity had increased via smart phones. He could still take or ignore calls from his wife Cindy, plus those from his other numerous female friends. He was a brazen outgoing officer, but he held his personal 'other life' close to his chest, knowing that jealousy could be detrimental. He always carried his personal and work phones. This way he could always be one step ahead, including with his employer.

Peter resentfully pulled on his jacket whilst frowning. He strode quickly to the hastily erected temporary gazebo that was anchored down to the metal railings in the car park. It was being battered by the wind but remained secure and offered some respite from the rain. He looked like the weather – miserable and in a hurry. Jackie and he arrived at the same time. Peter's face had a stern appearance as this incident had interrupted his well-planned weekend away in the sun. Jackie had watched him march from his car with a face like thunder. She thought, *Same old Peter, here we go again!*

Peter spoke to Jackie with a snarl. "Well Sherlock, what have you found?"

Jackie thought, *Yeah, got out of bed late! And flippant with it too, calling me Sherlock.* She mustered her reply. "Good morning Guv." She knew Peter liked to be called Guv, so she'd played along just to keep him happy. She continued, "Well Guv, we had a call at 6:15 from a witness, a local farmer, Betty Smith, out walking her dogs. She came across the deceased, Petra Kline, on the beach about 300 metres along from here. The initial witness was soon joined by her spouse, Alan, neighbours to Petra. They knew her well and apparently the hubby tried CPR unsuccessfully. When PC Landy arrived at the scene, he found Petra unconscious and bleeding with the two witnesses next to her. The initial thought was Petra had fallen from the cliff above, some 40 metres high. Paramedics soon arrived and confirmed Petra was dead. However, upon checking, the senior medic noticed suspicious marks around the deceased's neck, lack of clothing and underwear. She reported these to PC Landy who then called the job in. I arrived at 7:37. I conducted a search on the deceased, looking for ID and whilst doing so I saw what appeared to be unnatural marks around her neck, and suspicious circumstances in that she was naked beneath her coat, apart from jeans. That's when I called in to ask for forensics. Uniformed are now securing the scene. Susan and I then went to the clifftop to see where the deceased may have fallen from. Susan found two pairs of shoes or boot prints above where we think Petra fell from. These may indicate some sort of struggle, even a push, and thereafter a fall."

Jackie watched Peter's reactions as he listened carefully. His eye openings narrowed to a slit, like in spaghetti westerns where the actor surveys the surroundings. All that was missing was his cigar. Jackie thought Peter was going to light up a cigarette, instead he discreetly took a vape from his pocket and sucked on the mouthpiece as though it was his final dying breath. His inhale seemed to last forever. When he could suck no more he looked away and slowly exhaled so the vapour wasn't too noticeable. He knew this was against the rules, but like a child, he misbehaved. Jackie caught a whiff of the exhaled vapour. Even though she had never smoked the smell was enticing. It had a strange, captivating odour that she thought was pleasing. He then replaced the vape into his pocket and pulled out a lip balm pen that he used to liberally wipe over both lips until they glistened. His squinting eyes now looked at Susan whilst he thought, *Look at her waddling across the beach like a daft duck!* Jackie had noticed that Peter wasn't looking at her face and thought, *Here we go, same old-same old-fashioned bloke looking at Susan's backside.* She'd assumed Pete – who didn't like to be called Pete, it had to be Peter – *was* looking at Susan's inverted light-bulb shape. Jackie had thought the same earlier, but she soon realised she wasn't actually that shape. Susan's appearance was work overload, simply caused by her regular police officer equipment and now with the additional CID paraphernalia tucked into any of her many pockets in her overlarge hi-vis jacket.

Peter responded to Jackie's feedback with a sarcastic tone and a shrewd smirk, "Well done Sherlock! And to your partner Watson! I've yet to meet that ugly duckling!"

Jackie was used to this type of remark; it was meant sarcastically rather than praise. She thought, *Peter definitely is old school, he has a chip on his shoulder the size of a potato.*

Peter continued, "So, Sherlock, what about the initial witness and her husband, not related to you are they?"

Jackie didn't know quite what he meant so asked, "Sorry Guv, I don't quite understand?"

Peter smirked again, slyly, "They have your surname! How do you know the farmer and his wifey weren't involved?"

Jackie paused. He was now becoming arrogant and sexist. She bit her lip and said, "They aren't related, I don't know them, and I don't know if they were involved, and yes, they could be. I've yet to interview them, they're on my to-do list. PC Landy has taken statements from them; he didn't think they were involved but wasn't 100% sure. Forensics and the pathologist's investigations may well find DNA samples and other evidence that could incriminate them … or not."

Peter had heard enough to satisfy himself. He abruptly asked, "What's next then, Sherlock?"

Jackie bit her lip, just a bit harder this time. She replied, "With your approval Guv, I want to visit the deceased's address first. Uniformed have already sent Dawn, the liaison officer, to pass on the tragic news to Petra's boyfriend, Alex Munro. I'll give her a call to see how the visit went, assuming she gained access." Jackie thought, *I was going to end my sentence with your honour, but I won't. I'll also use the word approval rather than permission as the latter implies subservience, and I'm definitely not going to be lesser than him, particularly where I've come from … the Met.*

Her thought ended as Peter barked, "Well, get on with it Sherlock, don't just stand there, it's POETS day! Oh, by the way, watch those farmers, the Smiths, particularly Alan.

He's been in trouble before with younger women, plus he gambles and drinks." He then abruptly turned his back to take another long inhale of his vape. He held his breath so the contents of his vape soaked into his lungs. He surveyed the scene as though he were master and commander of his patch. He slowly exhaled, knowing the rain and wind would disguise his vapour trail. Again, he used the lip balm pen. His attention then focused on Susan.

Jackie was very familiar with male colleague responses. She thought, *They could be rude, sexist and old-fashioned. Equality is still a long way off. Whilst in the Met I've endured belittling comments from above, below, and sidewards. I've had frequent abusive language from the general public, been physically attacked by both men and women. I have a thick skin but still I've never liked the abuse, who does? I feel for Susan, here in her infancy with the police, she has it all to come. It's still a tough world for females. Change is happening but at a slower pace than is often publicised. And Susan has to work for some idiots like Peter.*

Jackie left the gazebo just as Susan arrived. Jackie walked towards her. The weather still remained unpleasant and could hamper the investigation.

"Hi Susan, did you get photos?"

"Yes I did!" Susan replied whilst wiping away the rain from her face. "And guess what? I'm not a forensic expert but in my opinion the tread patterns on Petra's boots are definitely the same as those we saw on the clifftop! I'm not sure, but I also think the other tread patterns are remarkably a similar style."

Jackie smiled as she replied, "Good work, Watson!"

Susan looked quizzically at Jackie and asked, "Eh?"

Jackie replied, "Doctor Watson, as in the Sherlock Holmes stories, Sherlock's sidekick, Watson!"

Susan laughed but didn't really understand as she replied,

"So, you're the great Sherlock and I'm the doctor?

Jackie smiled and spoke. "Well, you and I have been elevated into the high ranks of detective sleuths! Anyway, that's what our illustrious 'Guv' is calling us. I'm taking it as a compliment. Go careful cos he's watching us! He's rude and arrogant!"

Susan didn't quite see it that way and was quite angry with Peter's flippancy. Jackie then said, "The Guv has said its POETS day and we're to get a move-on!"

Susan didn't understand so asked, "*POETS* day?"

Jackie said, "*P*iss *Off E*arly *T*omorrow is *S*aturday!" They both laughed as Jackie added, "I wish it were POETS day for us ... somehow I don't think it will be!"

As they walked away from the gazebo, their infamous Guv stood, smirking at them. He nodded as they passed. Jackie realised Susan was just about to say something she might later regret, so she pulled her arm without Peter seeing. She turned to Susan and discreetly placed her finger over her lips to indicate a shush. Now wasn't the time to remonstrate with their boss. Jackie led Susan away to her car. She held Susan's arm all the way, but not before Susan smiled falsely at her new boss. Peter smiled and nodded back. Jackie explained the conversation. They got into the car and Susan said, "What the hell is that guy on, he's so misogynistic?! He could be the most arrogant bloke I've come across in my two years of service, and I still haven't met him properly! I wish I hadn't asked for this secondment!"

Jackie was sympathetic with her reply, realising Susan's inexperience. "Susan, the force *is* changing, as is society, but slowly. It's sadly still a male-dominated environment, as are a lot of workplaces."

After a few moments to digest Susan responded, "I remembered 'kudos' as one of those words that had done the rounds several years ago, everyone started to use it, it became part of a catchphrase, but then it disappeared. Nonetheless, I don't like sexism in its raw form, just as much as I dislike racism and criminality. And I think Peter *doesn't* really hate me in the context of the true meaning of misogyny; he's just a bloke!"

Jackie smiled back with her reply. "Peter would find no kudos in that, would he?" They both laughed as Jackie continued, "Steady Susan, 'just a bloke' could be misconstrued as a misandryist comment!"

They both laughed out loud together knowing that they wouldn't put the world right today … but they could at least move closer to finding Petra's murderer.

Jackie called Dawn, the liaison officer, with her hands-free steering wheel button. Jackie didn't expect an answer as that team were always busy. It was ringing and surprisingly Dawn answered after two rings.

"Hello Jackie, how's you?" They knew each other from previous encounters at work.

Jackie replied, "I'm fine, how about you?"

"Yes, all good with me. I guess you're calling about Petra?"

"I am, have you visited the address?" said Jackie with a quizzical expression.

There was a deliberate pause from Dawn. "Yes I have. The last job of my nightshift, I'm on my way home now. Shattered I am! I found it strangely sad as I met Petra's newlywed husband, Alex Munro. He's the local Farmer Combined representative around here and really well known. He's very upset with the news I had to deliver. He said he went to bed at 10ish last night and Petra went out for a walk, alone. I thought that was odd. He said it's something she does regularly as it helps with her work, she was an artist. He wakes this morning 5:30ish and she's not returned. He worries and goes out looking for her and comes home 7ish without finding her. Calls a girlfriend, Suze, who then appears whilst I'm giving him the sad news. They then support each other as though they are *really* good friends, and I mean *really, really* good friends ... *lovers maybe.* Am I making sense here?"

Jackie and Susan looked at one another. Susan lip-whispered, "Very strange?"

Jackie replied to Dawn, "Hmm, sounds a bit odd, doesn't it? Do you think there is more to it, like if they're lovers they may have a motive to remove Petra?" Jackie didn't explain what she meant as Dawn wouldn't have known about the clifftop evidence.

Dawn replied, "Well, that's what I'm thinking. They do appear very close, unusually so. I was going to mention it to whoever got the job and I'm glad you've got it, cos if anyone can smell a rat, you can! Note it when you visit ... the comfort they're giving one another. The number of kisses, and on their lips too! It just doesn't feel right. There could be motive, that's what I think. Anyway, see what you make of it. Let's catch up for a drink sometime."

Jackie replied, "Thanks for the heads-up and yes, let's fix a date sometime. Cheers."

The call ended. Jackie looked at Susan and said, "It takes all sorts to make liquorice and when you open a box of chocolates you never know what one you'll get if you don't look. In other words, let's not judge anyone until we have more than motive. We need evidence!"

Susan smiled at Jackie as they drove out of Tamorna Cove to visit Petra's home. Susan said, "Mmmm, that does sound weird. Even very close siblings wouldn't kiss on the lips, would they?"

Jackie concentrated on her driving along the windswept lanes that had a covering of autumn leaves moving wildly in the wind. She replied, "Let's arrive with an open mind. It's always a traumatic time when we inform someone about death. I've seen some really strange things that turn out to be 'normal' in the recipient's mind, but they are actually so wrong. It's different things to different people. It's the law breakers we need to find."

As they drove, Jackie enlightened Susan about the resentment she'd received in Cornwall from certain members of the CID team. "I took a demotion from the Met to get this job, but my previous position was a DI, Peter's equivalent. I think he resents me as does Sergeant Ian Walsh. I guess they both feel threatened with me being here, they may think I'm after their jobs! I've worked for the Deputy Chief Constable here, DCC Tony Martin who has also recently arrived. He was very good and got his promotion to Cornwall through hard work and determination within the Met. We were assigned several cases that we cracked when no others could. I've heard on the grapevine that he wanted me here and was waiting for the opportunity to do just that. I think he was hoping one of his DIs here would go for redundancy sooner, namely Peter Drew. I guess I would have slotted into his place and then his boss's place when he retires next year. He would shed two of the old boys. By the way, don't repeat our conversations to anyone. Particularly what I've just said. No one knows about my connection with Tony."

Susan smiled at her and said, "Go girl, go! YTL"

Jackie smiled back and asked, "What does YTL mean?"

Susan laughed and replied, "You The Lady!"

Jackie smiled back and said, "That's SO yesterday, I prefer YTW, as you are for finding the footprints!"

Susan frowned as she asked, "YTW? WTF?"

Jackie laughed aloud. She knew Susan's WTF meant What The Fuck, so she replied, "YTW means You The Woman. It sounds better than calling us 'ladies'. That's such an old folk term for us females, we're women!" They both laughed out aloud. LOL!

CHAPTER 4
THE DOOR KNOCKERS

At Petra's home in Dartin, Suze and Alex were comforting each other; they felt terrible and were in a never-ending nightmare. They were both sobbing and oblivious to anything else other than Petra. Their needs were raw and basic at this moment in time … time was irrelevant, they just needed comfort and compassion. They found this with each other. Suddenly they were interrupted when there was a series of loud knocks coming from the front door. Alex froze. He turned to look out into the hall. Suze paused her pain as best she could and turned to look. There, through the opaque glass of the front door, was a darkened figure that became brighter with continual movement. Again, three loud knocks were heard as the silhouette could be seen banging against the wooden door frame with a clenched fist. "Who could that be?" whispered Suze quizzically with her soft sniffling voice as she looked at Alex.

He replied as he wiped his eyes, "I don't know … I'll go to find out."

Alex approached the hall slowly and stiffly, whilst he recovered from what he now knew was an uncomfortable sit on the cold kitchen floor. The only warmth had come from Suze's hug, and she now wasn't close by his side. He switched on the hall light as he passed it, the gloomy weather had darkened the space. He used the tissue that Suze had given to him to wipe his eyes and nose. At that moment he frowned, as there was an additional figure, this time carrying something very bright, something fluorescent yellowy green. Alex arrived at the door and slowly opened it to find Jackie and Susan struggling with their jackets; it was now raining harder than before. Jackie, who banged on the door, was pulling up her jacket zip as the door opened. She politely asked, whilst simultaneously showing her ID, "Hello, are you Alex Munro?"

Alex looked startled as he replied, "Yes?"

Jackie continued, "Do you know Petra?"

Alex's eyes welled with water, "Yes, Petra is my wife – was my wife." A comforting arm slid onto his shoulder; it was Suze. Suze had seen the visitors whilst brushing dust off her jeans. She made her way silently from the kitchen to be by Alex's side. Her face was blushing red and both eyes were swollen with the crying. He gave a minimalist smile showing his appreciation and then pulled her with a gentle hug. Jackie replied to Alex with a neutral look, although she had noted the *so* obvious body language, and an atmosphere filled with intensity from the consoling couple.

"I'm Detective Constable Jackie Smith, and my colleague is Constable Susan Hill." She briefly glanced at Susan, whilst introducing her, but could see Susan struggling to put her arm through the jacket as the wind was gusting. The gusts kept blowing the jacket's armhole away from Susan's approaching hand as she tried to insert it into the sleeve. Susan looked up with awkward embarrassment as she grappled with the situation. Jackie tutted and steadied the jacket to enable Susan to insert her arm into the hole. Susan then acknowledged Suze and Alex from her slightly stupid position with an embarrassed smile. Alex hesitated as he watched. His blurred mind didn't fully understand why he now had two police officers on his doorstep with one who looked foolish as she couldn't even put a jacket on. He also couldn't make sense as this horrid nightmare continued to play out in his mind. Without warning, cold rain spat against his face as the wind gusted; it suddenly woke Alex as he flinched with the unexpected splashes. This was like a bucket of water being thrown over a boxer after being felled by a thumping great punch to the head. Alex, like the boxer, semi-conscious and without full control stuttered, "Hello … can … can I help?" His blurred vision, behaving as if it were an auto-focus camera, was oscillating to and fro whilst adjusting from the fuzzy to sharp image of the two officers now standing before him. His focus settled. "Can I help?" he repeated. Realisation that the two women were police officers hit Alex, but this time with reality as he said, "Do … do come in, the weather is horrible." He opened the door fully and beckoned Jackie and Susan to enter.

"Thank you," said Jackie as she and Susan entered. Suze beckoned to take their wet jackets, which had only just been put on. Susan closed the door and followed Jackie to Alex and Suze as they walked towards the kitchen. No words were spoken as the group walked through the now well-lit hall. Jackie and Susan looked in admiration at the decorated walls with the bright photographs and excellent pieces of artwork. Susan noticed the pair of familiar-looking muddy walking boots on the floor, and the damp coat hung next to hers. She assumed both were Suze's. As they entered the kitchen it was obvious that Suze and Alex were terribly upset.

Jackie asked, "Alex, if I may call you that?"

Alex replied, "Yes, please do."

Jackie looked sympathetically towards him and Suze as she said, "Thank you. Please call me Jackie and my colleague is Susan. May I ask who you are?" Jackie was quizzically looking at Suze.

Alex replied, "Oh, er, sorry … I should have introduced

you to our dearest best friend Suze Barnard." Alex didn't realise he had said 'our' meaning Petra and himself. "Sorry, I … I mean, Petra has gone." He started to weep. Suze put her arm around him. Alex continued whilst sobbing, "I meant … well, I don't really know how to say it now, *Petra's* gone, Suze was … is our … I mean my best friend."

Jackie recalled Dawn's comment and immediately thought about what Alex had just said, *he means my dearest best friend and lover Suze*! Suze smiled as best she could with Alex's awkwardness and held out her hand to shake it with the officer's.

Suze said, "I'm really sorry for the state we're in. It's been shockingly horrendous." As she finished speaking a tear began to run from her eye. Alex was holding his tears in, as best he could, but they came out and soon fell down his face. He slouched onto the nearby sofa. Suze joined him as they embraced again to console each other.

Both Jackie and Susan were taken aback and began to feel the pain that may be real or false. By now Suze had run out of tissues from her pockets. This had become obvious to Jackie who asked Susan to get tissues from their car, but Alex replied assertively, "No!" as he waved a pointed finger towards a kitchen drawer.

Jackie thought, *Crikey! His abruptness and actions were immediate. Could it be he's a controller? I wonder if he's role playing and pretending he's innocent?*

Suze got out of the chair to get the new tissue box whilst snuffling and asking, "How about a nice cup of tea or coffee?"

Alex smiled and replied, "That would be great, thank you. I was about to make one earlier but couldn't as we both succumbed to the upsetting news."

Suze looked at Jackie, "Would you both like tea?" She

wiped her eyes whilst looking at the two officers.

Jackie replied, "Yes please, that would be very nice, thank you." Jackie had another thought, *Suze is very accommodating to Alex, is she subservient to him?*

Susan used the moment to politely ask if she could use the toilet. Suze replied, "Of course you can, it's back through the hall, on the left." Susan nodded a thank you and walked into the hall pulling the kitchen door closed behind her, deliberately. She hadn't needed to pee; she had noticed the wet and muddy walking boots on the hall floor and wanted to discreetly take photos and check their size. They looked very similar to the ones Petra had been wearing. In particular she wanted to take photos of the tread pattern to see if they matched those from the clifftop. She was aware her actions could be discovered at any time. She talked to herself in her thoughts, *OK Susan, be quick and quiet. Look and listen for movement coming from the kitchen. Don't disturb the scene. Don't touch anything as you haven't got gloves on!* She then discreetly took photos of the boots and also placed her booted foot next to the corresponding boot and took another.

This, she thought, *will enable me to compare the sizes on the clifftop footprints, and these with my boot size.* When Susan had finished her covert operation she flushed the toilet. At first glance she thought the tread patterns matched. Although excited with the comparison, she wouldn't talk about her assumption right now. She'd relay it to Jackie when the opportunity was right, and that may not be now. She double-checked that her bodycam was still operating as she couldn't remember switching it on when she arrived. It was, so she relaxed. After rinsing and drying her hands, she innocently walked back into the kitchen with confidence that she had learnt from Jackie earlier.

Susan entered the kitchen as Jackie asked, "So, Alex,

when was the last time you saw Petra?"

Alex was taken aback; he rolled his eyes and blew out "Phew!" It was only a short time ago that Alex had seen Jackie's colleague, Dawn Tew, and he had already answered similar questions.

Jackie realised and apologised. "I'm sorry about the repetition but we need to be very precise and clear, so we get the facts right." She finished with a soft polite look. "Dawn is a police *liaison* officer and we're *investigative* officers. We need to ascertain the circumstances that led to Petra's death."

Alex, clearly upset, answered, "The last time I saw Petra was yesterday evening about 10:10pm."

Jackie promptly asked, "What frame of mind was Petra in, was she OK?"

Without hesitation Alex asked, "Why ask such a question? She was fine. We had a conversation about a TV programme we'd just watched and afterwards she said she'd go for a walk."

Jackie responded, "Didn't you think it was rather late to go out alone and in atrocious weather?"

Alex was getting perplexed and became anxious. He tried to rationalise and then thought he'd answer the question more fully. He took a noticeable deep breath in through his nose and replied, "No, I didn't think it strange. She'd regularly go out in the evening to walk. It cleared her head and helped her sleep, plus it was good for her work. She's an artist. Walking anytime, day or night, gave her inspiration. She'd go out in all weathers, with a head torch if needed. She'd walk a few hundred yards, or several miles ... sometimes she'd be gone for hours. One time I did worry ... I had gone to bed, I usually did if she went out late at night, but for some reason I awoke about 2am to find she wasn't here. I got up and went out looking for her. A few miles away I found her asleep in a cave above the beach where we, or she and Suze, would sometimes swim. The cave gave her inspiration for her work, and she just fell asleep. She was fine. After the first time, she often stayed out all night. Sometimes in the cave, and other times wherever she found a good place to be in. She liked the Paidwick Castle ruin, and would often walk through, or come back that way. She would sometimes sleep out there too. As I said, her nocturnal walks gave her inspiration and escapism. The solitude helped her mind. She would sometimes sleep out anywhere that felt good. In the early days of our dating relationship, I would walk with her. But after a few years I tired of the walks and random sleepovers. It was Petra who needed the space for her thoughts, not me. So, I gradually withdrew from accompanying her."

Jackie immediately picked up that Alex mentioned about the beach cave, just above where Petra now lay and that she wore a head torch. She had noticed the cave whilst on the beach when she looked up to the clifftop. It was also noted in her mind that Alex mentioned the precise location where Petra was found. She'd visit the cave at the next opportunity. At first Jackie thought Petra had strange behaviour but 'escapism' resonated with her. She had served in the Met. The harsh environment of city policing, with more intensive crime, ever-increasing workload and other aspects had led to Jackie's 'escapism' to Cornwall. She applied for a transfer to be at the end of the world. This, she dreamily thought, would allow her to unwind and work in a less-demanding environment where she could ultimately retire de-stressed. She didn't want to burn out or get seriously injured as some of her colleagues had. Plus, she had finished a long-term relationship with an officer who'd been having other relationships without her knowledge. It had felt very awkward working with him thereafter, and with the same colleagues who knew both her and the ex-partner, Steve. Collaborating with Steve thereafter had felt both weird, uncomfortable ... and not right. Jackie's escapism dream bubble popped soon after her transfer to Cornwall. The working environment was tainted with the same 'isms' as in the Met – racism, sexism and ageism. These had quickly shone through when she arrived. A new ism had appeared; jobism! This, she thought, was the fear people above your grade have about those highflyers below, like her, who could threaten those above. But she had wondered if Steve's behaviour was actually deliberate so she wouldn't get his job, *or* leapfrog over him with a higher grade job to become his boss. After arriving in Cornwall Ian Walsh and Peter Drew soon popped her bubble of work serenity. Thinking about Petra, Jackie had worked in some parts of London that were *definitely not* the type of place that females could safely go out alone for a late-night walk. To sleep out alone in the city was unheard of unless you were homeless and walking alone in some areas was also scary. But this was very rural Cornwall. It was a popular destination for holidays, particularly with the camping and surfing communities that were an accepted, and needed, part of the economy. Single women and men would frequently walk and wild camp near the various paths and places around Cornwall; it was the norm. Wild camping wasn't approved but it happened particularly with the coast path walkers. As for Petra's night-time activity it now didn't appear too odd to Jackie, given Alex's explanation.

Jackie's mind quickly returned to Alex, and she asked, "When did you become aware that Petra hadn't returned?"

Alex replied with a gulp, "I was aware she wasn't here when I awoke this morning at 5:30ish. I got concerned straight away so dressed and came downstairs to make a coffee. I made a cafetière optimistically thinking that she'd arrive home soon. I waited a while but then I saw it was raining heavily and had got a lot colder; I became worried." Alex sobbed and gasped, holding his hands against his face. He cringed, as could be seen between the gaps of his fingers. He took another deep breath, removed his hands, and continued. "I put some wet weather clothing on and went out to look for Petra at 6ish. I noticed she'd taken her red jacket and head torch when I put my gear on."

Jackie remembered where she found Petra ... *there wasn't either a torch or a necklace.* She continued listening to Alex.

"It was dark, but dawn was coming. Her favourite route was coming back via the Paidwick Castle ancient ruin. She'd walk amongst the disused tin mines and along the coast path to the cliffs above Tamorna Cove. It's a seven-mile route, there and back. It takes about two hours if you stomp it out. I figured I'd start the route in reverse as she would come home a different way than the way she started. By that, I mean she'd do a circular walk, so I set off in the direction she'd normally come home from. That was Paidwick Castle." Alex paused. Susan and Jackie were listening intently, with Jackie taking notes, plus Susan's bodycam was recording the interview.

Suze interrupted, "I've made tea, now seems a good time to drink." She passed the drinks around. Susan again noticed the intimate body language between Suze and Alex. Jackie had seen the same and her thoughts again alluded that maybe the two might be more than friends. She thought, *There was appropriate loving comfort in times of tragedy, but the comfort between Suze and Alex is way more than that, more like lovers' comfort. There could be motive here.*

Suze had been listening attentively too, some of this was new to her, it wasn't in such depth with detail when Alex had spoken to Dawn earlier. As she sipped tea, she held her hand out to Alex for comfort. He gently rubbed his thumb over the back of her hand in appreciation as he spoke. "I assumed Petra had either done the long circular walk, or as she loved the mystic of Paidwick Castle, gone there ... it was always her go-to place. She felt a connection with there as it's steeped in myths, which she loved. She preferred to go there at night. She loved the myth where there was the connection with King Arthur. Apparently his mistress lived there when it was a castle. Anyway, I walked there as I assumed she'd come through that way or even be asleep there. She had told me many times that she'd stayed over in the ruin. Anyway, she wasn't there so I walked further. After an hour there wasn't a sign of her anywhere, so I turned around and came home. By then I was more concerned as it was about seven this morning. The strange thing is, Petra knew Suze was coming to stay this weekend. The plan was for us three to go out for lunch." Alex gulped again. "That's why I worried when I awoke. She was never late for anything, especially if Suze was coming."

Jackie had a few more queries that were significant and important. She spoke before Alex continued. "Alex, did Petra have a phone?" She asked this basic question as Alex hadn't mentioned calling Petra.

Alex immediately replied, "Yes, it's over there on the worktop, next to mine. When Petra walks, she likes to be remote from the outside world, including work. If her phone isn't there then I know she's at work in her gallery at St Ives. If it weren't on the worktop I would have called her before I left to look for her." When Alex had finished, he took another sip of tea as he was thinking, *All these questions may have been asked to eliminate me from being involved with Petra's disappearance ... or they are to incriminate me!* He started to feel uneasy.

Jackie noticed as she asked, "Why did you stop after half an hour and then come home, why didn't you continue around the walk?"

Alex became noticeably uneasy, he wasn't making eye contact with Jackie, preferring to look at Suze. Alex replied, "Where I walked to, there is a high spot. From there I could virtually see the 360-degree route; I would have seen Petra because she was wearing her headlight torch, it was still dark. As I said, I left through the back door, her red jacket had gone, as were her walking boots *and* head torch. I couldn't see her head torch light in the darkness from the high spot, so I came back the easiest route, which was the way I took from here, half hour there, half hour back." Alex paused and then abruptly asked, "Why are you asking these questions, you're not suggesting I was involved with her disappearance, are you?"

Jackie was a seasoned professional who had come from the murky policing life within the capital city. She'd had dealt with all types of crime and criminals ... and had heard all sorts of alibis and stories made up by villains in the attempt to avoid arrest and conviction. She needed to know if Alex, or Suze, had participated in this tragic event. Petra's death could have been an accident, but Jackie's experience and intuition thought not, particularly with the two pairs of footprints at the clifftop *and* the mark around her neck. The forensic examination of Petra's body could indicate the cause of death. Jackie knew most murders are committed by known associates, including partners, spouses and friends. DNA samples would be taken from Petra's clothing and body. These would be matched against DNA from the police database and those samples collected as part of this investigation. Jackie needed to get Alex and Suze's DNA samples.

Jackie answered Alex's question. "Alex, I'm sorry but I have to establish the facts. I need to map out the events that led to Petra's death with a timeline. I'm not accusing you of anything and I really appreciate your answers." She had a serious look but smiled politely when she had finished.

Whilst the questions and answers were being asked and given, Susan drank her tea, but she was also observing Suze. She was thinking, *Suze looks quizzical at the questions but again the chemistry between her and Alex is shouting out and they do appear very close. I think there may be more than friendship between them; I wonder if they're in some sort of relationship, maybe friends with benefits, and if so, could they even be a murderous pair!*

Jackie didn't want to over pressurise Alex. She still had an open mind, but it was becoming skewed towards him and Suze. She just needed to ascertain what had happened, and if they had a role in Petra's fall. At this point she turned to Suze and was about to question her when Suze was quicker off the mark and said, "Would anyone like more tea?" This momentarily threw Jackie's thoughts; she realised her mug was still full.

"No, I'm fine, I'll just finish this one, thank you."

Susan and Alex didn't want any more so they shook their heads when Suze looked at them.

Jackie finished drinking her tea and asked Suze, "Suze, how were you contacted and what time did you arrive here?"

Suze now felt the pressure, as had Alex earlier, but she knew the questioning was relevant, so she replied, "Alex called me just after seven, he was distraught. I was staying at Petra's gallery apartment in St Ives. I caught the train to St Ives last night on my way here from London. I thought that would be better than arriving too close to lunchtime today if I had caught the train to Penzance this morning. The three of us were going out for lunch today and I was to stay over here for the weekend after lunch. I often come here to stay over, I have keys to both places, such is our friendship. I arrived here to be with Alex just after eight. I was asleep when Alex called me, so by the time I was dressed and had arranged a taxi it was 7:30ish when I left St Ives."

Jackie listened to Suze and thought she spoke far more eloquently than Alex. Alex's voice had a definite Cornish accent, that she thought was lovely and very masculine, whereas Suze sounded eloquent and more refined. Her voice also had a particular soft feminine sensuosity that Jackie admired. Jackie could just hear a very slight West Country burr to Suze's accent that came out in certain spoken words. She carefully chose her next question. "How frequently do you visit Alex?"

Suze felt apprehensive as she answered, "I come to see *both* Petra and Alex as often as I can but generally come here every other week. Petra and Alex are my best friends." She said this and started to cry and then said, "But now Petra's dead!" She began to wipe her eyes as tears welled.

Jackie paused whilst Suze recovered. Alex had again put his arm around Suze. Jackie realised that enough had been asked here for now, apart from one last question. "Alex, did Petra have any relatives?"

He replied, "Yes, her mother and father, they live in Germany, and you've reminded me that I must inform them. They have no other children. Petra was the only child. Petra has dual nationality, UK and German." He sobbed again.

Jackie was looking for both evidence and motive. She saw a great show of compassion, and maybe a love affair, *more than maybe* she thought. There didn't appear to be great wealth in the cottage and Alex drove a company 4x4 utility truck, which was seen on the drive. The cottage wasn't lavish or expensive looking with its contents. In fact, Jackie thought it just looked a typical country cottage with comfort rather than expensive items. It appeared as a home that was lovingly lived in, and the great arty feel was obvious. Jackie, however, remained uneasy about the relationship between Suze and Alex. She still had some doubts. But their explanations did seem plausible … for now. She was slightly reassured that there wasn't anything jumping out at her to warrant further questioning. She also needed to talk to the witnesses, Betty and Alan. She had noticed Susan's fidgety body language and wondered if she had something to say. Jackie looked at Susan and asked, "Susan, I think I've covered everything I want to for now, is there anything that you'd like to ask?"

Susan replied, "I just want to check some details about Petra, if I may?" Susan was looking at Suze and Alex.

Alex spoke, "Yes, yes what would you like to know?"

Susan had been taking notes throughout the visit but wanted to clarify some points. "Thank you Alex. Is Petra spelt 'P e t r a'?" She spoke one letter at a time. Alex nodded. She then asked, "What is Petra's date of birth?" Alex gave the date and said she was 36. "Could you spell Petra's former surname?"

Alex said, "K l i n e." He spelt it one letter a time and said it was German.

Jackie then interrupted, "Actually, I'd like to take statements from you both, given the gravity of our investigation, and your DNA, OK?"

Both Suze and Alex looked bemused. Suze said "Why?"

Jackie had a serious appearance as she looked Suze in the eye. "Petra's death is unexplained at this time, so we need to build a picture from all those connected to her. DNA is a routine process that helps our investigation to be thorough."

Suze nodded with a better understanding as she replied,

"OK, thank you, I now realise. I worried that you were thinking we were involved with Petra's death!"

Jackie smiled at Suze as she said, "As I said, we need to fully investigate everyone as part of the process."

Suze smiled back, "Yes, that would be a good idea. I get the way you are asking questions and the way you appear to be uncomfortable with us both comforting one another, there may be some doubt about us. Well, *we* have nothing to hide, *we* are innocent of anything untoward against our beloved Petra. The sooner you eliminate us from any sort of foul play the better!"

Alex looked at Suze and appeared pleased with her response. He too wanted to show his innocence and believed that science could help eliminate them from further undue pressure. Suze and Alex were separated into different rooms to give their statements and DNA mouth swabs.

After the statements and DNA had been taken they reconvened in the kitchen. Jackie spoke. "Thank you both for your help in such tragic circumstances. Please do accept our sincere condolences. Oh, did Petra wear a wedding ring?"

Alex immediately replied, "Yes. A lovely gold one with a single diamond." He gulped again. "It's upstairs in our bedroom."

Jackie continued, "OK, didn't she wear it regularly?"

"No, she hardly ever wore it. It interfered with her painting. I nearly didn't get her a ring as I knew she wouldn't wear it. She does like it though and keeps it as a token of our love."

"Oh, I see. She could have worn it around her neck attached to a chain."

Suze looked and smiled to Jackie. "What a brilliant idea! We'd never thought of that."

The word 'we'd' stuck with Jackie as she immediately thought, *There most definitely is more to Suze and Alex's relationship!* She replied, "Thank you. We'll leave now but will be in touch with you again as we progress our investigation. Should you have any further questions then please contact either myself or Dawn, the liaison officer."

Jackie gave her official Cornish Constabulary business card. Suze and Alex stood to see their visitors out. Susan led and again became fidgety as she walked through the hall. Suze opened the door; they were met with the wind and rain. Jackie and Susan said their goodbyes and walked through the rain at speed to the car.

Jackie sat at her steering wheel and quizzically looked at Susan. "Are you OK, do you need another pee? You're awfully fidgety."

Susan looked pleased with a smile that showed off her pearly white teeth. "I think I've got a lead!"

Jackie quickly replied, "What is it?"

Susan said, "You remember the tread marks we found on the clifftop?"

Jackie frowned. "Yes?"

Susan's smile enlarged, "And did you notice the wet muddy boots in the hall? ... I did! And I've taken photos of the treads! Guess what? They match with the ones on the cliff! And they're the same style and size as Petra's!"

Jackie's face immediately lit up. She looked at Susan with an 'oh my God' expression and said, "Outstanding Watson, well done!" She continued, "Well, I'm thinking aloud now. We could go back and ask more questions. We could take the boots as evidence. We could ask both to come to the station. Or we could go to the cove and await the initial forensic report?" She hesitated. She wanted to check out Susan's ability to prioritise the situation.

Susan was put on the spot but had already thought the processes through and assertively said with another beaming smile, "I would take the boots as evidence! Leave out additional questions for now and go back to the cove."

Jackie was impressed as she smiled. "Well done Watson! Now get those boots into an evidence bag!"

Susan went to the door and knocked. A short while later Suze opened the door with a quizzical expression, "Hello again?"

Susan looked down towards the muddy boots and said, "Hi Suze, I need to take those boots as evidence."

Suze frowned as she spoke, "Why?"

"Part of our investigation has shown footprints near to Petra. I noticed your boots were muddy and wet. We need to confirm that *your* boots weren't those used to make the prints."

Suze looked shocked as she put her hand over her mouth and opened her eyes wide with disbelief. She moved her hand away and replied, "You cannot be serious? You don't suspect that I've been involved? Or are you? You do ... don't you?"

Susan kept a calm serious look as she spoke. "Suze, this is helpful for our investigation. We need to get facts and evidence. Taking your boots could assist with our investigation to understand what actually happened to cause Petra's death." As she was talking, she grabbed the boots and put them into her large evidence poly bag. She wrote a receipt and gave it to Suze who stood and stared with her hand over her mouth.

Alex could be heard crying from the kitchen; he had listened to the conversation. Susan didn't want to prolong the experience so politely thanked Suze and suggested that she may want to phone Dawn, the liaison officer, for assistance.

Susan quickly made her way to the car. She sat with a solemn face as Jackie asked, "How did it go?"

Susan turned. "Suze was shocked when I asked for the boots. It could be she's totally innocent, or *she* was at the crime scene. And do you know what?"

"What?"

Susan replied, "Our job is shit at times. We have to make awkward decisions at difficult times and rarely get thanks for doing such a crap job. Suze could be totally innocent, but now she's under immense pressure as we're indicating that she is a suspect. If so, she could do anything … she could commit suicide! Alex is bawling his heart out. He could do something irrational." Susan looked eye to eye at Jackie as she continued, "But, either, or both, *could* have played a part in Petra's death."

Jackie replied, "Yes. That's why we do our job. Innocent until proven guilty. We must be sure and certain. With our investigations people can get awfully upset and offended where, if innocent, no offence was intended. But, by proving the guilt the guilty will get caught and pay for their hideous crimes. We do indeed have tough jobs."

Susan smiled and nodded. Her first day with CID was an eye opener. One that she wouldn't forget, and it wasn't even lunchtime. "I'm hungry, what about you?" she said.

Jackie smiled back with her reply. "Actually, let's go back to the cove and see how forensics are getting on. We could get a snack there if someone's got any spare. And who knows, Peter may have organised something, or not!"

Susan replied, "Thank you Sherlock. And there's more! I'm going to do a web and social media search on *their* three names. It's surprisingly easy to find information about people on social media. And did you note, Petra was an only child?" She got her phone out and started to research the names. Jackie smiled and thought, *Work has just got interesting with my sidekick, her confidence is coming through along with an obvious inquisitiveness. I may enjoy working with her more than some others in the department!* She started the car and drove to Tamorna Cove.

CHAPTER 5
HEAR NO EVIL, SEE NO EVIL

As Jackie approached the cove she noticed a police roadblock with two officers standing by. Jackie was still relatively new to this constabulary and not yet well known. She slowed down, and as she was in her own unmarked car she and Susan showed their IDs to pass through the block. The controlling officer smiled and beckoned them through. She slowly drove down the slight hill to the cove's small car park that was now full of police-related vehicles. The weather was still rotten, and the temporary gazebo had been removed. There were now several larger vehicles; a Mobile Command Unit (MCU) and a Habitation Vehicle (HV). The HV had a kitchenette, table, seats, a sandwich selection with an honesty box plus a pair of unisex toilet cubicles. The investigation was now well underway with busy officers beavering around. They were dressed in their distinctive personal protective equipment (PPE) adorned with clear plastic covers as it was still raining.

Jackie and Susan entered the MCU to find out who was in charge. She met the Communication Officer, Sally Newton, who said Peter the Guv had gone back to the station. Jackie was pleased to hear that he wasn't on-site so she and Susan could freely check out what had happened in his absence. Sally gave Jackie an update including the arrival of Forensic Pathologist, Dr John Smedley who was with Petra.

"Good!" replied Jackie.

Susan asked if Sally could run checks on the police database with the names and addresses that Alex and Suze had given. She then looked at Jackie who smiled and said, "Right Susan, are you fit, well and ready?"

Susan smiled as she replied, "I sure am Sherlock!"

They put on PPE with the protection plastic covers. They carefully walked towards the erected shelter that was over Petra's body. They noticed the tide had come in and was nearly at the structure. Forensic officers were conducting a methodical search on the remaining section of the beach for evidence whilst they could. They were assisted by a line of uniformed officers slowly trawling across the stones and rocks. The leeward side of the canopy had an entrance flap that was blowing wildly in the wind; there was a uniformed officer standing by to guard the scene within. Jackie, in plain clothes, showed her ID. Inside stood the Forensic Pathologist, Dr John Smedley, along with the Crime Scene Photographer, Brian Ludlow. They were discussing items of interest with their backs to Jackie. Jackie hadn't met either of them before so politely introduced herself along with Susan.

"Hi, I'm DC Jackie Smith and this is PC Susan Hill." The noise of the wind on the fabric skin was very loud, almost unbearably loud. John and Brian hadn't initially heard Jackie. Jackie realised and repeated her introduction, but shouted, "HI, I'M DC JACKIE SMITH!"

The two looked around and John replied loudly, "Hello Jackie, we've been expecting you. Peter said you may well look in. I understand you found Petra earlier?"

John spoke in a very eloquent manner and smiled warmly as he finished. He was an older chap with large grey bushy eyebrows that protruded over his spectacles. He was balding and looked well-groomed with a clean-shaven face apart from his hairy ears that matched the intensity of his eyebrows. Both he and Brian wore PPE suits with their hoods now folded down as they had completed their initial examination. The way John spoke with his smile lessened any apprehension that Jackie may have had. She could do without another arrogant Peter type.

Jackie replied, "Yes that's right. PC Landy was the first to the scene. PC Hill and I followed soon after." She introduced Susan, who smile and nodded. Jackie continued, "We both saw the suspicious marks around Petra's neck, as well as the other injuries, with the neck marks not fitting too well with Petra's fall."

Petra lay, now uncovered where she fell. John closed her eyes after completing his examination. He was still peering at Jackie over his spectacles as he answered, "Absolutely right! The neck marks appear to have been caused by a garrotte, particularly on the rear of the neck where bleeding occurred. I think the marks were made from a chain, maybe a strong necklace chain, and it could be one worn by Petra rather than a third party. Forensics are searching for it now in this awful weather, but they haven't yet found a chain or necklace. There also appear to be finger bruise marks indicating some strong force was used, like hands being gripped around her throat in a regular strangle hold. If the necklace were strong someone could have grabbed it in each of their hands and used it like a garrotte wire. There's a small cut in the front of Petra's throat; it could be the chain snapped with the force applied as strangulation took place. We've taken DNA samples from the neck marks and the wound where those hand marks were; they may be caused by the perpetrator's nails. Our biggest problem right now is all this rain; evidence may have washed away or be covered in mud; plus, the tide is coming in fast."

Jackie looked at Susan, to check out she was OK. She was attentively listening to the conversation. Susan, in her mind, wished *Petra rest in peace.* She wanted to cry as she looked at Petra's awkward body positioning, but managed to hold it in. Jackie couldn't hear Susan's thoughts or know her feelings so assumed she was OK.

Jackie turned and replied to John, "Do the other injuries match with a fall from height?"

John took his spectacles off as he looked into Jackie's eyes with seriousness. "Yes they do … but some of them don't. I need to examine her further, there's only so much I can do inside a tent with these horrid conditions. We're about to take Petra to the morgue, it's being organised as we speak. The tide is coming in faster than we thought!"

Jackie was perturbed at not knowing what John meant about the non-related fall injuries and she wanted him to clarify. "What do you mean?"

"Well, her upper body clothing is missing for one thing, including a bra, if she wore a bra. Her jean fly zip was undone; I couldn't see a how fall could cause the zip to open. Again, I think she either hurriedly dressed because, we know not, *or* someone else dressed her. She isn't wearing pants and again that is if she wore them. This makes me think all her clothing had been removed and hurriedly put back on, either by her or someone else, for whatever reason. There are so many what ifs. She may have been under the influence of drugs or alcohol, either self-induced or administered by another … there also could have been some sexual overtone with the way we found her scantily clad. I need to conduct a proper autopsy in the morgue to confirm all these thoughts. As everything is sodden wet here, I don't want to contaminate anything unnecessarily."

Jackie and Susan listened attentively. Jackie broke the intensity. "OK, I understand, thank you."

John spoke in a softer tone. "There is something else. Petra, I think, and tests will confirm, died as a result of her fall or strangulation. But ... I think she had an experience of something *before* her fall. What I mean is she may have been the subject of intoxication ... alcohol, drugs, self-induced *or not*."

Jackie bravely looked at John and then to Susan, to check that she still appeared OK. Jackie hated these processes from a personal perspective but whilst at work she had to try and see these sad events just as that same four-lettered word – work. It was difficult to leave work at work, particularly this type of work. The seriousness played out in her mind, again and again. It was difficult to block out any deaths by murder when she was tasked to find closure for the deceased. She couldn't let go until the case was resolved, no matter how long it took.

Jackie turned to Brian the photographer and asked, "Brian, have you been to the clifftop and taken pictures of the footprints that Susan found?"

He smiled as he spoke. "Yes, I got to those before it rained really hard. I quickly found your evidence markers. I have some good images. We've covered them to try and preserve them for when the weather improves. We'd like to take impressions from the tread patterns."

Jackie responded, "Could we look at your images of the footprints?"

Brian walked closer towards Jackie and Susan whilst fiddling with his camera to find the images. "Here, these are the pics!"

He stood with his camera so both Jackie and Susan could view the images. Susan quickly got her phone readied and quickly toggled to the images she'd taken of Suze's boots and those from the clifftop. At this point Jackie said, "It was Susan who found the imprints and subsequently lay the markers."

Susan smiled as Brian replied, "Well done you! If they

weren't there we may have lost them due to the weather. Thank you!" They then compared both their albums of photos. The tread patterns did appear to be the same.

Susan spoke. "These images are the boots that Suze had taken off at Alex's home, he's Petra's husband. They had the same tread marks as seen indented in the mud on the cliff above. Your images look remarkably similar to mine. On the clifftop there were two sets of footprints that had walked towards the cliff edge, both with similar tread patterns. One pair turned around and faced the other pair. The prints facing away from the edge were those that Petra is wearing." Brian nodded to her as Susan looked at him. She continued, "Petra was either pushed or naturally fell, hence the slide marks off the cliff. Whatever happened, someone wearing identical boots to those Suze wears, that we now have as evidence, was there. There is now a suspect … Suze." The four of them looked at each other. Susan continued, "We have Suze's boots as evidence in the car … I'm guessing you'd like to have them?"

Brian replied with a beaming smile, "We most certainly will!"

Susan commented, "Wow! We've definitely made quick progress!"

John followed her comment, "Yes, excellent progress Susan, well done you! Let me move Petra to the morgue where I can examine her thoroughly without being hampered by this poor weather! I need to categorically prove all that we've discussed here."

Brian followed on, "Forensics are still on the cliff doing a deep search. There could be additional evidence, hopefully the chain, or segments from it. I'll ask for samples of the footprint soil, as well as plaster casts of their imprints and will keep you posted. It's great you've got Suze's boots as evidence for us to analyse. We'll compare the soils on the boots to see if there's a match."

Jackie was as pleased as punch, given the pace of events that only arose this morning. She mentioned the missing head torch that Petra was wearing, but it hadn't yet been found. She thanked John and Brian for their good work whilst Susan copied her photos to Brian's album.

Jackie and Susan walked back to the cove, pleased with their meeting. As they neared the MCU they saw Mr Grumpy, alias Peter Drew. Susan had called him this discreetly under her breath when she saw him standing there, peering through the window whilst they haphazardly made their way to the van.

He'd watched his duo as they came across the beach from the forensics tent. He muttered, "Here they come, *now* both like a pair of waddling ducks, quack quack!"

Jackie and Susan entered the MCU dripping wet. Peter turned to Jackie and spoke abruptly, "OK Sherlock and you Watson, what do you know that I don't." He then sat casually in a swivel chair whose backrest allowed him to lean backwards in a relaxed style. He clasped his hands together behind his head, elbows swung backwards with his legs provocatively outstretched wide apart.

Jackie replied ignoring his bold posture. She looked directly into his eyes. "Well Guv, we've made some significant progress. We have a person of interest in Suze Barnard, Petra and Alex's *best* friend. I'd like to interview her again sometime after forensics have examined her boots that we've just handed to them. We've compared the tread marks on the cliff, and they matched very well to Suze's boots. The footprints on the clifftop indicate there may have been a struggle and maybe a push."

Peter said, "Good work! I'm impressed. I might start

calling you Puss in Boots, referring to the boot evidence and the fairy tale of the same name!" He laughed out loud and slapped his right thigh with the palm of his hand whilst saying, "Boom-Boom!" in a joke manner.

She ignored his joke and replied, "I need a search warrant, could I have your approval?"

"Yes you have! And I've just thought of your new name! Pussy Galore!" He laughed so loud he started coughing and spluttering like a smoker's cough. He was now referencing the saucy character in a James Bond movie.

Jackie didn't think his sexist comment was funny given the gravity of the investigation. There was a hint of sexism in that his word 'pussy' could have a sexual connotation. She said nothing but noted it. Hopefully, his behaviour was being caught on Susan's bodycam. She humoured him with a pert smile whilst having a dumb look as she rolled her eyes upwards, like the dizzy stupid stereotype he envisaged *all* females were. She'd play his game.

As he continued to chuckle, and when he had stopped spluttering, he spoke. "I'll call the magistrates office right this minute! Now piss off and solve this case!" He laughed out aloud and spluttered again.

Jackie thought he was a very sad man but managed a smirk just to humour him. She was going to curtesy but thought that may make Peter feel he was a king. He definitely wasn't, he was more like the court joker. She didn't want to play his game; she knew it would provoke more of his same outdated and unwanted humour. Susan stood behind Jackie. She kept quiet throughout but was fuming. They both left the MCU angered by their boss's sarcasm and outwardly sexist posture. Plus, he seriously crossed the line during this murder investigation where the victim's anatomy was being used as a joke.

When they had closed the door Susan said, "If wit were shit, he'd be constipated!"

Jackie laughed and replied, "If that man were also a mathematician *and* constipated, he'd be full of shit ... he'd have to work it out with pencil!"

They both laughed aloud and followed up with giggles. When they had regained composure, they walked to the HV for their lunch break where there were sandwiches and coffee. Jackie thought, *Crikey, it's alright for us women to joke rudely and take the piss out of a bloke, but not for Peter to have the same option back to us women ... is that OK?* She left the thought for another time. She was concerned whether his behaviour was recorded on Susan's bodycam, if so it would include hers and Susan's jokes thereafter.

Jackie spoke. "We could report his lewd comments. We will report them, but not now. If we do, we'll lose our momentum. The fallout could hamper our investigation. Petra deserves justice. Was your bodycam recording in there?"

Susan replied, "No, sorry it wasn't. I switched it off before we entered to see the pathologist and Petra."

Jackie replied despondently, "Good! It'll be our words against his, but an uphill struggle. Just as well we didn't record our own jokes about him. Let's leave it for now, he'll have his judgement later. The warrant should be a straightforward process as he's in the MCU. Only a DI or above can request the warrant. Once the request has been made and the magistrate has approved and signed it, the warrant becomes valid." She hoped there would be a magistrate available. As luck would have it *there* was in Penzance, some 30 minutes away. Jackie was too junior in her current rank of DC to collect it and protocol had to apply. She now relied upon either DS Ian Walsh or Peter, both who were not particular buddies of hers, to make the journey to Penzance.

As they finished their refreshments and vacated the HV they heard, "Oi, you two!" They turned to look at the MCU. There stood Peter yelling from the doorway, "Oi, you two! Get your arses back 'ere!" The sarcastic DI knew he was going to be asked for the warrant. The duo walked to see Peter. He smirked, "I know Pussy, I want me to collect the warrant. Well, I will, but it'll cost you a pint, or two, in the tavern next to the court ... OK?"

Jackie was bemused. It was against police rules to drink alcohol whilst on duty, including lunch breaks. She smirked back toward Peter; he may have been trying to catch her out. She replied, "Actually, I'll get us tea and cake from the café next door!"

Peter smiled. "OK, it's a done deal, let's go before I change my mind." He got up and reluctantly put his police logo jacket on. The trio left the MCU and walked to their cars. Peter spoke as he approached his car, "We'll go in the two cars, I need to see the magistrate about another case. Once you have the warrant you can go and issue it, OK?"

"Perfect, good idea," replied Jackie. They got in their respective cars and drove in convoy to Penzance.

They arrived at the magistrates not long after Peter. After a short time inside, Peter appeared holding the long-dated warrant. "Here you are ladies, just what we need. Now let's get some cake!"

The café was nearby, they entered, sat and ordered refreshments. After some general weather chat Peter said, "Jackie and you Susan, my new A team, let me tell you something. I really don't mean to be sarcastic, sexist or rude. I'm sorry, please don't take what I say as personal insults. I've been in this job too long, old habits die hard and they persist. Some of the old school ways are difficult to shake off. We're moulded from our experience and change isn't easy the older we get. Jackie, I was aware you were my rank in the Met, and I really thought you'd come here full of bullshit, but you haven't. In fact, I'm really pleased with how you've settled in and that you haven't got an axe to grind. I realise it must seem strange for you reporting to Mr Happy, aka DS Walsh, but that's how it is. I don't make the rules, we have to abide by them. But, and I mean this, your experience and persona shine through thick and thin. You're a good copper and I like that. You have great intuition and know the processes well. Plus, you can smell a rat, that's what we need. I'm really pleased how this case is going and I'm happy to let you run with it. Just keep me in the loop and don't do anything over your current grade without clearing it with me first. We have protocols that we have to follow, as you well know. Neither of us must overstep our grades, but a little bit here and there could go unnoticed, if you get my drift?" He finished with a sly look. He continued, "I called John the pathologist on my way here. He's given you both glowing praise with your speed and investigative prowess. He said you'll both be a credit to our constabulary. He's thinking Suze is our prime suspect and that Alex may well be connected. My money would be split on them, or Alan Smith, the farmer. We've had run-ins with him before. He's a dimwit with no brain. So well done you two!"

Jackie was taken aback with this out-of-nowhere positivity. Suddenly she realised Peter was, just maybe, OK after all. Perhaps he was just tired of the routine, disgruntled or had been passed over for promotion. *Whatever*, she thought. Jackie guessed he had nearly done his time, his '30', and that would leave him with a good pension. Maybe he just wanted a quiet life. She smiled as she replied, "Well thank you Guv.

I really appreciate your comments. I hope we can now work together on an even keel, without the need for sarcasm or sexist jokes?"

He nodded in acknowledgment along with a smirk. He then looked toward Susan, smiling as he said, "Susan, I know you've only just finished your probation. We were planned to meet this morning, but you had the call-out with Jackie. Your induction to the department most definitely has been rapid. You've been assigned to the best DC I have. You'll learn a lot from Jackie. Your records show you performed really well during probation both on and off the job, you came top in your class at college. Yes, a few gaffs on the way, as we all do, but nothing serious. Keep up your good work and you too could go far. From what I've seen from you this morning I'm extremely pleased. Well done!"

Susan appeared delighted. Peter's comments were the icing on her cake as she chomped into her lemon drizzle.

Jackie responded, "We've yet to see the Smiths, they're on our to-do list."

The trio ate their cakes and drunk their tea, the atmosphere between them had significantly improved following Peter's earlier rude comments. The café meeting had a positive vibe about it. The obnoxious Peter had shared a personal insight that showed he could be a nice person, and just maybe be a good boss. *Time would tell*, thought Jackie.

Peter gave her the search warrant. Jackie asked, "If we have reasonable grounds with either Alex or Suze we'll make an arrest. If not, we'll wait for forensics to produce some additional evidence?"

Peter looked at Jackie shrewdly as he narrowed his eyes. "Jackie you're as experienced as me, if not more so. You decide, I'll back you with whatever you do. Just keep me in the loop. I think either of them need to be high on our watch list, and don't forget Alan Smith!" He smiled pleasantly. "I even have a new name for you both, you're now my Rottweiler Team! I know you're both strong-minded and that you can look after yourselves."

Jackie took this compliment, and she too smiled back appreciatively. "Thank you Guv!"

The day wasn't yet over but she accepted this as a huge 'pat on the back.' Susan was delighted that within hours of arriving in the CID she'd already made a significant impression after her wobbly start early that morning.

Jackie and Susan finished the lunch at the café and departed to re-visit Suze and Alex. Peter went back to the magistrates office for his other business. Jackie had another twang in her head, a nagging feeling. It was similar to the one she felt earlier on the beach when she had the call-out to Petra. The feeling worsened when she thought about Peter's nice comments ... but she still thought, *He's a sly old fox. Maybe a wolf in sheep's clothing. Why has he suddenly changed his persona?*

CHAPTER 6
THE SEARCH WARRANT

When Jackie got into her car she took paracetamol for her head. As she set off, Susan asked, "Are you OK Jackie?"

She replied, "Yes, I'm fine just a headache. Maybe this depressing weather with its low pressure."

As Jackie drove Susan spoke. "We have to put up with so much crap. If only the men could understand what we women have to cope with! What with bloody monthly periods, the dreaded PMT, the pill, pregnancy, childbirth, HRT, the menopause and then the men! Sometimes I wish we could turn the menopause on and off like a switch, as and when *we* wanted it. Why? I hear you ask, well menopause is Greek for 'men pause' we could then pause the men as and when we wanted it like full stop, no, end of or period, as the Yanks would say." They both chuckled. She continued, "Wow, Peter really did show he has a better side to him. Perhaps he's realised you are the real deal and good at your job.

Jackie replied, "*We're* the real deal. You have been outstanding, and I'm so pleased you're doing fine. Well done you!"

Susan thought about what Jackie had just said. "Thank you. My life has been a struggle. I've had to work really hard coming from a non-white UK background. I'm UK born but as I have Asian parents and I look Asian I've had to put up with so much crap in my life. The racial taunts at school and now as an adult. The bullies, being beaten up … but I've made progress and I'm getting through it. The sad thing is it still happens now even though I'm an adult. It's everywhere. It's sad. That's why I joined the police. I want to represent *all* peoples and help *them* fight injustices from the bad guys ....and girls, no matter what colour skin they have, what disabilities they may have, where they live, poor or rich. We should all be respectful to one another as equals. We all deserve justice for wrongdoings. We're all human irrespective of our differences and we all live here, on this one planet. We are sisters and brothers. We should all respect all religions and all races. Respect disability and disadvantaged people. Respect people's choices with their genders and choice of orientations. As long as there is respect, understanding and law abidance, then we'd all get on better with far less hate and crime."

Jackie looked amazed, "Well done! I'd vote for you if you stood for election! Well done you for persevering and holding your head high. As Peter said, and I agree ... you'll go far!"

As Jackie drove she was thinking about the sudden change with Peter's persona. *From rudeness and arrogance to respect and apology. This had happened to me before within the Met, from another senior officer. The officer was herself a criminal and was identified during an investigation.* With that thought, her mind was nagging again, her slight headache had returned. She changed her thought to relieve her nag and focused on the weather. She thought, *The tree and bush leaves are changing colour from green to vibrant copper shades. The brownie red shades remind me of Petra's magnificent russet hair colour.* Jackie was abruptly back in work mode, she didn't care as her thoughts continued. *When I first saw Petra's body, this morning on the beach, her beautiful hair, even though it was soaking wet, was swirling and dancing about in the wind, like a free spirit.* She gulped as she thought, *She is now a spirit in the sky, gone away forever. Petra didn't deserve to die like this. Someone, or some people with evil intent took her life away. That evil person, or persons, need to answer for their hideous crime and we need to bring justice for Petra. I'm thinking it could be Suze or Alex ... or both, but I need more evidence and motive. I've yet to interview the Smith farmers and I've had a tip-off from Peter about Alan.*

They arrived some 25 minutes later and parked in the lane out of sight of the cottage. The weather had changed to heavy drizzle rather than rain. Alex's utility vehicle was still in its same position on the drive so they guessed he would be home. Susan switched her bodycam on. Jackie spoke before they got out of the car.

"Right, I'll knock on the door and you be prepared to give chase if we have a runner. If Suze or Alex are guilty, and they suspect we're onto them, they may well run to avoid arrest. Have you got cuffs?"

Susan was familiar with the process and was prepared. "Yes, I'm all sorted with kit and ready to go! I'm nourished, hydrated, fit and keen to run!"

They smiled at each other as they quietly left the car, closing the doors silently. Jackie crept to the cottage door with Susan deliberately several metres behind. Susan readied herself, standing back near the gate where she had visibility over each side of the cottage and to some degree the rear garden. She would be the runners' chaser.

Jackie stealthily approached the door and pushed the bell button. It still wasn't working so she knocked on the door with her knuckles in the common *tapeti-tap-tap* sequence. There was no answer. She peered through the opaque glass; it was dark in the hall. Jackie knocked again; she was firmer this time. Suddenly, light appeared through the hall as the kitchen door opened. As the door opened further a figure could be seen walking through, at the same time the hall light lit.

"Someone is in!" whispered Jackie in a surprised but satisfied way whilst giving a thumbs-up gesture in case Susan couldn't hear. *This is good*, she thought because if Suze and Alex weren't in it could be that they may have absconded, inferring their guilt.

The hall figure was Alex. He opened the door, his face red and puffy eyed. "Oh? Er, hello again. I didn't expect to see you so soon?" He had a curious expression with a frown.

Jackie had a serious look but politely smiled. "Hello Alex, may we come in?"

"Ye … yes please do," he nervously replied, moving backwards whilst holding the door open.

Jackie passed him and went into the hall, followed by Susan who nodded at Alex as she passed.

As they started to walk, Jackie asked, "Is Suze here?"

Alex answered, "Yes, she's in there." Alex opened the kitchen door and there on the sofa was Suze. She too had a sorrowed red face and a tissue in her hand. As Jackie entered, Suze had a look of surprise on her face.

"Hello Suze," spoke Jackie in an assertive way.

Suze wiped her nose, "Hello again Jackie, I didn't expect to see you again today. Come in, would you like tea or coffee?"

Jackie replied, "No thank you."

Susan looked at Suze and thought she was simply one of two things, innocent or guilty. Susan was getting anxious in her mind that here, sitting on the sofa, could be the murderer of Petra. She thought, *Suze, you do act rather well, and you have more confidence now … I wonder if it's you we're after?* Jackie calmly sat at the end of the sofa away from Suze, just in case blows were thrown at her. Susan watched and remembered her college training. She moved to stand on the other side; Suze was now sitting in the middle of the two. Susan discreetly checked her handcuffs were easily accessible.

Jackie spoke firmly to Suze whilst Alex stood nearby listening attentively. She didn't produce the search warrant at this time. Jackie said, "Your boot tread marks match those near to where we found Petra."

As with the earlier visit there was a sudden 'oh my God!' expression on Suze's face, that then immediately blushed. She gasped with both hands over her mouth. She slowly removed them and spoke firmly. "We've already had this conversation. You *really* don't think I was with Petra this morning ... do you?" She started to cry. "*You do*, don't you?"

Alex rushed towards the sofa, but his sudden movement caused Jackie to quickly stand to be less vulnerable. Susan had stepped forward to intervene. Almost immediately Alex slouched onto the sofa to comfort Suze by putting an arm around her, holding her safely. Jackie and Susan relaxed their stances with facial expressions of seriousness. Susan let go of her baton; her hand was ready to retrieve and use it. She thought, *Here we go again, lovers in need ... indeed!*

Jackie sat again at the end of the sofa, she spoke. "Suze, we've found something that we needed to check out further. At this moment in time there is a photo match with the clifftop footprints with the tread on your boots. Given this evidence we now need to search this property." She looked at Alex as she finished the sentence. "Alex, I have a search warrant authorising us to search this property." She produced the document and handed it to Alex.

Alex spoke. "We gave you the boots and our DNA sample earlier, why did you want our DNA?"

Jackie knew exactly why she wanted their DNA. She had thought, *If the DNA from Suze or Alex closely matched any that may be found on Petra's neck wound, then either or both could become prime suspects. If Suze's boot mud analysis produced a sample that matched the clifftop then it could be valuable additional evidence to help with the conviction. We still need motive for another piece of the jigsaw, that's what I need.*

Alex said, "I can't believe what I'm hearing!" He appeared stunned and was awaiting Jackie's answer to his DNA question.

She replied, "DNA helps us to eliminate persons of interest from further investigation." She stopped there rather than inflaming the issue by adding her thought, *DNA could also identify those connected with the investigation.*

Alex replied, "OK, but you do realise that Suze and I are extremely well connected with Petra. *We* sleep with her; *we* were a threesome. Suze and Petra are the same size and share each other's clothes, they both have the same boots and are the same foot size!"

Both Jackie and Susan raised their eyebrows with what they'd just heard. They glanced at each other; their hunch now had a twist in that there was a threesome relationship. Things had suddenly become complicated with the investigation. They had understood that Alex and Petra would sleep together, they were married. But there was now a permutation in that Suze would regularly join them. Jackie thought, *This is a key aspect. If* Alex *were part of the process that wanted Petra out of the way he'd then have Suze without interference. The same would be true from Suze's perspective. I did wonder at the previous visit if the threesome were sexual partners, as well as just good friends. My hunch has now been confirmed. Perhaps jealousy had crept in ... maybe Petra didn't like sharing Alex with Suze ... maybe Suze didn't want Alex to be with Petra. It is all maybes. I need motive and more evidence.* She looked at Alex and spoke assertively. "We want to search your home now, please!"

Jackie hadn't alluded that she wanted to find the necklace

chain that was used as a garrotte around Petra's neck. Suze appeared shocked, it wasn't her home to disapprove, or question the reasons, she just sat and stared at Alex. Jackie continued, "Alex, I'd like you and Suze to remain here with Susan whilst I conduct a search. If I need your help with anything I'll ask for your assistance, OK?"

Alex replied, "OK, go wherever you want, I, *we*, have nothing to hide. We just find this really upsetting." He slouched next to Suze, cuddling her. They quickly kissed each other.

Suze spoke. "Our secret is out, we were embarrassed to mention it earlier. Please do respect our privacy."

Jackie thought, *This could be an alibi fib to cover their dreadful deed.* Or *I must remember they're innocent until proven guilty.*

Jackie had PPE gloves and evidence bags; she started the search upstairs by going from room to room. She was very particular, methodical and curious with the new slant on the three-way relationship. Jackie soon found various necklaces in the main bedroom, she assumed this was Petra and Alex's room. The chain links appeared strong enough to function as garrottes and she took them as evidence. She noted that the very large bed wasn't made, and it had the appearance that two people had slept there recently and assumed they were Petra and Alex, although there were three sets of pillows. As she went through the drawers and wardrobe it became clear that two women were using the room. The wardrobe had three distinct sections of clothing, two women's and a man's. Jackie found photograph albums that had photos of the three. As she flicked through the pages the images showed them in happy times. They all looked joyous with each other's company. The closeness and warmth between the three shone through. There did indeed appear to be a lot of love equally split between the three. Jackie thought, *I see love between them, but I'm envious that I don't have* that *love, the love I lost by betrayal from Steve, my partner.* Another album had nude erotic photos where the three shared embraces, images showing the three in bed, in the bath and on the beach, enjoying each other's company and closeness with one another. As Jackie flicked through the pages she thought, *These aren't lewd pornographic images; they show the intense love between the three. They're warm sensual portrayals of their good relationships. What stands out for me are the smiles, joy and laughter the three to have for each other. There doesn't appear to be any negativity between either of them, they appear as equals.* She stopped her thoughts as her mind nagged again. *I need paracetamol again!* Jackie now had some doubt with her previous thoughts ... *There doesn't appear to be motive for Petra's death within these images of joy between three consenting adults in love with each other.*

Jackie went into another bedroom that she assumed was a guest room or Suze's room, where she found similar gothic pendants attached to strong necklace chains on the sideboard. She bagged these and shouted down, "Alex, could you please come here?" Alex proceeded up the stairs. Jackie asked, "Is this the bedroom where Suze sleeps?"

Alex replied, "No, she sleeps in the main room with us."

Next to the made-up bed there was a bag. Jackie asked, "Are these necklaces and this bag Suze's?" Alex nodded.

Jackie searched Suze's bag. There were clothes and other items associated with a stopover but nothing Jackie felt relevant with her investigation. She looked under the bed and through the drawers and wardrobes, as she had done in the main bedroom. The third bedroom was more a storeroom and home office rather than a bedroom and nothing unusual appeared to be there, just a chair and a desk without anything of interest within. The bathroom didn't produce any evidence.

Jackie had called Alex as she wanted to go up into the attic, this being the final upstairs check place. Alex lowered the loft ladder and switched on the light. Jackie had a look, but nothing was there apart from the very well-insulated small and large water cisterns. She quickly looked in the cisterns with her torch. These, she had learnt, were very good hiding places to stash cash, drugs and other illicit items inside waterproof poly bags. There wasn't anything inside apart from a dead mouse that had drowned. Jackie didn't stay in the attic too long as she didn't like spiders or other such crawly things. Cobwebs were abundant, Jackie noted, *Cobwebs are good indications that spaces haven't had human movement, so there isn't likely to be suspicious items of interest.*

Jackie and Alex made their way down into the lounge and then into the remaining rooms. The search didn't produce any further evidence. As they returned to the kitchen Jackie dangled the bags in front of Suze. "Suze, I've got your gothic necklaces as evidence, along with some more of Petra's. I've also taken some photo albums. I'll give you a receipt later."

Suze went bright red again. Jackie noticed and thought that this could be a guilt blush. She'd seen it before on criminal faces when they're embarrassed … or guilty. Suze was aware that Jackie had viewed their private personal and very intimate images. "I trust you'll keep the album images private?" Jackie didn't smile. "Trust me, I'm a police officer."

Susan had realised Suze *wasn't* going to do a runner so she searched the utility room, pantry and kitchen whilst Jackie and Alex were upstairs. She didn't find any incriminating evidence, that is, until her eyes glanced at the calendar next to that loud ticking clock, which continued with its obnoxious *tick-tock, tick-tock, tick-tock.* That morning Susan noticed the calendar showing the month of October, and the two photos of Petra and Suze, with the word **Myluv** handwritten in a blood red colour over Petra's image. But now she could see another **Myluv** handwritten below Suze's photo. They appeared as **Myluv & Myluv**. She wondered, *Was this significant?* Susan didn't know but she took the calendar as evidence. Suze had watched but said nothing.

Jackie looked at Alex. "OK. I've had a thorough look around and we've taken some items that may help our investigation. This is usual when a crime of this magnitude has been committed. You and Suze *are not* under arrest. We'll be in touch as the investigation progresses. I'm sorry for both your loss and the apprehension that you have. It's a really awkward time for us all. As you can appreciate, Petra has died in unusual circumstances and we must therefore investigate fully all aspects."

Alex and Suze looked extremely upset and both nodded, they could do nothing more. They again hugged one another.

"Finally," said Jackie, "please don't go anywhere without letting me know first, we may need to talk again."

Jackie and Susan left, with Alex showing them out. They walked to the car carrying their haul of bagged evidence with expectations that forensics may find something to link Petra's death to either Suze, Alex *or both*. As they drove away, they shared with each other what they had seized. Susan was intrigued about the photo albums and was desperate with her naivety to look at the images.

Jackie spoke firmly. "You can't open the evidence bags once they've been sealed, unless you have a valid reason. If you do, you have to document it. The images are private and personal property and show the love between three consenting adults. They have altered my opinion from my initial thought that there may have been upset between Suze, Petra or Alex. In fact, the opposite is displayed. There appears to have been a huge amount of warmth between the three. Nothing within the albums leads me to think there was any animosity between any of them. However, I'll keep an open mind until all the evidence has been checked. Also, and I'm not suggesting you would, there have been incidents where officers foolishly share images to colleagues on social media apps. They've lost their jobs through stupidity. Beware of such things and don't you ever do anything like that. There will be an opportunity for you to see the images under supervision of a senior officer, as the case progresses. The learning experience will be beneficial."

Susan wasn't miffed, she understood fully what Jackie had said. "Jackie, I hear what you say. Thank you. I have heard about these unscrupulous officers that have done such things. Some have even shared corpse pictures with their mates! Disgusting! They bring all that we try to do down to the gutter. We lose public confidence, and yes, they should be sacked and convicted like any other criminal!"

Jackie replied, "We walk a fine line and must always endeavour to serve the public."

Susan replied, "I remember the horrendous PC who selected random people from bars and clubs. He'd engage in conversation with them, spike their drinks and take them to car parks where he molested them. They were unaware as they were drugged. He took pictures of his victims whilst molesting them. It was only by chance that one of the victims realised she was being chatted up by a stranger who was coming on to her in a very lewd way. She rightly asked the bar person, *Is Angela there?* He was familiar with this coded request and mentioned it to his manager, who called us. The perpetrator was named and shamed in the media with lots of other victims, women and men, coming forward after seeing his photo. He was convicted and jailed."

CHAPTER 7
BACK AT THE RANCH

Jackie drove to the base at the cove. The rain was easing, the wind had lessened. Leaves were falling but not at the rate they were earlier. It was becoming calmer until Susan began to fidget whilst reading her phone.

"Are you alright?" spoke Jackie as she glanced at the uncomfortable looking Susan.

"No! I'm bloody not!" She continued to fidget whilst violently pulling her trousers one way, and then the other. She pushed her trousers away from her backside with a hand on each thigh. She lifted her buttocks forward then up off the seat whilst tugging her trouser legs down.

Jackie laughed, "Have you got a wedgie?"

Susan stopped and froze. She looked uncomfortably and quizzically at Jackie.

Jackie laughed again, "Have you got a wedgie? That's when your pants get stuck in your bum crease!"

"Well actually, yes and no! I cycled at the gym last night, spinning, I did 40 miles. My backside is SO sore now and the bones within ache!" Susan laughed back at Jackie. She rummaged again with her trousers trying to free her pants from her buttocks. "That's it! I'm sorted"

Jackie responded. "When we knock-off you could go to the bike department at Brook's. They have those hideous cycling trousers with the built-in silicone bum pads. Next time you go spinning at the gym they'll make the ride experience so much more comfortable. You'll feel you're riding on air; but you'll look like a right idiot when you dismount. The pads make you look like you've pooed yourself! All baggy around your bum cheeks!" She roared with laughter; Susan joined in too. Jackie said, "It'll be the end of your megasoreass!"

Susan looked at Jackie with a beaming smile and said, "What? You mean the dinosaur ass?" They both laughed out loud.

It was now getting dark; it was 4:55pm as they arrived at the cove's car park. It was well lit by spotlights that showed a hive of activity with officers and forensic-suited personnel moving about. As they parked, Peter walked over to them.

He spoke. "Hello my team, how are you both? Found anything useful?"

Jackie thought, *The cake stop in the café really has given us a different boss, a different boss compared to the one who had been extremely rude to us just a few hours earlier, amazing!* Or *is it false?*

Peter continued before Jackie had time to answer. "Forensics moved Petra to the morgue. She's in Penzance for the autopsy. Additionally, they've found other related items of interest that can be checked at the lab."

Jackie smiled, she replied, "Good progress then! Plus, we've got some more evidence. We've got a few thick gauge necklace chains that may match the one that John Smedley thought may have been used to garrotte Petra. Suze and Petra both appear to wear them."

Peter said, "Excellent!"

She continued, "Bizarrely there's a calendar with some anomaly that just doesn't sit right with us."

Peter looked puzzled, "What do you mean?"

"Well, it's a photo calendar with two photos. October has a beautiful photo of Petra with **Myluv** handwritten below it in red."

"What's strange about that?"

"My point is that Alex calls his wife **Myluv** as her cute nickname, he loves her. But now she's dead he has another **Myluv** in Suze. Since our earlier visit this morning, he's written **Myluv & Myluv** over their images. It's complicated, I know. I may actually be thinking this through too hard. Actually I am. We've just come from their home, and I've got photo albums that show huge amounts of love between three people. And I mean true, raw and uninhibited love. A threesome that isn't kinky, lewd or purely sexual. Oh OK, there is tons of sex, but not in a pornographic context. The gratification jumps out as true love. Love that we can only dream about! Suze has confessed that she, Petra, and Alex were in a three-way love relationship. So, the calendar and his additional **Myluv** for Suze isn't such an issue. These albums show their love graphically."

Peter was showing great interest in the album information as his dull face lit up.

Susan excitedly came into the conversation. "There's more! I've done a web and social media search on The Trio, as we call them. The results have just pinged onto my phone in the car! Petra is the only child of extremely wealthy German parents; they own a massive industrial concern worth millions!"

Jackie and Peter looked at Susan with curious frowns. Both were taken aback with the revelation of wealth, Peter's expression more so. Jackie jumped into the conversation before Peter could say anything.

"Aaaah! So, here's a potential motive for the murder! Alex had only just married Petra. He could now become the beneficiary of her potentially huge estate. With the three-way relationship, maybe Alex or Suze or both are connected to Petra's murder. Suze would benefit from the estate wealth too if she were involved with Alex."

Peter needed to raise his voice and take control of his excited Rottweilers, "Outstanding! Well done ladies ... I mean women, sorry ... females. Or is it people, persons ... oh, fuck it, whatever! Well done Jackie and Susan. And don't you get upset Susan; in my book it will always be age before beauty! There you go, I've fucked up again, that last saying is a sexist comment in *some* people's eyes!"

The three then simultaneously roared with laughter at the often stupidness of morality.

The seriousness returned. Jackie had wondered whether or not to arrest Suze and Alex. She said to Peter, "Although there now appeared to be a motive, potentially a large inheritance, it was purely speculative at this time. Could you arrange background checks to see if Suze and Alex are married? Or if anyone knows about any plans to get married? If they are currently married, they've committed an offence. My thought is that Suze would definitely benefit from Alex's inheritance if she were his spouse, which is assuming Alex does inherit Petra's wealth. It isn't a given at this moment that there could be a payout. I think we should bide our time. We have some useful evidence for now and we've yet to get the full forensic results. I think we should get these background checks."

Peter nodded. "Yes, good thought. I agree, let's wait before we make an arrest. Are you two available to work tomorrow?"

Jackie looked at Susan, who nodded.

Jackie replied, "Yes Guv, of course we can!"

"Perfect, thank you. Have you seen Alan Smith yet?"

Jackie looked at Susan. She looked tired. Jackie replied to Peter, "Guv, we've had a full-on day. Let's pack it in now. We'll see Alan tomorrow; we haven't forgotten him."

Peter looked slight despondent but replied, "OK, we can

nab him tomorrow! We're on a roll. Excellent work today and thank you! I'll see you in the morning here at eight!"

Just then Jackie's head twanged. She put her hand over her ache.

It was getting late, darkness had arrived and the tide was in, the decision was made by forensics to close down their activity until daylight the next day. Peter suggested to the CID team that they meet again tomorrow morning. Uniformed officers would remain to keep the area secure. Peter was a happy man. He was smiling. Good progress had been made in a very short time. He had potential prime suspects virtually in the bag and another yet to be interviewed. This he'd report to his superiors ... who were always awaiting updates. He deliberately took the albums, calendar and necklaces to put with the evidence held at the station. He said his goodbyes and strolled to his car. As he did, Jackie called out to him.

"Peter, I'd thought I'd go to see John on the way home, I could drop the evidence there to save time?"

Peter frowned as he turned to look. By then Jackie was almost next to him. "OK Jackie, take the necklaces, I'll take the albums to the station, here you are."

Jackie took the necklaces, and they said their goodbyes.

Jackie wanted to take the evidence to the laboratory and hopefully see Dr Smedley the pathologist to get the latest about Petra. Susan needed to be dropped off at the police station that wasn't much of a detour for Jackie as it was near the laboratory. As they walked to the car Jackie said, "Wow! We've had a busy day but just look at what we've achieved! Absolutely amazing! Well done Susan!"

Susan responded, "Pete's a different man. This morning, he was an asshole, but now he's suddenly normalised. Perhaps we should take him for cake more often?"

Jackie chuckled. "What? As a threesome? No way! He's better ... but tomorrow is another day. Leopards don't change their spots overnight. Let's just wait and see what he's like in the morning. I know his job is like a pressure cooker, I've been there. Your bosses always want immediate results for any case, especially one's like Petra's. And at the end of the day, we still haven't got categoric evidence to say Petra was murdered. It could just be the fall, and that could be a tragic accident. Her necklace may have caught on a rock during her fall. The clifftop footprints may have a time difference in that someone else was with her but left way before she fell. Also, I know many men and women who scantily dress, for whatever reason. I've had friends who take their clothes off as soon as they get home from work. They go around starkers as it feels natural. The same as naturists behave, and they aren't perverts." Susan smiled.

The chat continued as they drove to the police station. Jackie dropped Susan to her car. "There you go Susan, I hope you don't mind coming in tomorrow, Saturday?"

Susan replied, "No problem at all. I'm going to the bike shop and then the gym to get my fix, and I hadn't planned anything particular for the weekend."

Jackie smiled with her reply. "Perfect! I'll meet you at the station for 7:35am-ish ... I hope you don't get to see another dinosaur ... you don't want another meeting with a megasoreass!" They both laughed.

Susan then offered, "Hey! We could meet up for a drink and get something to eat over the weekend, like a takeaway ... if you'd like to?"

Jackie smiled with her reply. "Maybe. There are a few things I've lined up this weekend, but they've gone tits-up now with us coming into work. Perhaps we could do something tomorrow evening, or Sunday if we're not working. I'll text you later, if not we'll chat tomorrow. Thanks for the offer!"

Susan smiled, "Great, just let me know."

They said their goodbyes and went their own ways. As Jackie drove away she immediately thought back to Peter wanting to take the evidence to the station, he could have dropped Susan off there as it was a dog-leg journey for Jackie to get home. Also, she thought, *Why did he keep the albums and take those to the station?* She looked around the car park but there wasn't any sign of his car. *Perhaps he's been and gone home already?* she wondered. Her head twanged again. She thought, *I wonder why I'm getting these funny few seconds of head issues. Perhaps it's the damp weather and cold wind?* came her answer.

Jackie's thoughts wandered as she drove to the morgue. She spoke to herself within her mind, *I remember the past and the harsh reality of mixing socials with work buddies. It was OK, fun and everything else that goes with work colleague friendship. But there were complications that ruined my work environment and colleague friendship, and it didn't happen immediately. Steve was both my work partner and lover within the Met. We lived together almost immediately after having met on the job; he was love at first sight. I really thought our personal relationship was solid and long term, until I found out he was admired by others from within our workplace. He explained to me he couldn't read the signs of the advances from the other females. He said he was led astray – yeah right! He blamed the pressure of work and different shift patterns. We didn't see each other for extended periods. He needed and found the additional stimulus to cope … other women. He had more than one close personal relationship, all of them officers. Our relationship began to falter. Other women were his drug. One session wasn't enough. His hunger grew as did his dependency to feed his habit. Ultimately he was found out. I was blind to what was going on as work was so full on. In the end it was by being nudged and hinted to by one, then several other female colleagues. That's when I realised. At first I didn't believe it, it couldn't be true. I was in denial. I still feel that excruciating pain when, finally, I confronted him. I really hoped there wasn't any truth in the rumours. I thought they were malicious jealous lies. But Steve admitted to his playing the field immediately after I asked. In fact, he said he'd enjoyed the fix he was getting with his several bed buddies. Sex with them was varied and better than with me.* The bastard, *I hate him. He walked out and dumped me the same day. I was mortified. I cried and cried. I went sick for two weeks and was getting depressed. I had hoped he'd at least text. But there was nothing. I stayed in, embarrassed and alone. I felt I was guilty of finding out. I started drinking as a coping strategy. I didn't do any washing, didn't shower or do my hair. I just moped around in a drunken daze. After a week of the booze, I collapsed on the floor. I was out for hours. When I woke I saw the broken glass so dangerously close to my head. I had reached rock bottom. I got up to get another drink. As I made my way to the booze I looked around and saw the state my home was in, it was a shithole. I passed a mirror and saw the sad reflection of me. It was that image that frightened me. It scared me as with work I'd seen many people with addiction ... I looked like them.*

Jackie was driving and all the time she was conscious and aware of her surroundings and other traffic. At roundabouts and traffic lights her attention had to be paramount, so she drifted in and out of her thoughts. After she navigated a roundabout, she continued her thought.

I didn't want that reflected image to be me. It wasn't really me. It was my reflection. It couldn't be me. But it was. *I needed to get back to who I really was. I was a victim, a victim of betrayal. I was a loser. I was trash, a sad no one. I needed to become who I was and that was me. To do that I needed to have hope, belief and confidence in myself. I didn't do anything wrong. I deserved better. With those thoughts I pulled myself together, skipped the bottle and I showered. It was the first time in a week. I stunk. I stood in the shower and cried. I cried until I could cry no more. I dug deep and I washed. I washed all traces of that bastard off my skin. When I finished, I threw the clothes I'd worn since the day he walked out away. I changed the bedding and threw that out. I washed anything he touched. I threw anything related to him out. I removed him. I is me, I am now stronger. I can survive and* I will survive!

I returned to work with a manager's interview with my boss's boss, Tony. He was good and understood my problem. I think it helped as he listened. He didn't judge me. He knew I was a good worker. He seconded me to another CID section at a different station where I regained my confidence. I soon realised I couldn't stay with the Met. News travels and although there weren't any backlashes, or jibes, I *still felt uncomfortable.* I *felt people were looking at me and* I *felt* I *was a loser. Tony contacted me to see how* I *was getting on, we met in a café,* I *couldn't face a pub or wine bar. It was he who suggested* I *apply for the CID vacancy here.* I *put in for transfer and here* I *am. Lesser rank with a ranker of a boss!* Jackie laughed at her own story and thought, *You sad bitch you ... get on with it.* I *am you, and* you're *doing fine! GGG – Go Girl Go! The pain I went through back then continues to this day, but it's in my mind and not happening now. I know it's history and it's gone. Steve really ruined me, some would say he really fucked me up. But* I *say he's fucked himself up.* I *had to endure not only a dishonest partner but also had to collaborate with those bitches who had also been fucking my man behind my back. That's difficult. Work had become intolerable, so here* I *am in glorious Cornwall. Baggage left behind in the Met and in my mind's compartment.* I'm *in a different force, a lesser role, and now with a twat of a boss, who may just be redeeming himself ... or not.* She smiled and chuckled to herself. I *do like my new trainee Susan.* I *like her wit and professionalism, and that made today enjoyable. She'll go far, she's one to watch. Perhaps* I'd *better keep on her good side as one day she could be my boss!*

Jackie continued with her mind. *There were other incidents where I've found mixing workmates and social life didn't always map out nicely. Mixing workmates as friends and then socialising with the same, was slightly incestuous. It seemed every other officer that had set up shop with another officer had separated or divorced. Ha! Just like loser me! Those that had a relationship with a civilian, a non-officer in other words, went through the same process. I wonder what the statistics were actually like for separation and divorce within the entire force over all people, no matter how the individuals classified themselves. In other words, for my un-informed mind, a simplified option is to say, inclusive of everyone. Everything in the police revolved around three foul four-letter words ... work ... fuck ....kids. Now let's say partner to be inclusive of everyone, all types, colours, religions, etc. It continually rotated through those three words with the relationships. So, forgetting work, but looking at relationships it goes, partner ... fuck ... kids. I had thought, if you cocked up at work the repercussions continued into the social life where there could be continual jibes, barracking and piss-taking. Psychologically the banter seemed to hang around forever, like a badge. Being a police officer was difficult enough so having an independent and separate social life is the way I want to proceed. Nice as Susan is, I don't really want to mix with her socially. Not yet. It'll end in tears ... it always does.*

Jackie had other intentions for the weekend, and that was now. She was still curious and didn't want to finish work, just yet. Her mind was spinning with angles of inquiry that she needed to make. She was driving to the morgue with the necklaces but without the photo albums. She wanted to see Petra again.

CHAPTER 8
THE AUTOPSY

Jackie drove to the Royal Conwillian Hospital in Truro where the forensic autopsy was being conducted. It was 6:37pm. She showed her ID to the security receptionist and made her way into the laboratory section. Senior Pathologist Dr John Smedley hadn't signed out yet as shown on the staff notice board. *Phew! He's still here, great!* thought Jackie as she walked to the laboratory where John and his assistant were tidying the area around the cloth covering Petra.

John looked up over his spectacles and removed his surgical mask showing a warm smile. "Hello Jackie, nice to see you! I'm glad you've come. I can share what I've found. It is rather complicated and not an easy task for us in forensics!" His pleasing smile came from the satisfaction he had gleaned from his investigations.

Jackie smiled and said, "Great! What *have* you found?"

He carefully and, with great respect for Petra, gently pulled off the sheet covering her fragile body.

Jackie looked at Petra and had a moment of silence. Jackie's mind rolled with thoughts, *Even in death I can see the natural beauty that's still radiating out from her bruised and battered body. John and his assistant have made an excellent job with their suture. They've removed and replaced her brain, heart, liver and lungs to find the cause of her tragic death. Petra, rest in peace. I'm here to help you, I will find the guilty who have taken you away.*

John knew Jackie was familiar with the processes. Visitors tended to want some quiet time to allow their thoughts to get into the right place for the often ugly and unsettling details that led to the autopsy conclusion. These would include the graphic details about the inflicted injuries that caused the death.

After a few moments with her thoughts, Jackie looked at John. This was to signal she was ready for his narrative.

"Jackie, Petra's injuries *are* significant with a fall from a great height, I'm sure she fell from the adjacent clifftop. I reckon it's at least 40 metres high; my forensic colleagues will confirm the actual height tomorrow. Petra *could* have died from the fall upon landing. We could have easily assumed her fall was a tragic accident, end of story. *But actually she died before the fall.* I'll come back to that in a moment. I'm confident she tumbled onto ledges during her fall hence the bruises across various parts of her body. She also has broken bones, here and there, that indicate a rapid tumbling down and across rocky structures rather than a free-fall impact. Petra's actual cause of death was asphyxiation before she fell. She suffocated from strangulation by a garrotte around her neck. The garrotte marks appear to be similar to those made by a necklace. A necklace with large strong chain links. We haven't yet found the said chain." At that moment Jackie held the bagged necklaces up for John to see. He nodded with acknowledgement and continued, "The chain wasn't snagged on a rock during her fall. If it had broken there would have been different marks around her neck, for example, marks that were only on a certain area of her neck as the chain tightened there. Her necklace chain was tightened by someone's hands from the front across her throat. The chain marks go completely around her neck with specific indentations in certain areas, namely the throat area. It appears to me that the chain was stretched tightly as the fingers and hands grabbed and pulled the necklace around Petra's neck from the front throat area. I suspect as the assailant continued the tightening process their hands crossed over one another. There are definite indications, bruising and cuts from thumbnails, being pushed in towards her windpipe. I've got DNA samples from what appear to be the fingernail cuts in the windpipe area ... they're being analysed as we talk." He paused to enable Jackie to comprehend and think about his explanation.

They both looked compassionately at Petra's naked dead body; cold and motionless she lay. Jackie held her evidence bags showing the necklaces that were collected from her earlier search. John instantly recognised them as having a chain link size similar to the type that may have been used around Petra's neck.

"They're very like the size I imagined caused her death!" said John in amazement.

Jackie replied, "We found them in Petra's home. You can have these to analyse."

John replied, "We haven't yet found *the* chain on the beach. Forensics are going back tomorrow at daylight to continue their search." John continued with his report. "There is an indentation at the rear of Petra's neck that infers the chain broke, it snapped apart. If it did and it fell, we should be able to find it. If it didn't fall the assailant may still have the remnants."

Jackie was picturing in her mind what had shockingly happened to Petra. She'd been with other pathologists in mortuaries during autopsies and had witnessed the unfolding facts that had caused death. She could form a series of pictures in her mind of how the final moments of life were taken away by the perpetrators of hideous crimes. The pictures transformed in her mind as a timeline where they were pieced together like a movie clip. From the clip she could try to map out the 'how' and 'why' the deceased person's life was terminated. Some of the corpses she'd seen were criminals, killed by other criminals. She had less sympathy for these dead people, but their murder *was* still a crime, and her role was to find those guilty of breaking the law. Petra's death was different as she appeared to be an innocent person, in the wrong place at the wrong time, murdered by someone unknown to her ... or maybe someone who knew her, as is often found.

John continued, "The neck wounds are consistent with a slow death over several minutes. The attack needed a tight grip to be applied, tightly. Hence these chain marks."

Jackie then asked the question that she knew would give an answer she wouldn't like to hear. "Petra wasn't wearing many clothes ... have you found any reason why?"

John became suddenly intense as he looked at Jackie. His bushy eyebrows fluttered with motion as they protruded above his spectacles, as though they were wanting to take flight like fledglings from a nest under attack from a predatory bird. His serious looking eyes, now wide open, peered at Jackie from above his spectacle frame. "I *have* found indications that Petra was abused."

Jackie took a deep breath. She did this to counter the sigh of upset and shock that came when she'd previously attended similar autopsies. She asked, "What makes you say that?"

He replied, "Well, look here and here." He continued by showing numerous bruises and teeth marks across Petra's body with explanations of how they got there. "We've taken photographs of these marks and imprints of the tooth indentations, plus samples of DNA. If we find the culprit we can then compare them against one another."

Jackie needed to know and so asked, "Was there intercourse, or anything else?"

John looked at Petra again, his face still full of dignity.

He astutely replied, "Yes. She's had intercourse in the past 24 hours. We've found semen traces, and the samples are being analysed."

There was a time for thought.

After a few seconds John spoke. "Look here." As he pointed to faint red marks around Petra's wrists and ankles. They were so faint Jackie hadn't noticed them on the beach or here. He continued, "She's been tied with a soft material, some sort of cloth methinks. I've managed to get tiny fragments, and I've sent these to be analysed. We had a quick look under the microscope and the material appears to be red fibre, like the colour of the jacket she wore."

Jackie noted the bright red colour and needed to know so asked the awkward question, "Do you think this was part of her sexual abuse?" Jackie was trying to formulate a picture of the events. She imagined Petra could have been bound, either with consent, or without. The fact she had been murdered suggested to her that she may have been bound and then raped.

John spoke in a lesser voice. "In my opinion the said bondage marks, as you can see, are very minimalistic, in fact almost hard to see. Death has brought these faint markings out. I think whilst she was alive these marks may not even have been too visible, given normal blood circulation. Therefore, I've been thinking about these marks and I'm not sure that they are related to her death … or with any sexual abuse. They may have been caused by regular self-bondage of some sort over a period of time, maybe months or even years. And they happened before death. Again, I'm getting DNA samples analysed that I've taken from those areas. In my opinion, I think the marks could be caused by frequent repetition as they are almost in layers, as though some type of activity is happening on a regular basis. I have come across this type of bond activity before, from my peers in their medical reports. It has been noted during several other autopsies from leading pathologists. I would hazard a guess, Petra self-bonded."

Jackie frowned as she didn't understand what John was alluding to. He realised and continued, "Jackie, you know we live in a strange world where there is normal and not normal, acceptable and unacceptable. Well, some people can't cope with various things in their daily life. They explore their surroundings and environment as well as their bodies. They can explore their bodies for self-gratification by having tattoos, piercings and other such things. They can also use their body to self-harm, like scratching their skin in one place until bleeding occurs, cut or hit themselves. Some can induce vomiting after eating if they're weight conscious. In Petra's case, I think she self-bonded to restrain from something. Like smoking, taking drugs or anything else she wanted to abstain from, including shopping! This has been proven by peer autopsies and the many reports worldwide. Social media feeds the world's population with all sorts of ideas and fads. Think of the many different types of cosmetic surgery that now happen. If I have a wild guess before we get the results, with Petra's age of mid-thirties, and her obvious fine body without an ounce of excess fat, she may have wanted to keep herself fit and thin to maintain her need to remain in her prime, to continue with her youthful appearance. She was, as you can see here, a very well-maintained female specimen, almost perfect and maybe too good to be true, in some minds. She had well-defined muscles that come from an exercised body, with no other signs of self-harm or body pleasure. There aren't any body piercings. The only piercings she has are in her ear lobes. She hasn't any tattoos or other body art anywhere.

In my opinion I think Petra self-bonded to prevent herself from eating."

Again, John paused. He did this deliberately as he knew Jackie was different from other officers who had attended autopsies. He knew she was far more experienced than most after his initial meeting with her just hours before. After she and Susan had left the crime scene he had spoken to Peter, the DI. Peter gave glowing feedback about his new prodigy explaining her role in the Met and how quickly she had ran with this case. John had soon realised that Jackie being here some 12 hours after she started work, and with the questions she was asking, indicated she was indeed living up to her previous role. He had optimism that Jackie was the right person to solve the mystery and the misery of why Petra was murdered.

Jackie looked bemused, not because she thought his feedback was strange, she'd come across all types of behaviour. With Petra it now appeared she had felt the need to maintain a strict body type. Petra, she thought, had everything going for her. A good well-paid enjoyable job, wealthy parents, a loving husband – *or not* – and a very good girlfriend ... *or not.*

John continued, "I don't think Petra was bulimic as the continuous vomiting erodes tooth enamel and hers looks fine. However, we'll check her blood electrolytes as these could indicate imbalances caused by starvation or purging. She definitely isn't emaciated and there were no signs of organ damage. She would have been very adept at masking her condition, knowing exactly when to eat or not. The indications are that she ate the correct foods, high protein and low fat with good vegetables and fruit intake. I think Petra couldn't self-control her eating with willpower, she needed a physical barrier to stop eating. By tying herself to something she'd be anchored and that could prevent her raiding the pantry."

Jackie responded, "So, Petra conducted self-bondage to ensure she didn't eat, or whatever it was she wanted to refrain from. She used a soft bright red fabric, perhaps a rope, or something else to do so. We need to find that evidence!"

John paused whilst he listened to Jackie's summary and nodded in agreement. His face then lit up with a smile. "Petra was wearing a smart watch! It was the latest lightweight model that was almost invisible. I've sent it off and I wouldn't be surprised if it shows a lot of exercise taking place. It'll record all her activity and rest periods; it will also show when and how far Petra travelled. It is a high-end version that tracks the movement and maps the routes taken, so we'll see where and when she travelled. The dates are recorded and that would be most beneficial. We'll know how she got to the clifftop!"

Jackie knew this could be a key piece of evidence. Her mind was deciphering the explanations that John had given, and his pauses suited her rationale of the events. She then asked, "John, I'd like to share my thoughts with the progress we've made today and add it to my understanding of what you've said. Is that OK?"

John smiled as he wanted to hear the thoughts of this new very keen officer on his patch. He knew she was extremely diligent and someone he'd enjoy working with in the future. Jackie gave her summary from the beginning, where she and Susan had their first contact with Petra, up to John's last comment. When she had finished his face was lit up with expectation that Petra's death could be solved. John spoke, "In you, Jackie, I sense a wealth of experience, keenness, integrity and an urge to get things done correctly."

Jackie was pleased and smiled. "How soon will the DNA

results arrive?"

John replied, "Well, it's Friday evening and most people have finished for the weekend, but given that this is a murder investigation, I'm hoping in just a few hours. The lab is open 24 hours. We have an experienced forensics team who will put the evidence together with us. There could be more important cases than ours, we'll just have to wait and see. I will, of course, ask for priority with the laboratory. As soon as I have the results I'll let you know. Just be aware that the results may be drip-fed back to you as we've sent items as soon as we've received them from your team. Oh! ... I nearly forgot to mention. Petra has some redness around her breasts with soft tissue damage. I'm not quite sure how this was caused. There was a presence of beach debris, specks of grit that couldn't have got there from a fall, her jacket was zipped closed. It's weird as both breasts have the same sort of hand indentations, illustrated by the soft tissue damage." He pointed to Petra's breasts and stomach. "None of her ribs are broken in the breast area, just some lower down her abdomen caused by the fall. No compressions appear to have been made near the breastbone. It's just weird."

Jackie said, "OK, strange. Could they be caused by something sexual?"

John replied, "Maybe. I'm just not sure, but again, I think I've managed to get a DNA sample from her left breast, there is a slight fingernail indentation. I'll let you know."

Jackie and John had finished their discussion and had some general conversations about the atrocious weather that had hampered their investigations. She thanked John for his time and made her way home, it was nearly 7.30pm on that fatefully stormy October Friday evening.

CHAPTER 9
YOU SHOULD BE DANCING

Jackie travelled home with thoughts of John's excellent autopsy feedback. She had answers and ideas to follow up. She was hungry for food and drove via the Indian takeaway in Penzance. As she arrived a flashback hit her; it was Petra's body in the morgue and John's rendition of her eating disorder. Jackie now didn't want to eat, but she was *SO* hungry she shouted out as she opened her door, "Bollocks! *I am going to eat!*" An older man misheard her first word as he walked out from the takeaway; a carrier bag was brimming with his order.

He smiled and said in a geeky matter of fact way, "Ha! Yes I can recommend those! Get the tandoori tikka ones … Mmm! Yummy! Chewy and juicy!"

Jackie smiled and nodded back to the OAP.

As she chose from the window menu she had an idea, she called Susan. "Hello Susan, what are you doing?"

Susan had returned from the gym and was just about to shower. "Well hello Sherlock! What can I do for you at this late time on a Friday night?"

Jackie laughed aloud. "How about joining me for a curry takeout?"

Susan laughed. "I've just cycled 40 miles and worked off my cake and sarnies, plus a bit more, and you now want me to put it all back on plus more?"

Jackie laughed as she replied, "You'll be fine! Did you find your dinosaur?"

Susan laughed. "My pet megasoreass? No, he wasn't

available tonight! The built-in silicone pad in my new funky trousers you suggested I get worked really well and kept him away, thank you!"

Jackie laughed as she said, "Would you like you to come over and share some good healthy Indian food!"

Almost immediately Susan said, "Perfect! That'll remind me of home with my folks and my ancestry. I love Asian yummy food! It's a deal, where do you live?"

Jackie said, "Ambrose Cottage, Naylings Lane, that's opposite Tamorna Lane. Straight on for four miles, I'm on the left, I'll leave the light on."

Susan replied, "OK, I'll be there 8:30ish if I come right away, or a bit later if I shower. Get me anything, I'm starving!"

Jackie said, "No need to shower, come as you are, you could stay over and shower here?"

Susan replied, "Perfect, only if you're sure, and that I won't be an inconvenience?"

"It'll be fine, just come as you are."

"OK, will do, see you soon. Bye!"

The call ended but the conversation left an awkward uneasiness within Jackie's mind. She ordered a variety of foods and whilst she sat and waited she thought, *Crikey! I've just realised Susan, and me too, are really so self-conscious about our sizes. Petra was too ... to the extent of some weird self-bondage technique to assist in abstinence.* The thought stayed with her as she returned home. Another niggle played out in her mind. *What have I done! I've asked a work colleague to visit my home who I've only just met today. I wasn't going to get too close to work buddies after the issues I had with Steve. But Susan likes her job, so we'll talk shop about Petra, I'm sure she'll like that ... I hope!*

Jackie's home was a very smart rental property. She had an employee relocation package that included a rent contribution for up to a year until she found a permanent home. It had recently been refurbished and was very homely. Like Petra's home it was in a small hamlet with just a few properties along a quiet rural lane. Jackie needed something isolated … just like her blank mind when she finally realised her London partner was messing around with other females. The rural remoteness helped her to compartmentalise the upset he caused her. She had space to think without the external noises from traffic and people. She could close her mind's door to shut out the horrible thoughts, pain and distress that his selfish actions had caused. She wasn't ready to bury or burn the trauma, she just couldn't let go and still wanted to analyse every thread of the pain. Strange as it was, the pain was a drug … she just wouldn't give it up. It became a habit as she fed her mind with twists and turns of the relationship as she searched within for answers. This, she thought, could make her stronger … but the answers never came. She was trapped in a whirlpool of horrid thoughts that circled in her mind. They were forever dragging her further down below the surface. Petra's murder had focused her mind away from her self-doubt. Sad as it was, Petra was creating a much-needed diversion away from her whirlpool mind of both her ex-partner and Peter her obnoxious boss. Susan and Petra were that diversion.

Susan arrived dressed in her sportswear, carrying flowers and her backpack. She was met at the door by Jackie who smiled as she held both her arms out to gently hug her new work partner. It was 8:39pm.

Susan apologised for her sweaty appearance. "Hey, don't get too close, I'm a bit wiffy! I've brought clothes so could I shower before we eat?"

Jackie replied, "Surely"

Susan frowned. "Don't call me Shirley, its Susan!"

They both burst into a laughing fit; they'd seen the same hilarious movie. Jackie was thrilled as Susan was only the second invited visitor to her new home.

"Come in, and welcome to my space!"

Jackie unconsciously glanced up and down Susan's body as she followed her into the hall, noticing the skintight fit of Susan's gym clothing. It glorified her true slender physique; unlike the work clothes she'd worn earlier that made her look frumpy. They entered the kitchen where Susan handed the flowers over and placed her pack on the floor with that familiar glass bottle chinking sound. She took out several bottles of prosecco along with chocolates and flowers that she placed on the kitchen table.

"Look, these are for you!" She smiled and kissed Jackie's cheek. They still had their price stickers on as Susan had gone to the local convenience store next to her gym. She had tried to remove them but gave up. They had some initial chatter, and both agreed they were ravenous, but Susan was desperate to shower before she ate. Jackie too needed to shower and said, "OK, let's keep the food warm whilst we shower. I've two showers, you use the bathroom shower and I'll use my en-suite."

Susan smiled. "Fabulous, get you for having two showers!"

Jackie replied, "If you want to stay over you can use the bedroom to the left of the bathroom. Go upstairs and you'll find it."

"Perfect, will do, I'll go now."

Susan made her way upstairs carrying her small backpack that also contained her essential stopover kit. This she kept in her car for emergencies, like working late nights and having to stay somewhere other than home. Jackie put the food into the oven and went to her bedroom for a shower.

As Jackie walked up the stairs she could hear Susan's

shower the nearer she got to it. The bathroom door was open, not fully, just ajar. She glanced through the gap and saw Susan sitting on the shower tray; she was wet from the falling water. She was sat, knees bent up with her arms wrapped around and her head resting on her knees. She was weeping, the sounds she made were very familiar to Jackie.

Jackie rushed in shouting, "Susan! Are you all right, what's the matter?" Jackie had thought Susan may have fallen or fainted.

Susan looked up with some shock. Her face bizarrely showed immense happiness with a beaming smile. She replied, "I'm SO pleased you're my mentor. I've had a rubbish life but here, in just one day, my world has begun to turn around. I'm just so happy to be here working with you!" She wiped her face and stood. Jackie grabbed a towel and hung it around her whilst turning off the shower. Susan continued, "I'm sorry … I've just got emotional, I'll be fine, it's coming out, thank you."

Jackie couldn't help but notice Susan's beautiful naturally bronzed Asian body. Her hair was no longer tied up in its work style. She had long glossy naturally black hair that now flowed like a beautiful water crowfoot plant. It reminded her of the long ribbon-like leaves swaying gracefully in the current that resembled streamers in motion. The shower droplets had mixed with the shampoo to make white frothy soap balls, they became like the plant's small delicate white flowers that floated, then they slid down the surface of her hair. Her face glistened under the light as the water droplets sparkled as if they were jewels, like priceless diamonds they tumbled slowly across her dark silky skin. She embraced Jackie. They hugged each other for a few moments that seemed like ages.

Susan whispered into Jackie's ear, "Thank you."

Jackie was now emotional with the outpouring but remained calm, even though she was still fully dressed and now soaking wet. Jackie gulped as she spoke, "Well, that's lovely to hear, I was worried you had fallen! Now finish your shower. We'll eat and talk about this later ... if you'd like to."

"Yes ... I will. Sorry ... I feel embarrassed now."

"Don't feel embarrassed. You're happy and that's fine now."

"I had thought you were upset."

"No, I'm just very, very pleased."

Their embrace slowly ended as Jackie released her hug. She pulled back and smiled as she carefully released and touched Susan's hand in a comforting way. When she was satisfied Susan was genuinely OK, she left her to finish the shower and went to have hers. She also now felt embarrassed, awkward, but pleased Susan was OK.

As Jackie finished her shower, she looked at herself in the full-length mirror and spoke quietly to herself, "Mmmm, my figure isn't so bad either, not for my age anyway! I still like me and my appearance. I still don't understand why that fucker of a partner Steve cleared off with those other ugly bitches, the bastard! I hate him!" She thought back to the shower incident with Susan. *Crikey! I felt really helpful just then, as though I was Susan's older caring sister.*

It was just after 9:30pm as they met in the kitchen, both wearing their nightwear. Jackie had a huge smile as Susan came into the room, as did Susan for her. There was an air of uncertainty between them. The awkwardness of Susan and embarrassment of Jackie during their shower encounter showed on both their faces. After a while, Jackie turned and went to the fridge.

"I've got just the thing we both need!"

She popped the cork off a bottle of prosecco. There was

music playing in the background, chilled music that was easy listening. As she poured the bubbles into flutes, Susan was admiring the kitchen. Jackie turned and their eyes met each other's. Susan started weeping and her eyes welled. Jackie spoke softly with a comforting tone.

"Here, sip this, and cheers!"

Susan wiped her eyes, took the flute and chinked it against Jackie's. "Cheers and thank you Jackie. I'm sorry for my scene, I just feel so elated. I've never worked with or met anyone quite like you! You're just SO amazing, cool, calm and the full package. You personify what the police college say we newbies should be like when we're fully qualified."

Jackie replied, "And you are the trainee that officers like me need. Exceptional doesn't describe adequately enough how I see you after just one day. Well done. We covered a huge amount of ground today; I couldn't have done that without you!"

The emotional intensity subsided quite naturally between them.

As they chatted, Jackie stopped listening as Susan's voice became white noise. She was thinking, *It would be so easy for someone to take advantage of Susan or Petra whilst they were in that moment just now. Where innocence and little experience is treading its way along a knife edge. Learning about life and its experiences as they balance precariously. The naive and easily led immature could take the wrong path, or be led and guided by the unscrupulous who have ulterior motives. I wonder what really happened to Petra. It definitely wasn't suicide. John gave me his thoughts about Petra's death ... I wonder.* Jackie suddenly woke from her thought.

"Jackie, Jackie are you OK?" The white noise had become Susan's concerns. "Jackie, are you alright?"

"Erm, yes, sorry I'm fine, I'll just check the food!"

Susan was smiling, she hadn't realised Jackie was out of it.

They sat at the large oak table where they ate a feast of glorious Indian food. They drank their flute of bubbles as they spoke about their backgrounds, families, cultures and the highs and lows of their lives. Jackie focused on her failed relationship whereas Susan spoke about herself being an ugly duckling as a child. She had received much racial abuse for being Asian, abuse for wearing tooth braces and glasses, being bullied at school as she was scrawny, and other nasty things. She was breastless until she was 18 and had the sad jokes and taunts because of that, said by girls, boys and adults. It was only during her late teens that she developed into how Jackie described her in the shower.

"You're now a fully-fledged PC embarking on a role with CID. I think you exude great confidence."

Susan explained she had practised taekwondo from the age of ten and had worked through to becoming a black belt. She gained self-confidence and belief in herself. She was bullied no more. She had acquired an indomitable spirit. Her family sponsored her education, so she qualified for police training college where she excelled. She had found her confidence along with a career of choice. She had realised she was heavy-footed, but this enabled her martial art combat kicking skills to be powerful.

Gradually the chat drifted to their work.

Susan was now very outgoing and, being relatively new to the force, hadn't yet become stereotypical. "I'd describe myself as determined, hardworking, but at the same time I'm optimistic, bubbly and buoyant!"

Jackie laughed; the bubbles were having an effect, so she didn't offer any more. "I agree totally! From what I've seen of you today I sense all of those things, and more!"

Susan smiled, "My family and I haven't always had it easy here. Because we're Asian we sometimes get treated differently, rudely and without justification. We're often categorised by some as not being UK citizens, as though we are illegal immigrants, or boat people crossing the Channel. When we're amongst other Asian folk, life is normalised, and I suppose that's why we appear to congregate in communities. Family is important to us, as is community, maybe that's why other ethnic minorities tend to congregate. We're mixing and blending with white UK citizens but it's still sometimes troublesome. I was born in the UK, and my language is English, but the colour of my skin defines me to some as an alien. Life *is* getting easier for people of colour compared to when my folks first arrived. Times are changing as the world has got smaller, and there is gradual recognition that different cultures of people are blending better than say 50 years ago."

She had a look of optimism as Jackie replied, "Yes, I get what you're saying and envy how community is important for you. I wish we could all live together as one big happy family, a community without crime and hate. That's why I joined the force, to try and influence change. Sometimes though, I do bash my head against the wall with how slow the progress is." She finished her sentence looking perturbed.

Neither planned to talk about Petra as this was a social meeting, but inevitably the chat changed to discuss her. Susan asked, "How did Petra's autopsy go?"

Jackie immediately changed to work mode as she spoke. She relayed the details of her meeting with John and his subsequent findings. Susan listened intensively.

After relaying the autopsy meeting, Jackie tapped onto her phone for the music app to change the music. There were Bluetooth speakers around the cottage that began to play music from the 80s. Then came the track that they couldn't sit still to, the 'Good Boys (Blow-Up Mix)' by Blondie. Jackie ramped up the volume and started to nod her head to the rhythm. They continued chatting and nibbling at the feast of food whilst dance music played.

It was just before midnight when Susan sang, "I'm tired so show me the way to go home. If I don't get home I'll change into Cinderella!"

Jackie burst out laughing, she too was happy. "OK, but you're not going home, you've had a drink. You're staying here."

They walked up stairs and, without warning, Susan grabbed Jackie's arm and flung herself onto the large guest bed, pulling Jackie at the same. They both laughed and giggled. Susan shut her eyes and within seconds was asleep. Jackie slowly got up and carefully pulled the duvet to cover Susan. She walked quietly to the door, turned and smiled at Susan blissfully asleep. She had a final look as a mother does to their daughter at bedtime, then switched the light off and gently closed the door behind her. She went into her bedroom and crawled into bed. She lay there maternally thinking, *In that shower moment I was SO motherly towards Susan. I need to know if I could be a mother. I'm sure I could. Trust that ass Steve who ruined it for me!* She awoke from her thoughts about Susan to those about Petra. *Petra could have been totally innocent, inexperienced and naive, more so than Susan. Petra could have been under the influence of someone, not a parent, but someone, or some people, who controlled her like a parent. They deliberately led her, trained her their way, they fooled her. Enchanted by their control, she died as a result of them.* She ended there; her nagging headache reoccurred. She took paracetamol and needed to sleep. She set the alarm and within seconds she fell asleep. It was 12:15am on Saturday morning.

Jackie awoke to her alarm. It was 6:30am. She could have used the weekend to recharge her body's battery but given the nature of work she thought, *Needs must!* She quickly dressed in her work clothes and then went to Susan's room and politely knocked on the door. Within seconds it surprisingly opened with Susan beaming a smile. She too was fully dressed ready for work, her long dark hair now neatly tied ready for the day.

Susan spoke, "Right Vera, what next?" She burst out laughing.

Jackie looked bemused. "What do you mean by Vera?"

"Well, you were called Sherlock yesterday, he's a bloke, and you're most definitely not a bloke, so today you're called Vera."

"Who's Vera?"

"God! You are so out of it! Vera is that TV female sleuth who solves all the crimes, like Miss Marple!"

Jackie looked bemused, "But I don't watch TV."

Susan replied, "It's a well-known television series that my mum watches, a bit like Midsummer Murders, or Miss Marple!"

They both laughed out loud as Jackie replied, "I prefer my own name rather than Vera. Call me Jackie!"

Susan smiled. She wound up Jackie further by saying, "OK boss!"

Jackie had a sense of humour too and said, "Enough, enough said!"

Susan replied, "Sounds like the phrase in that romcom movie!"

They both walked downstairs giggling to find a horrific scene, as though a full-on party had taken place within the open-plan kitchen and on into the living room. There was an empty bottle, rubbish and empty soiled takeaway containers, plus the dirty crockery and cutlery.

Susan loudly said, "Right, come on! Let's tidy up before

we go, we can't have you coming home to this mess!"

After the tidy-up they travelled to the cove in Jackies car. The weather had improved from yesterday; dark clouds prevailed but it wasn't raining, and the winds had lessened. They arrived just before 8am and went straight to the MCU.

Peter smiled as they entered where other officers were waiting for the briefing. "Good morning Jackie, and to you Susan."

The two were pleased with their welcome from Peter. Jackie and Susan both smiled and simultaneously spoke, "Morning Peter."

Peter suggested they sit around the table with the team as he wanted to talk about the overnight DNA results and developments.

"John contacted the coroner yesterday given the circumstances of how Petra was found on the beach and her suspicious death. John asked for direct preliminary feedback to be granted to us in CID whilst the documentation is being formalised. We need to ensure that this deviation from the normal chain of command does not compromise the chain of custody, or the evidential integrity required for any potential legal proceedings as per the coroner.

"Some of what I'm going to say is known to Jackie who saw John last evening. I've received more of the DNA results from John and can confirm Petra *wasn't* strangled by Alex or Suze. *Their* DNA doesn't match. Someone else strangled her; we have a DNA profile from cuts their fingernails left in Petra's neck. It isn't someone on our records ... so, we need to find *that* person. I can also confirm that sexual intercourse had taken place twice within 24 hours of death. There were in fact two different semen samples. One of the samples matches that of Alex's DNA. We need to establish from Alex if his intercourse was consensual, given also that very slight bondage marks were found around Petra's wrists and ankles. She may have been bound whilst Alex had intercourse ... with consent, or not. The tests found strands of a bright red cotton fibre left on Petra's wrists and ankles, so we need to look for something that matches that at her home. The fibres come from a different garment; they are not from her jacket. The second semen DNA sample comes from an unknown person. Again, our records don't have a match for that person. We need to find that person." Peter paused. He knew this was complicated so wanted to evaluate the understanding from Jackie. "Jackie, any questions?"

Jackie and Susan were suddenly on the line after their long day and late night. Jackie responded, "Well, this is a complicated case. We now know there could be more than one suspect. Two are male because there are two DNAs. One is from Alex, the second is unknown to us at this moment in time. We need to check back with Alex about his DNA sample and if intercourse involved bondage. Thinking about boots, Suze could be implicated if her boot DNA confirms she was at the clifftop. Have you any other feedback from forensics?"

Peter continued, "The first boot imprints found on the clifftop were those as worn by Petra. The second pair of imprints from the clifftop are virtually identical to the pair collected as evidence from Suze. They are the same brand and size as Petra's." Peter paused. He looked at Jackie and Susan who were optimistically thinking they were Suze's. He maintained a serious expression as he knew that a conclusion had been formed in both their minds. "Jackie, what are your thoughts?"

She replied, "Well, where we are at this moment is that the clifftop boot prints were those of Petra *and* Suze's." Susan nodded in agreement.

Peter replied, "Good try, *but* forensic tests have confirmed one set *was* Petra's and the others were *most definitely not* Suze's!"

"Crikey!" said Susan as both she and Jackie looked at each other with a miffed expression.

Jackie quizzically asked, "How do they know that?"

Peter replied, "Forensics managed to take a cast of the said prints from the clifftop and upon analysis there is a small part of the tread missing on the right boot of the second pair. Suze's right boot *doesn't* have that part of the tread missing, and neither do Petra's."

There was silence, Jackie and Susan stared at each other. Jackie spoke, "Right then, we need to find the owner of matching boots to Petra's and Suze's that have a piece of the tread missing from the right boot. Suze could tell us where she got hers from and the retailer may have a list of those who purchased the said boots. Next we need answers from Alex about his sexual activities with Petra and whether he was responsible for her bondage marks. And if not him then who. We need to find some sort of bright red garment that matches those bondage marks. Delicate as it is, maybe we need to ask Alex about the other male whose semen has been found. Alex may know. We also need to find the missing necklace chain."

Peter hadn't yet mentioned the chain but did now. "Forensics at the lab have checked the chains you took to John last evening. The DNA matched Suze's with hers and Petra's with her necklaces. There doesn't appear to have been any swapping of chains from one person to the other. But their chains are indicative of the type and link size used to strangle Petra. They appear to be solid gold, but they are good imitations that are gold plated. Forensics will be on scene today to keep searching for a particular necklace chain, or parts thereof that were used to strangle Petra. So, where to now?"

Jackie spoke enthusiastically, "I would like to interview Alex and Suze now and have another look around his home. I'd like to have a search warrant to visit Petra's gallery and apartment in St Ives. This is where Suze allegedly stayed Thursday night. We need proof that she did in fact stay there. Finally, I still need to interview the two witnesses, the Smith farmers that found Petra's body."

Peter replied, "Yes, do visit the farmers. That Alan is a character; he's most definitely worth visiting!"

Susan listened and joined the conversation. "Given that we may make arrests, would it be appropriate if we travelled with uniformed officers in a police car or two? I'm thinking if we were to make an arrest, or more, we've got uniformed officers to assist and secure cars to manage their arrests."

Peter liked the idea. "Yes, good idea. Given it's Saturday, St Ives can get very busy. The police cars could park anywhere as the public car parks could be full. Leave it to me, I'll sort it."

Jackie then spoke. "John mentioned some bruising marks around Petra's breasts and bite marks. I'll talk to PC Landy and check his findings."

Peter frowned. "That's strange as he didn't mention that aspect to me."

Jackie replied, "He almost didn't mention it to me either, he added it at the end of his narrative as though he forgot."

Peter, still frowning, added, "He's past retirement, maybe he should go now! Yes, do talk to Landy, he may be here now. I'll get another search warrant for Petra's gallery apartment organised and given to one of the uniformed officers who'll accompany you with their cars. Now get back to work and solve this hideous crime! Oh, by the way,

I've heard the press are aware, so you two beware! Don't get ambushed into saying something you'll later regret. Jackie, if you're approached refer them to me, unless you feel confident saying something. I know you've spoken to the press in your previous role."

Jackie felt pleased with the recognition from Peter that she was previously his equivalent but also knew the protocol was for senior officers to talk to the press after they were sanctioned by their superiors. The CID team planned the day's programme of movements and responsibilities.

After the meeting was over and the other officers were tasked, Jackie and Susan waited in the HV for their uniformed colleagues and transport.

It was now just after 9am. As they waited they drank strong black coffee. At 9:31 two marked police vehicles arrived with a male and female officer in one of the vehicles; Jackie and Susan chose to sit in the rear. The first driver was directed to visit Alex and Suze's address with the second car following behind. They arrived a short time later. The second of the officers waited near the cars whilst Jackie and Susan, accompanied by the female and male officer, knocked on the front door.

As they waited for an answer they heard Suze shouting from behind the closed door, "Who is it?"

Jackie replied, "Hi Suze, it's Jackie and Susan from the police, can we come in?"

The door unlocked and opened just slightly with the security chain stopping it fully opening. There stood Suze peeping out from inside.

Suze spoke, "Oh? What do you want ... I thought you may have been that horrible man from *The Cornish Daily News*! He was prowling around outside last night and he's back again this morning, knocking on our door regularly.

Alex told him to clear off when we realised he was peering through the windows last night. As the night progressed Alex was telling him to piss off when he saw him around the back. Later on, we saw him in the front garden, so Alex then shouted *fuck off* so loudly one of the neighbours came out as they were concerned about what was going on! He's been here again on our property just after eight this morning." She then removed the chain and opened the door.

Jackie replied, "I'm sorry to hear that, can we come in?"

Suze invited them in. Susan stalled as she asked one of the uniformed officers to ask her colleague with the cars to remain outside of the property boundary to fend off any trespassers. She didn't want or need any prying eyes hindering the investigation, whether they be journalists or from the general public.

Suze led the team into the kitchen where she offered seating. Alex appeared from upstairs.

"What's going on?" he asked with a frown.

Jackie said, "Good morning Alex. We need to ask more questions and would like to conduct another search. Our original warrant specified we could conduct multiple searches here, as per the copy you received yesterday. You can voluntarily answer our questions here or accompany us to the station for the interview."

There were looks of disbelief from both him and Suze. She put her hand over her mouth and began to cry.

Suze sniffed as she asked, "I thought we'd answered your questions yesterday?"

"You did," replied Jackie. "But as the investigation is evolving more evidence has arisen, and we need to ascertain facts."

Alex was annoyed; he wiped his tired eyes from an obvious sleepless night. "What evidence have you got now that you didn't have yesterday?"

Jackie calmly suggested they sit down so the process could begin. She knew standing at each other's throats antagonised situations, plus being interviewed in their home could be less stressful than the perceived formality within the police station.

Jackie knew she had to get Alex and Suze's full cooperation and felt that could be better achieved if the process was as informal as possible. If she conducted it more formally they may react in a different way that she didn't want or need just now. She wasn't yet convinced they had murdered Petra and needed conclusive evidence; all avenues of investigation had to take place.

After a while, Alex and Suze realised they needed to cooperate. Their beloved Petra was dead and gone, but neither liked the idea of strangers, including the police, going through their possessions and private affairs. It could be embarrassing and humiliating at the least ... or incriminating at worst, that that would most definitely be awkward and life changing for both Suze and Alex. Jackie seized the moment after they were all sitting, less the two officers who remained standing. She asked both Susan and the female officer to start the search, room by room. She asked the male officer to accompany and wait with Suze in the living room behind its closed door. Jackie remained in the kitchen with Alex. She closed the door for privacy, and both she and Alex sat at the table.

"Alex, I need to ask you some personal questions about Petra. The autopsy has been conducted ... the pathologist has found indications that Petra's death wasn't an accident."

Alex gasped.

"There is evidence showing marks around her neck that indicate she was strangled with a chain, like the strong necklace chains we took from here yesterday. What do you know about this?"

Alex began to cry, he wiped his eyes. "I told you everything I know yesterday."

Jackie responded, "Where did Petra get the chain from?"

Alex said, "She had several and gave some to Suze. I don't know where she got them from. Suze may know. They are a gothic design, I think."

Jackie said, "We know that you or Suze didn't strangle Petra as it wasn't your DNA around her neck."

Alex replied, "There you go! You're making out we killed Petra but there's no evidence as we didn't kill her … can't you see we loved her; she was our **Myluv**."

Jackie then pressed deeper into Alex. "And now the Suze is your other **Myluv**, as you wrote on your calendar after Petra's death?"

Alex looked at Jackie dumbfounded.

Jackie continued, "If Petra is dead, who gets her inheritance, who gets her gallery and apartment? You and your second **Myluv** … Suze?"

Alex's face reddened. He took a deep breath and stood. He looked down at Jackie and spoke. "You really don't get it, do you? We three loved each other. We never thought or cared about possessions. All we wanted was each other. Neither of us have wills or stuff like that. And as far as I know Petra isn't entitled to inheritance from her parents." He sat down when he finished and cried.

Jackie listened and wanted to believe what he'd just said. She needed to know about his and Petra's sex life. "When did you last have sexual intercourse with Petra?"

Alex froze with disbelief and embarrassment as he stared open mouthed at Jackie. His face grimaced as he replied, "That's really personal, I don't want to answer!"

Jackie continued, "Was it on Thursday, the same day that she walked out?"

He replied, "No comment!"

She asked, "What caused the very slight red marks around Petra's wrists and ankles?"

"No comment!"

Jackie immediately thought she was onto something. The savvy guilty who had things to hide would often use this phrase 'no comment' to defend their position. She thought it strange that he suddenly used the phrase.

Alex was weeping. His privacy and personal life were being torn apart and were now being embarrassingly opened and analysed by a complete stranger, and *she* was a female who wanted to hear very intimate details about his sex life. He was awkwardly shirking the question and had blushed, even though *she* was a police officer.

Jackie hadn't finished, she wanted more. "If you didn't kill Petra, then who did?"

Alex gasped again and blurted out, "I don't know! It definitely wasn't me!"

Jackie continued, "Was it your other '**Myluv**' … was it Suze?"

Suddenly Alex stood again and raised both his hands into the air with an angry growling appearance; his face reddened as he looked down and stared wide-eyed at Jackie. He grimaced, and shouted, "No it fucking wasn't Suze!"

Jackie sat motionless. She became concerned and frightened. Anger erupting this way could quickly turn to aggressive attacks. Jackie retained her exterior calm appearance whilst within she was shaking with fear. She slowly stood and stepped back. She quickly thought, *This, I hope will leave me in a less vulnerable position where I can try to defend myself from an impending onslaught of punches, kicks or headbutt.*

I've deliberately stepped back to remain away from Alex's boot reach. If a kick can't reach me then neither will his fists. My training and experience at this distance will keep me safe from a headbutt. I'll have time to counter the attack. Alex, being male, has a weak, very tender part of anatomy ... his testicles. I've played both rugby and football ... I know how to take accurate spot kicks. With my mean and powerful right foot, I could easily plant my new shiny black boot directly into his unprotected groin. I know it's his pleasure dome, which can excite and erupt like a volcano. But I also know it can easily become his damp squib in anticlimactic moments, such is its vulnerability with my good kick; I was saving this for Steve.

Jackie sensed quickly that her standing had a cooling effect on Alex; he now didn't have the high ground from towering over her seated position. She calmly and politely asked Alex to sit. He did, begrudgingly, as could be seen from his body language as he shook his head side-to-side whilst shrugging his shoulders up and down. Jackie relaxed too; her boot-to-ball guided missile counterattack didn't need to be launched. Jackie sat soon after he was seated. She continued, "Alex, I really don't intend to upset you but please realise I'm doing my job to establish why Petra is dead. Evidence is indicating she was strangled with a strong necklace, similar to the one she and Suze wear. She has marks that indicate she was bound in some way and there are a lot of unanswered questions. Did she have any enemies, people she didn't like? Anything that would help our enquiries is really important. Is there something you want to tell me?"

By sitting Alex had reduced the build up of intensity within his sore head. It felt like a pressure cooker that was about to explode as the safety valve had stuck, and it hadn't been able to release the steam. He answered Jackie's question. "Look, I loved Petra, as I do Suze. We three had a very special loving and open relationship with one another. We shared and knew everything about each other, including the intimate parts of each other's bodies. If I could have married both Petra and Suze at the same time I would have. Such is the love between us. And I'm sure they felt the same way about me, as they did for each other. Petra and Suze were in a relationship before I met Petra, and it became a normal extension that we had a three-way relationship when I met Suze. It was mutual. We three wanted it to be that way. It was extremely special. It was heaven. We were equals and in love. We never ever argued, nor did we hold grudges against each other, we fully respected one another. In fact, Suze is handing in her notice at her London job and relocating here. We were to live together full time with her moving in here. There is no way I or Suze had anything to do with Petra's death."

Alex stopped to wipe his eyes. He looked at Jackie who was listening attentively. She was beginning to believe and understand what she was hearing. Alex continued, "On Thursday evening Petra and I had watched an erotic TV programme that had made us feel good and turned us on. We made love on the sofa whilst watching the programme, as you do, or as *you* may not. When we'd finished, just after ten, Petra wanted to go for a walk as she could hear the patter of rain on the windows, and she loved to walk in the rain. Being out with nature gave her inspiration for her work. She didn't want me to go as I had a busy day ahead and was tired. She didn't mind going alone. This is a safe rural area. She didn't always dress fully when she walked, she liked to be free in nature and so went out without much clothing apart from her jeans, coat and boots. I know that's all she wore as we'd had a romantic bath together earlier. We never dressed after baths, there was no need to. We sat here starkers, lying together watching the programme. It's our home and that's what we do behind closed doors. Is there anything wrong with that? We don't think so. That was ... that was the last time I saw her." He broke down again, crying aloud.

Jackie was emotionally moved by his description of events on that fateful night. She wondered over the explanation. *But I still didn't have an answer about the bondage marks that John had uncovered during the autopsy, or where the second DNA analysis of semen came from. Should I tell Alex about it? No! I won't. If he offers to tell me then that would be OK, but it could be more upsetting if he was unaware. With the evidence John gave, with the signs of sexual abuse, it could be Petra was raped. That isn't what Alex needs to hear right now assuming he is innocent. I feel compassionate and want to put my hand on Alex's shoulder in a comforting way, but I won't. It could be misconstrued.*

When Alex had recovered a little Jackie asked again about the bondage marks. She had John's theory but needed to know if Alex, or Suze, had been involved with the bondage, in whatever context. She needed to check John's theory about food abstinence, maybe he was incorrect by saying others self-bonded. Jackie had wondered if they were caused by some type of torture. She needed to ask. "Alex, do you know how Petra's marks were caused, those on her wrists and ankles?"

Alex spoke in a soft voice. "Yes. Petra has been a troubled soul for many years. She's always had an eating disorder since I've known her. Initially she would disappear to vomit her food after eating to try and keep her shape. But this became awkward and uncomfortable for her and us. She would diet unsuccessfully when she never needed to lose weight. She weirdly found, from the internet, that self-bondage was a way that could help her by preventing her from eating. She would bind herself to a chair, sometimes for hours, where she could meditate and have self-enforced abstinence from food. Her body was self-imprisoned. It *was* bizarre, *but it worked* for her. She didn't do it in front of me or Suze. She felt embarrassed. We didn't interfere. She said it worked better if she was sitting in front of a mirror. She'd stare at herself. She'd talk to herself, questioning why she ate. We'd often suggest she see a doctor, or go to a clinic, but she declined. Suze and I categorically did not assist her in any way. It was us trying to get her to seek medical help, but she didn't. It was another way of dealing with her mind problem. She'd do it at her apartment, and here in the spare room. Suze and I never spoke about it to her as we respected Petra's wishes to keep it amongst us three. And that we did. Another thing was she often struggled to be creative. Like writer's block, but with her art. I think it started when she moved to St Ives and Suze wasn't around so often. When I first met Petra she craved for something, she would get the shakes and be irritable. Maybe she was obsessed with weight gain. She'd walk for miles daily, or just walk and sit, staring into space for hours. She needed to be alone, so I left her to it. She'd return happier. She opened up after a while and said she'd been taking herbal calming medication, initially in St Ives, with someone she'd met there who had a similar problem. When she moved in here she continued with her long walks. After a while she told me she had met an older man who had similar concentration issues with his work. As days and weeks passed, being like-minded they bonded and walked together. She said it was therapeutic for both of them to meet and chat about their problems. Apparently he was on the same herbal remedy. She sometimes came home in the early hours. When she did, she was revitalised and good to go. She had her bubbly persona and was the Petra I first met. It never really bothered me as I loved her for who she was, habits as well. I think she and the chap outlived their company and the regular meetings fizzled out. She continued with her walks and solace, arriving home in the early hours at least once a week. She always came back happy and refreshed; that was good. In the early days, I'd walk with her and wild camp. But over time my job became more demanding so I needed a regular sleep pattern. We three had our secret in that no one knew about our three-way relationship. It was our private relationship. They wouldn't understand and we'd become a target for jokes and jibes. We never interfered or imposed our relationships, or private stuff, with anyone else. We just simply loved each other and therefore respected Petra's problem ... is there anything wrong with that?"

Jackie too had personal secrets that were for her alone. If what Alex had said was true, then who was she to judge? She asked herself, *The Trio's life was different to some people's idea of normal, but that difference had appeared to work for them, so why not? I can't keep up with the new fashion of people types and what they like to be known as. So, if a threesome want to be known as a Trio, that's fine too. Inclusiveness is on the agenda in our modern society!*

She continued in her mind, *I'm still short of motives, evidence and answers. I know, I'll ask,* "Does Petra have a smart watch?"

Alex became more attentive. "Yes, she never takes it off, it's waterproof, virtually invisible, and I'm guessing you've found it. It isn't here."

Jackie was pleased to hear this as she replied, "Yes, we've found it, it's being analysed."

He said optimistically, "Good! It has a tracker so it will have mapped her route! We'll know where she walked, with the times and other useful stuff!"

Jackie smiled. She sensed Alex was as keen as she was to

establish facts. She continued, knowing her next sentence wouldn't go well. "We need to take your phones, along with Suze's, as evidence to be checked over. They will be returned as soon as we've finished with them. This will be inconvenient for you, but remember the reason, we're trying to find the clues. Something insignificant to you could be a clue we'd like to follow and that may lead us to the answers we all seek."

Alex became compliant. He just wanted Petra to rest in peace and have closure for both him and Suze. He gave the phones to Jackie without quibble.

Jackie asked, "Did Petra have any enemies, people who may have threatened her?"

Alex smiled for the first time. "No, she was well liked by everyone who knew her. She never ever mentioned about enemies as she didn't have any."

She nodded. "The reason I ask is that we need to check your bank accounts, we need to see that everything is regular."

He replied, "Yes, do that. We have nothing to hide. We never got to say goodbye to Petra ... before she died. That's really sad and it hurts both Suze and I ... that we never said that final goodbye." His eyes welled and he dropped his head into his hands.

The raw emotion got to Jackie this time. She was beginning to believe everything Alex had told her. She felt a tear was welling in her eye, she fought it from flowing down her cheek and then quickly wiped it whilst Alex looked away. She then put her hand on his shoulder as she felt her mind tugging and nagging. She spoke. "*I really do* feel sad for you both. Why don't you write her a goodbye letter?"

Alex lifted his head and sorrowfully looked at Jackie as he softly spoke. "But she's gone, she'll never read it?"

Jackie patted her hand gently on his shoulder and said, "You write it as though she'll read it. You'll say all those things you loved about her. Those fantastic times you've had with her. And you'll say your goodbyes. If there is something greater than us, she'll read it and she'll be happy that you said goodbye. Suze could write a letter too, or you do one together."

Alex looked Jackie in the eye; this time he saw her tears. He felt it was Petra asking for the goodbye through Jackie. The empathy between Jackie and Alex was mutually shared, no words were said, they had a moment where nothing was said but their connection was special.

When the special moment ended, Jackie thanked Alex for his cooperation and asked him to remain in the kitchen whilst she swapped places with the uniformed officer in the living room. She knew in her heart that Alex wouldn't know where the other DNA semen came from. She didn't want to put him under even more pressure with him knowing that Petra could have been raped *or* had a secret lover. She'd wait and see how the investigation mapped out before she asked such an awkward question. Time would tell as she listened to the *tick-tock, tick-tock* from the kitchen clock as she passed it.

Susan and the other officer were still upstairs searching for evidence, as could be heard from the rummaging noises as Jackie walked through the hall. She let her held-back tears come out as she looked at the decorative art works on the walls. She wiped her eyes hoping they wouldn't appear reddened. It was an emotional raw time. She then entered the living room.

Suze sat on the sofa looking fretful. She may have heard Alex's anger. Jackie asked the officer to swap places and go into the kitchen with Alex. She closed the door behind him and then smiled at Suze as she sat next to her. She asked, "Suze, I need to ask you questions relating to Petra's death." She then went on to explain the circumstances why she needed to know and then went forward with, "You said you arrived at Petra's apartment in the early hours of yesterday morning and stayed there after a late train arrival. Did you go directly to the apartment?"

Suze now felt intense the pressure as though she was going to explode; tears began to roll down her face as she replied, "Yes I did. The train arrived in the very early hours yesterday morning. There weren't many people about and it's a short walk to the gallery and apartment."

"Did anyone see you go into the gallery?"

"Not as far as I'm aware."

"Did you contact anyone, like Alex or Petra, to say you had arrived?"

"No. It was too early in the morning; they would have been asleep. But the gallery is alarmed and the date and time of me switching off the alarm will be recorded. Plus, there is CCTV that will show my arrival time and movements within the gallery. I texted both Petra and Alex the night before to let them know I was definitely arriving early Friday morning."

"Once you went into the apartment did you leave before Alex called you with news that he was concerned about Petra?"

"No, I didn't leave. I had a shower and went straight to bed at about 1am. I slept through until Alex called at about 7am. The CCTV would have recorded my departure as I set the alarm when I left. The CCTV within the gallery continuously records 24/7 so everything is caught on camera."

There was a pause from Jackie whilst she waited for

Suze to wipe tears away from her face. She then asked Suze, "What time did you call a taxi, and what company was it?"

Suze gave the details. Jackie would have the details checked later as she was going to seize Suze's phone for evidence. This would confirm the calls and texts, along with their times and dates. She would also access her bank accounts for details of transactions. Now she knew there was CCTV at the gallery she'd get that analysed too. Jackie then focused on other aspects,

"Suze, your boots, where did you get them?"

"I got them in St Ives at the same time Petra got hers. They were an identical pair, same size and colour. We got them a few months ago; I still have the receipt if you'd like it? The shop isn't far from the gallery."

"Yes that would be very helpful, thank you. And your necklaces, they look the same."

"Yes they were. We were so alike in our fashion and other ways. Even the same size clothes! We'd share everything, like good sisters!" Suze had a very slight smile.

Jackie raised a discreet eyebrow; Alex mentioned their relationship just a short time ago. She asked where the necklaces were purchased from, and again like the boots, they came from a shop in St Ives. The jewellery shop name was given and noted by Jackie. Jackie now wanted to dig deeper into Suze's personal life. "Suze, what was your relationship to Petra?"

Suze replied, "Actually, Alex and I discussed your visit yesterday and we felt that honesty and openness was required, particularly with your investigation into Petra's death. We don't share our private lives with anyone, as you may appreciate some things that are personal should be kept that way, and it's awfully embarrassing. But with you we trust what we say is confidential, so I will explain. Petra was my best friend and lover ... as Alex is ..." She paused with slight embarrassment and then continued. "The three of us are in ... *were* in a three-way relationship. We were a Trio. We're not now ... as Petra's dead!" Suze wept. Tears rolled down her face. After a while she composed herself and explained the relationship, as Alex had done earlier, although she was unaware he had done just that. She then handed her phone over and confirmed Petra's addiction to exercise and abstinence from food. She explained, "When I first met Petra at college all those years ago, we just clicked and fell in love with each other. As I have done with Alex and he with me. As we three loved each other equally we wanted a three-way marriage, but as you know that isn't allowed here in the UK. So, we drew straws, the two longest drawn would marry. I drew the shortest. But it didn't matter as we three knew our love for each other wouldn't change. It was mutual and perfect. Petra told me years ago about her need to exercise to maintain both her fitness and athletic appearance. She wanted to look good for me, and then for Alex too. She said her mother's side of the family were quite large, particularly the females. The men liked their women, wives and partners big. Petra didn't want to be large. Gradually, as we grew older, Petra tried different ways to maintain her size, like vomiting after eating. She then found a technique – the bond method – online. She's used it since, which when you think about it, is really safe, tame, drug free and not disgusting like vomiting. The idea is you simply bind yourself to a chair until the desire to eat passes. You can't reach food. Petra actually found the process therapeutic and helpful for her mind; to wander away from the thought of food and the need to eat. Her wandering mind helped her to focus with creativity, as well as karma and mindfulness. She was a wonderful person when I met her as a young woman and she just became better with age, that's why I and Alex loved her *so* much. She wore a smart watch to maintain a level of fitness that matched her goal. It all worked out fine, *but* I do wonder if she focused too much on her fitness. I guess she became obsessive, but then don't we all obsess about something or other at some time? She really didn't have to diet or lose weight. She was just perfect; it was just in her mind. There is something else I need to tell you. We three have used drugs before. Alex way before he met Petra and me. He stopped some 12 years ago. Petra and I smoked it whilst at college. Not the heavy stuff like heroin, just weed. We both stopped when we left college. But I think Petra's bondage was also used to prevent her from taking drugs. I'm not sure, it's just a hunch. I never caught her doing it, nor have I come across any evidence of it. Needless to say, I felt she was floating some days. More so than her hippy-dippy way. Her art had changed too. It became far more relaxed; the images were blurry rather than sharp. They were still just as exceptional, but more intriguing."

Jackie felt Suze's relationship explanation was plausible. It could be a truthful scenario as it matched Alex's, *or* it could be a well-rehearsed plan to cover for their involvement. *The jury is out*, she thought. On the drug issue, she needed to investigate further. John would be the person to ask.

She asked Suze to rejoin Alex in the kitchen. She had heard enough for now. The officer stayed with Suze and Alex in the kitchen whilst Jackie searched the lounge and hall, she didn't find anything incriminating. What she did find was a lot of love as shown in the photos and artwork of The Trio.

As the seconds ticked away, like the annoying kitchen clock, Jackie was starting to think, *Suze and Alex* are not *who I had first suspected, being guilty partners. I am slightly envious of The*

Trio's relationship with one another, not because I want a threesome, that just isn't me ... well, not for now, maybe later! She chuckled in her mind with that thought. *My envy is for the love depicted between The Trio. It was the love that I wanted from a partner or spouse who I haven't yet found.* As she looked at the artwork it was evident to her, *The Trio's love for each other is immense. The images pour out with intensity from the three-way relationship that I didn't notice yesterday, but now I've had the story from Suze and Alex.* She blinked at one image and another tear welled in the corner of her eye; she gulped as the love shone out and blinded her. True love had yet to find her. The tear was both her emotion, having not experienced such love, and for the love that was projected by the pleasure and happiness shown by The Trio's affection for each other. Her mind said, *Sadly, that kind of joyous love has eluded you, I thought I had it, but it was stolen from me!*

Jackie wiped her eye and regained composure as she walked slowly step by step upstairs, passing the glorious art on the stairwell. She walked onto the landing where she found the uniformed officer coming out of the attic hatch. He shook his head as nothing had been found there. Susan appeared from the largest bedroom.

"Hello Vera. Sorry, I mean Jackie!"

Jackie smirked knowing Susan was being herself as she gruffly said, "Found anything?"

Susan stared at Jackie as she asked, "Are you OK? You look red in the face and upset; have you been crying?"

Jackie replied immediately, "No ... no, I had something in my eye." She didn't lie, she did have something in her eye, she just didn't explain that it was a tear.

Susan then beamed a large smile as she produced her find within the evidence bag. "Look what I have in my bag! There are two *red* dressing gown belts. Come in, have a tour.

The third bedroom is more a storeroom than anything else ... but I found this chair that I think Petra was using as her bondage frame! I've found two unused bright red bathrobes hung on the door that have their belts missing. The belts were under the chair. I've taken photos of how it was before I released the belts. I'm guessing you tie yourself onto the chair then use your imagination, the psychology of being restrained and out of control. Being helpless and alone, but at the same time being in control of the restraint. With Petra's technique I'm guessing she really wanted abstinence within her mind and the physical restraint of being bound removed her from actually getting to food, let alone putting it into her mouth. The robes are newish; they still have the shop labels attached. I don't think they've ever been worn. The belts are just slightly worn from being around her ankles and hands. I'll get a larger bag, so we can take the pair of robes. Forensics could identify if the belts are the ones that match the gowns, and more importantly if the fragments found around Petra's wrists and ankles match them!"

Jackie smiled. "Well done Susan. Excellent work! That technique could also stop the bound person from smoking or taking drugs ... have you found any drugs or herbal remedies?"

"No, we haven't found anything like that?"

Just then Jackie noticed a box of lip balm pens. She walked over to the box curiously as people tend to buy just the one or two pens, not two boxes. The label showed they each contained 30 lip balm pens. She asked Susan, who had gloves on, to check how many were inside. Susan counted 13 in the opened box; the other box was unopened.

Jackie replied, "OK, put the boxes in bags as evidence for forensics. Just a hunch I have." She continued, "I've interviewed both Suze and Alex. Their stories match and independently they both had the same scenario that pathologist John alluded to. Petra had an eating disorder, this weird self-bondage technique to enforce abstinence could be the reason for the marks on her wrists and ankles. Great! You've got the evidence that will hopefully tie in with John's analysis."

Susan discreetly chuckled and whispered, "Boom-boom! You said, 'tie in' Ha-ha, but I understand your context!"

Jackie had a shocked appearance. "Save your jokes. This is a murder enquiry! Show respect!"

Susan, red faced, immediately apologised.

They walked downstairs as Jackie spoke loudly so the uniformed officer could hear her plan. "Right, we've got some evidence for analysis. Officer, please collect new statements from both Suze and Alex, there are amendments from yesterday that need updating. We have no need to arrest either at this time. They don't appear to have been involved in Petra's death, but we'll keep an open mind. Susan and I will go to St Ives with your colleague outside. You two will remain here with the one car, one inside the property, the other outside. Be aware that a journalist could be prowling around, please keep any off the property. If you need back-up, request it. If there's any query, refer it to DI Peter Drew to sanction."

The officer nodded with acknowledgement, as did Susan with her reply, "Sounds good to me!"

The three entered the kitchen. Jackie relayed her plan to both Suze and Alex. Petra's gallery and apartment keys were handed over, along with the alarm code and their three phones. The officer remained to take the revised statements with today's additional information. Jackie thanked Suze and Alex for their cooperation, and she and Susan said their goodbyes to leave with a uniformed officer.

No sooner had they closed the front door behind them, than they saw a person taking their photos from behind one of the police cars. The officer standing by was trying to stop the journalist from entering the property. Jackie astutely walked to the journalist.

He asked, whilst holding up his press ID card and camera, "What's going on. I've heard there's been a murder, a female body has been found mutilated on the beach. I've been told that the occupants of this property are suspects, is that why the police are here?"

Jackie assertively replied, "Hello. I'm DC Jackie Smith. Sadly, yesterday morning, around 6am we found the body of Mrs Petra Munro on the beach near Tamorna Cove." She continued with accurate information but didn't yet say it was a murder enquiry, rather a tragic fall from the wet clifftop during yesterday's storm. She also asked for any witnesses and the public's assistance. When she finished, she politely asked the journalist not to trespass onto the property and to respect the mourners at this tragic time. He had taken a movie of Jackie as she gave the statement. She thanked him for his cooperation and walked away as he fired a barrage of questions at her. She ignored them as she made her way to the vehicles. The officer politely used his body to stop the journalist encroaching into Jackie's path. She and Susan got into a car. Danny, the officer who blocked the journalist, was to take her and Susan to St Ives.

As Danny drove off, Susan said to Jackie, "Well done you! That was a bloody good announcement. That should hopefully stop a witch hunt."

Jackie replied, "Thanks, I've had experience. We could have referred him to Peter, but it's now sorted. Just give out limited true facts, don't lie, and ask for the public's assistance via 101. No one knows what we know, the witnesses who found Petra don't know she was murdered, as far as they are concerned the death was as a result of the fall. They were asked not to relay Petra's death, although they may have, we'll have words with them later. They're the farmers Smith. Someone else from the public may have seen something suspicious about which we don't yet know. Hopefully, if they do, they'll contact us as a result of the announcement *if* the news gets published. We need as much help as we can right now." She looked Susan in the eye. "It appears Suze or Alex didn't strangle her, nor was it Suze's boots at the clifftop. I didn't tell her that just now just in case she's involved somewhere. Someone else was at the scene, and we need to find that person. Alex did have sex with Petra Thursday night, just before her walk ... so, our second semen suspect, whoever that is, had intercourse with Petra after that time ... after she went for her walk. I didn't want to ask Alex if he knew who the other person was. If I had I think that news would have broken him. Let's see what develops today. Also, remember that journalists are always looking for a scoop story. They can throw innocent headlines at you with the intention that you'll bite if their speculative questioning hits the mark. They are like us, questioning to establish facts, and some are quite subversive as to how they obtain their information. So, the tip here is, don't give out anything that may jeopardise the investigation as that could alert and assist the criminals. Stick to a plan that gives out enough truth, but *not everything* we know. And remember, no news is good news."

Susan smiled back in acknowledgement and then said, "I'm sorry for my bad joke back there, I shouldn't have said it, and I won't do it again."

Jackie looked pleased. "Apology accepted, just don't do it again! Look here's my phone, you call Dawn, the liaison officer, to ask her to revisit Suze and Alex to give them additional support, they both need it right now. This will be a good way for you to introduce yourself to her." She gave Susan her phone so Dawn could recognise it was Jackie calling, rather than Susan's unknown phone number.

Susan made the call to Dawn who answered quickly. "Hello Jackie."

Susan replied, "Hi Dawn, this is Susan, Jackie's trainee. I'm on Jackie's phone, she asked me to call you."

"Oh, hello Susan, how are you?"

"Fine thank you, and you?"

"I'm good too, where's your boss?"

"She's alongside me and has asked me to call you so I can introduce myself and to ask you to do a job."

"OK, pleased to chat to you! What's the job?"

"Jackie is wanting you to re-visit Alex Munro, Petra's husband, and Suze. We've just been there to interview them again and they're both really upset. Can you visit?"

"Well, its Saturday and I'm just finishing my weekly shop, but can do after I've taken it home. Hopefully, I can get overtime, or time off in lieu. I could get to them within an hour or so, OK?"

Susan looked at Jackie for agreement. Jackie nodded. Susan continued, "Yes, that's perfect. Thank you."

"OK, will do. And hey, Jackie and I need to catch up over a drink, why don't you join us? Then I'll be able to meet you in person."

"Sure, I'd like that. I'll ask Jackie to call you to arrange."

"Fab, I'll await her call, say hi to her, bye for now."

"Bye."

The call ended. Susan gave the phone to Jackie. "Well done Susan, nice one!" She then high-fived her.

Jackie explained to Susan the interviews she had with

Suze and Alex. Susan listened keenly. She replied back to Jackie to check out her understanding. "Well, the picture forming in my mind is that The Trio *were* in love with each other, they lived together as lovers, and all was good with them. There didn't appear to be an obvious reason as to why Suze or Alex would have wanted to kill Petra. If there was, it could be jealousy, or for money. But inheritance wasn't a given as we don't yet know what Petra's parents' provision is. We need to find that out. Also, Petra and Alex didn't have a will, but the fact they're married could mean Alex inherits Petra's estate. So, there could be motive. It appeared the murderer was someone else, a male maybe because of the sexual intercourse. It could be a small male as the boot size is five. He wore identical boots, albeit with a small section of tread missing. Also, someone who may now have Petra's strong necklace, the murder weapon."

Just at that moment, Susan's phone rang. She answered it. The caller replied, "Hello Susan, it's Sally Newton from the MCU. I've checked out the searches you asked for Petra's parents and have a direct number for her mother."

Susan eyes lit up. "Excellent! Thank you very much!"

Jackie got the gist of the call and, when the call ended, she immediately asked Susan to call Mrs Kline. After the call with Petra's mother Susan fed back to Jackie.

"Mrs Kline said Suze and Alex informed her yesterday about Petra's death. It was a shocking thing for her to hear. She and hubby are coming here today, on their private jet! They land at Land's End Airport 3pm today. I said we'll see them later and have asked her to call me back when they're available."

Jackie smiled. "Super. I like it when parts of the jigsaw fall into place. Now we'll get it from Petra's parents if there are any inheritance gains for anyone related to Petra. Motive plays a key part with criminals. Money could be that *big* motive here. And from what you found out yesterday, Mrs Kline *is* very wealthy. That's a twist in that we can't yet rule out Alex or Suze just now. Well done Watson!"

CHAPTER 10
ST IVES

The car drove to St Ives, an attractive tourist hotspot town on the north coast of Cornwall. It was a 36-minute drive from Suze and Alex's home, it was now 10:31am. Jackie and Susan stopped talking as they approached the town and admired the glorious sea views. They were mesmerised with the changing natural light that was casting itself over the sea. The sea was forever changing colour as it was illuminated by the alternative bright and darker clouds that were still racing overhead. The clouds were being backlit by the sun above, creating a magical appearance. The sun was trying its best to shine through and would occasionally find a gap between the clouds, nudging the bleak darkness away. When this happened Jackie's mind tugged again. This tugging felt unnatural to her, she was becoming more concerned with its frequency, she wondered if it was the bright light from the sun. The sensation ended as quickly as it started as her thoughts returned to Petra. She thought, *I must get this checked out, not only is it bloody annoying but it could be serious!* The clouds had created moody scenes with their different shades. The daylight changed from an angry gloomy darkness to a calm, warm and bright tone. When brightness did shine through, the sea had Caribbean colours, pale blues, turquoise and then jade green to crystal clear. At this moment it looked spectacular and very inviting but as the darker clouds reappeared the sea became dark grey and far more ominous.

Jackie spoke. "Look there, the railway line passes that beautiful sandy beach. There are several beaches here, all sandy. That's one of the reasons why St Ives is like a magnet for tourists. There are numerous holiday resorts, plenty of hotels, B&Bs plus other types of accommodation. Suze would have arrived at the station and then walked to Petra's studio early yesterday morning."

Susan was mesmerised with the continually changing light and how it lit St Ives. There was now the added attraction of many sandy beaches. She made a mental note to bookmark this town as a definite place to visit as she replied, "I'm a keen swimmer and mainly swim indoors, I'll definitely come here to try cold water swimming in the sea. I haven't really tried cold water swimming, but I understand it's *so* invigorating."

Jackie looked at her. "Well, when you do, let me know, I could join you!"

Susan smiled, "Really?"

"Yes, definitely! I need to do some more exercise, the older you get the lardier you get. I'm not ready to get too large, not yet anyway!"

Susan laughed. "You're not fat at all. Don't you go getting like Petra and become obsessed. The next thing you'll be getting is a smart watch to measure how many steps you're doing every day. You're as fat as you feel; believe me you don't look fat at all!"

Jackie laughed aloud as she spoke. "Have you heard of a jelly belly?"

"No. What's that?"

"Well, it's like a six pack but horizontal. Six rolls of fat that wobble."

Susan replied, "Yes, *we'll both* have those after last night's huge curry!"

They both laughed aloud as did Danny the driver. He had been making out he wasn't listening to his female colleagues up to that point. Susan had noticed and so asked the officer, "Have you got a six pack?"

He coughed and spluttered as he nearly choked whilst he laughed. "Yes, I have! They are six lagers, and they're in my fridge staying cold until tonight ... that's the easiest way to get a six pack!" All three laughed.

Jackie then had another silent thought in her mind as she her memory drifted back to last night and how she found Susan sat in the shower. *Susan has a younger body. A young nubile dark body that is lean and good looking. I recall the time when my body looked that way, lean and perfect! I wonder how Petra must have felt about hers as she became more and more conscious about her size. We are similar ages, 36ish. That's old compared to early twenties like Susan.*

As Jackie's thoughts rolled around in her mind the car arrived in the town centre. She snapped out of the unanswered questions as they made their way into the sometimes very narrow streets. Danny was adept with his ability to manoeuvre around the tight corners and after a short while, with splendid views of several beaches, they arrived near the well-known Tate gallery. The majestic Tate building overlooked a glorious sandy bay and was situated on a promenade road. Danny slowed to look for Petra's address. He stopped immediately outside the **Myluv & Myluv** gallery located in its premier position next to the Tate.

The gallery frontage looked extremely swanky with a huge plate glass window that was adorned with a huge sign above that surprisingly showed the unmistakable **Myluv & Myluv** logo in large bright red letters. Jackie and Susan got out and looked around to take in the ambience of the location. It was breathtaking. An artist's heaven with the natural light appearing uncannily different and more beautiful with every cloud that drifted over. When the sun shone the sea glistened and seagulls squawked as they flew overhead. The front of the studio caught the light and allowed it to pass through to the magnificent window display where the natural light lit the art. The art was beautiful, exotic and some of it quite erotic. It was Petra and Suze's artwork.

Jackie unlocked the door. The alarm countdown had started as she went inside, she entered the code to disable it.

"OK Susan, you find the apartment and have a look there, I'll check out the gallery. I was going to say I don't think we'd find anything, but that could *be* wrong. I always anticipate that things may not be what I think, and that we need to check, and keep on checking, to be certain."

Susan nodded in agreement as she made her way to locate the apartment.

The gallery was a lavish space. Jackie was impressed by the quality and nature of the images, despite not being an art expert. There were beautiful colourful paintings, pencil and biro drawings, photographs and sculptures that featured a mix of abstract scenes and the erotic. She wandered around admiring the art but also for evidence of any kind. She found none apart from the obvious love that was reinforced and displayed in some of the art. At that moment she again felt her head twang. It was becoming medically concerning. She needed paracetamol and would ask Susan if she had any within one of her many pockets. As she continued her search there were abstract images of The Trio to disguise themselves. They were obvious to Jackie, as was the three-way love between them. It was discreetly done so neither could be identified, but Jackie knew … she was familiar with their story. She glanced out of the studio window and saw many passersby who stopped to look in at the magnificent window display. Many smiled with obvious delight and chatted to each other as they pointed at the works of art.

Some had tried to enter but realised the gallery was closed. Jackie felt honoured by her private viewing.

Jackie finished her search and meandered upstairs to look for Susan in the apartment. As she entered she was met by a stunning panoramic view. The glorious sandy beach, stretching both left and right, and then to infinity, out towards the sea where its line met the sky. She spoke loudly as she couldn't yet see Susan. "Wow! If the view doesn't make you happy then nothing will. Absolutely amazing!"

Susan was still making her way around and her head popped out behind a door. She was smiling. "Yes, I totally agree. And for Petra and Suze to have their gallery below is just perfect. It would have been most inspiring to create art here."

Jackie shook her head. "I haven't found anything incriminating, how are you getting on?"

Susan smiled. "Look what I've found! Another heavy necklace!"

Jackie smiled. "Perfect! The more the merrier, goes the saying. OK, let's wrap it up here."

Just as she finished her phone rang, it was John the pathologist. She switched her phone to speaker so Susan could hear.

"Hello John, how are you?"

"Jackie, I'm fine thank you. Listen, Petra's smart watch has come back from forensics. Several things are evident. On Thursday evening she was at home in Dartin. Between 9 and 10pm her heart rate increased. At 9:45 it dramatically increased and subsided thereafter for around ten minutes. I think this could be due to Petra having sex for that duration. This period fits with the lab analysis of the semen's age profile."

Jackie spoke. "That also matches with Alex's admission

to having intercourse around the same time!"

John replied, "Good, that answers one aspect. Just after 10pm she went for a walk, she walked to Paidwick Castle arriving 10:39. She was there until 1:37am yesterday morning. From there she slowly walked to the clifftop, arriving 2:42am, her pace had increased somewhat during the latter section of the walk, compared to the initial slow pace when she left the castle. At 2:53am there was a very rapid acceleration ... that would be due to her fall. The watch stopped recording at 2:55am, that would be the time of her death as her heart finally stopped at that time."

Jackie had a quizzical expression as she listened and then replied, "So she was at Paidwick Castle for three hours?"

John's voice enthused, "Yes! And there's more. At 10:45pm, a short while after arriving at the castle, her heartrate rose dramatically and stayed high for over an hour, as though she was on an intense gym workout, then for two hours it dropped to a resting pace, as though she was asleep."

Jackie immediately said, "Right, we're in St Ives but will go there very soon. Anything else?"

There was a pause from John. "Yes, there sadly is. Petra's other semen result indicates the second sample, from its age analysis, suggests it was introduced sometime between 12:20 and 1:20am. She had intercourse with an unknown male during this time, and that *was at* Paidwick Castle. Strangely, at this time her heart rate slowed as though she was in a resting state. I can't yet prove it, but I think she may have been drugged into a relaxed state ... and the intercourse took place then. It could be, given her bite marks, she was abused."

Jackie interrupted, "Do you mean she was drugged and then raped?"

John's tone lowered. "The indications are suggesting that. If she orgasmed with Alex, she didn't with the perpetrator at the castle." There was silence for a moment. John continued, "We think Petra had small traces of a drug substance. We haven't been able to identify it yet as, whatever it is, it rapidly disappears into thin air. It shouldn't degrade as her body isn't functioning. It could be a new synthetic drug, or some other substance that could explain her relaxed state of resting, this could be when she was potentially abused. As soon as I know I'll be in touch."

Jackie replied, "Well that's very interesting. We found something that seems rather odd, but I've a funny feeling about it, we've included it just in case … it's a box of lip balm pens."

John replied, "Any evidence is good, I look forward to receiving it all! My assumptions about Petra's food abstinence have been reinforced. Her fitness obsession was obvious within the history section of the watch whereby her daily fitness activity amounted to abnormal amounts. She would have needed food to supply her fuel for the energy expenditure. Overeating could soon add bulk and weight gain. If she were weak-willed she could easily overeat. My theory of self-binding to prevent this, if willpower is low, could be true."

Jackie enthusiastically replied, "Yes! John, we have found red robe belts as potential evidence to confirm your theory. We'll get them to you for analysis. Alex explained Petra's eating disorder and the self-bonding was to enforce abstinence. There wasn't any sexual implication with her bondage."

They summarised their conversation and said their goodbyes, the call ended.

Jackie looked at Susan. "Right Susan, let's finish here,

go to the shoe retailer, the necklace shop and then onto Paidwick Castle!"

Just at that moment Susan saw a kitchen table chair in the bathroom. It was the last room she had to check. She quickly marched into the room and saw two familiar red dressing gowns, which looked new, hung on the rear of the door but without their belts. *They* were hung on a different hook, and *they* looked used. She replied to Jackie, "OK, but first I'll take these two belts that look remarkably similar to the two we've taken from Alex's home. John can have these for analysis as well. Also, I found another box of lip balm pens, look."

Susan smiled. "Don't you think a second box of 30 is excessive? There's only five pens in here."

Jackie replied, "Well, what's your point?"

Susan replied, "Just seems strange."

Jackie said, "OK, my thoughts too! Put them in an evidence bag and we'll get those evaluated too."

Susan wore PPE gloves and quickly opened the cover from a balm to have a closer look. It looked like a regular balm. She twisted the handle and the balm head appeared. She sniffed the white-coloured balm tip; there was a strange alluring smell. She was tempted to try it on her lips.

Jackie abruptly shouted, "No! Don't you dare! That could be dangerous for your health, and more importantly you'll be interfering with evidence. Put the lid on and return it to the box. Bag and seal it!"

Susan obeyed sheepishly with an apology.

Jackie replied, "Good find, well done, now let's go shopping!"

They left the apartment and gallery, securing it at their exit with the alarm.

"Susan, can you put a call out for forensics to call in

here to obtain the CCTV recordings for Thursday and Friday, plus conduct a thorough search in case we've missed something. They'll validate Suze's arrival and departure times."

"Noted, will do," replied Susan.

Danny was waiting next to the car. Jackie spoke. "Danny, we need to go to Daltons Shoes and then on to a jeweller nearby. And thereafter Paidwick Castle!"

They set off on the next leg of the journey, again winding their way through the very narrow streets of the town. They soon arrived at Daltons Shoes. It was a small shop but with a long history going back to the 18th century as could be read on the prominent aged frontage sign.

Susan remarked, "This place reminds me of one of those shops depicted in a Dickens novel. Quaint and quintessential!"

They entered to hear the old-fashioned 'ting' of the bell attached to the wooden door. There in front of them was the most amazing and historic old-fashioned shoe shop with a marvellous display of footwear on antique wooden stands and shelves. An older balding man with thick curly sideburns approached, he smiled as he spoke eloquently.

"Good morning, how may I help?"

Jackie replied whilst showing her ID, "Good morning, we're making enquiries about a specific style of woman's walking boot. Susan, please could you show your phone pics to the gentleman?"

Susan obliged and presented her images to him.

He smiled. "Yes, they're our very popular 'Stellar' model. We sell them to local people who like to walk, agricultural workers, and such like."

Jackie's expression lit up as she asked, "Do you keep your clients' names and addresses?"

"No, sorry we don't as purchases are predominantly made with debit and credit cards these days. We have no reason to take anything other than the card details that are not stored here."

Jackie asked, "So you can't list the size fives to the card numbers, as from that we could identify the names and addresses of the customers?"

He laughed. "No, I can't do that, but the card issuers could. You'd have to speak to them."

Jackie knew this but asked as some traditional retailers *did* take names and addresses as they wrote out handwritten receipts, maintaining the old-fashioned ways. She looked at Susan, "Right, your next task is to get onto the card issuers."

Susan nodded whilst immediately thinking she'd task Sally, the MCU communications officer, to conduct this aspect. That she did.

They thanked the gentleman and left. As they entered the street, a shop a few doors down caught Susan's eye. It was a jewellers.

"Look!" Susan pointed to it and started to cross the street heading towards the shop called Gothic Jewellery. As they neared the frontage, they noticed a sign hanging within the window reading 'New and Used Jewellery' and below another read 'Items Bought and Sold for Cash'. They peered through at the window display. There were all types of jewellery, including chains, some of which appeared to be similar to those already collected as evidence.

Jackie spoke. "Well spotted Susan, let's go in, this looks promising."

They entered the shop to the smell of roll-up tobacco smoke, plus something else. The second smell was far more enchanting and alluring. Susan thought, *That's the smell of the balm!* Music was playing, not modern, but an old type that one associates with the genre court jesters would dance to in medieval times.

A strange tall older man and younger shorter woman were chatting behind the low sales counter. The two ignored Jackie and Susan. Jackie and Susan pretended to be perusing the stock but at the same time were watching the strange couple. The man and woman were more consumed with each other. They were, at first, standing sideways to Jackie and Susan, where they continued with their conversation with each other in a flirtatious way. They laughed and joked as they continually touched each other as though they were *very* familiar. His teeth were browned with tar and nicotine stains; hers were brighter and every now and then something glistened within her mouth. She appeared to be considerably younger than him. He had grey, tightly swept back hair, as it flowed from his forehead, up and over down to his neck into a ponytail at the rear. The flimsy ponytail wafted around the side of his head with small bows tied at the ends. These looked like dark small butterflies, or even moths, as he nodded and laughed aloud. His long grey goatee beard had a bell at the end of it that rang every time he moved his head, or when he chuckled, as he did often. His ear lobe hung horribly low as it was stretched with the heavy weight of a large metal earring – which may have been a fishing line weight – dangling from its pierced hole. The hole was the size of a 10p coin with a gold ring within to prevent the lobe from tearing with the excessive weight. Even more bizarre was a neck tattoo that mimicked necklace chain links. Jackie noticed this and nudged Susan. She discreetly pointed to her own neck and made it obvious as she glanced to her right towards the man's tattoo, hoping Susan would see it. Susan did see it and casually nodded with acknowledgement. There were red coloured spatterings around the chain tattoo and a ghastly red dribble that imitated blood weeping from cuts the chain had made. All very similar to Petra's wound. He wore a very tight-fitting, and far too short, grubby egg-stained vest that looked stupid for the six-feet plus height on his tall skinny frame. Wisps of curly grey chest hair could be seen above the vest's neckline and below its bottom; it only covered his lower ribs. His protruding belly button was pierced and stretched by another heavy metallic weight. Jackie thought, *This could be his navel tongue and looks like a work in progress. Its ghastly and looks horrible!* Long curly pubic hairs protruded above his loose-fitting jeans that were worn far too low and only just held up by his bony hips.

The woman, if she were, could easily pass for being a young girl less than 18. Susan was thinking, *She looks at least 30 years younger than the old man. Her shiny long thick black plaited hair with striking red and blue colour tones throughout hangs neatly from her head!* There was a piercing through her nostril that she repeatedly fiddled with as though it itched and was annoying her. Periodically, and unhygienically, she twiddled and played with the piercing. There also appeared to be some piercings throughout the side of her tongue, which glistened as she spoke. Susan thought they resembled sharp ominous shark teeth but also diamonds that sparkled in the light. She too was flimsily dressed in a very loose-fitting and *so* obvious see-through t-shirt that showed her full breast form to be without a bra. Her erect nipples were clearly visible as were the attached piercings within. There was a snake tattoo, with its tail starting from her left wrist. The image increased in size from its lower body as it snaked up around her arm and on across the top of her shoulder. The thoracic section of the snake had increased its girth as it disappeared provocatively from her shoulder down the front of her chest neatly between her voluptuous bosoms. She deliberately *and* sensuously pulled her shoulder down and backwards to make her breasts appear larger. Their volume appeared to increase as she glanced from the corner of her eye toward Susan. She wanted to be watched. Susan *was* watching her. Susan had become magnetised and attracted to the woman's performance, which she found bizarre, but also quite erotic. The two strange characters suddenly became silent as they turned to face Jackie and Susan.

Jackie had seen most things, but the pair before her were unique. They both shocked and calmed her. Their graphic visual display of the extraordinary within the relaxing effect of their performance left her amazed. Jackie felt a good mood of serenity that made her feel comfortable, at peace and satisfied. She couldn't explain why she felt lightheaded. She took another deep breath of the pleasurable atmosphere. She could taste an addictive scent that had wrapped itself around her, like a warm love-filled caress. The aroma again entered her nose where it fuelled her desire for more, her sensory receptors were flooded with delight as the smell swam within her body. It was so alluring it wanted, and needed, to be breathed in again and again. Unknowingly to her, the air she breathed in was tainted. It slowly and successfully anchored in her mind as it became addictive; she wanted more of the musky oud fragrance. She had become happy as her head felt lighter. She glanced at Susan who was fixated with the female. Jackie smiled; Susan's jaw-dropping mouth resembled the dog that her sister owned. At its feeding time it would have long sticky drool strings of saliva hanging from his jowls that resembled hot wax falling from candles. Susan's wide-eyed appearance and her open jaw was replicating the said dog; she too was salivating at the side of her mouth. Susan, Jackie thought, had become intoxicated with the woman's presence, and the strange but *so* pleasant atmosphere. Jackie felt she was floating. It was a surreal and very weird time, but now it felt *so* good to be here. There was no urgency now. This was a relaxing space, and it all felt good and warm within. Jackie was unaware she and Susan were slowly and surely being trapped by the mesmerising odour.

The man and women had turned around and were now facing Jackie and Susan. Their visual appearance had suddenly and quite dramatically changed. If they had been shocked at first, their look now escalated to that of shock horror. They both had completely half-shaved their heads bald. Seeing them sideways on hadn't shown this anomaly; they had one side with hair, and the other side without. The female stared at Susan and cutely smiled, as though their attraction was mutual. She glided with a mesmerising movement from behind the counter and appeared to float towards Susan. Suddenly her tongue flicked out, like a snake gathering information about its surroundings. She had mimicked the use of her tongue where snake tongues are sensory tools. She was detecting if Susan was a predator … prey … *or* a mate. Her tongue flicked up and down as she proudly showed the sharp silver studs on either side of her waving tongue. She lifted the tattooed-snake-adorned arm and put her hand behind her head that then exposed a thickly haired armpit. As she slithered from behind the counter, she raised her opposite arm to deliberately show its armpit was shaved bald, like the opposite side of her head. With both arms raised, her breasts pushed forwards as her chest naturally lifted up and forwards. Her t-shirt raised up exposing her bare stomach to just below her breasts. Her low-slung Lycra skin-hugging shorts were just above her pubic area. On her stomach the snake tattoo could now be seen arcing down towards her studded navel to then disappear down under the front of her shorts into her mons pubis area.

The man followed the woman; he too appeared to glide provocatively. As he moved, his short vest showed that one half of his chest was shaved, as was his opposite armpit. He smiled, showing shiny gold caps on some of his dirty rotten teeth. He spoke with a gravelly voice.

"Wot can we *do* to you two?"

Jackie needed her ID but couldn't remember where it was; she was intoxicated. She slowly felt around her pockets but forgot why she was doing so. It was found by chance as she casually produced her ID.

"We'd ... we'd ... we'd ..." She didn't finish. She giggled.

The man spoke. "Yeah, yeah, my dear, we'd all like some weed. Is that wot yor arfter?"

Jackie giggled. "Nah, we'd like to ask you some ..." She stalled before she finished her sentence. Her thought process wasn't quite working, she felt tipsy and happy. Again, she smiled and giggled. She started again with a beaming smile, although she assumed her appearance was the usual serious interview look. "We'd ... we'd like to ask you some questions."

The odd couple immediately changed their smiling provocative deviant mannerisms to quizzical, frowning looks with some angst thinking they were under investigation. He retorted with a deep London twang, "Well, your 'onour, we ain't guilty of nuffink."

The woman spoke. "Onest Guv, we ain't dun a fing, not fuckin nuffin!"

They both laughed out loud and high-fived one another.

Jackie tried to keep a straight face; Susan laughed loudly but then bit her lip as she wanted to laugh too. She got the humour but thought she'd better not, not in front of Jackie. *They're taking the piss*, Jackie thought. She fought back as her senses drifted and asked the man, "That tattoo around your neck, is there any reason for it?"

He simply replied, "Yea mate! I likes it mate, I luvs it, alwight. Anyway, wots it got to do with you two?"

Jackie asked Susan if she had the chain she found at Suze's apartment. Susan fumbled dizzily through her pockets and dropped the evidence bag on the woman's feet. As Susan bent over to pick it up, she stumbled onto all fours. She giggled but as she lifted her head her face was just inches away from the woman … she couldn't stop herself from looking at the woman's legs. The woman both deliberately and quite slowly slid her feet wider apart. She now stood very provocatively astride the bag. *Wow*, thought Susan, *I need to stretch my arm forward to get the bag.* As Susan moved her body forward, her face came within inches of those tight Lycra shorts. There was a different odour, which was even more alluring and very inviting. One that magnetised her more so. It was better than any perfume she'd ever smelt. She didn't know it, but it was oud, liquid gold. As Susan collected the bag from the perceived provocativeness, she slowly stood from being on all fours. As she did, she glimpsed *that* elusive snake. It had reappeared high on the front of a thigh from below the skimpy shorts. There it had rotated and was fiercely looking up towards her mons pubis with its mouth wide open, tongue out, and with two large fangs ominously protruding. High on her other thigh was a tattoo that read, 'Beware – It Bites First And Asks Question Later!' Susan slowly stood, feeling more lightheaded and very woozy. As she got to eye level the woman smiled politely and winked at her.

Jackie waited patiently for Susan to hand her the bag.

She didn't actually mind as this show of distraction was both comical but also really quite erotic to watch, plus it appeared to play out in slow motion ... and that added to the exciting anticipation that Jackie felt for Susan. After Susan stood, Jackie was forcing herself to concentrate as she finally showed her ID to the pair of extroverts. She asked, "We need to know if you stock this type of chain, that actually looks a very similar size to that tattoo around your neck!"

The man became nervous. He fidgeted and his beard bell began to ring, 'ting, ting, ting, ting' sounds as he started shaking his head.

Jackie asked, "Do you sell this type ... maybe you even sold this one?" She thought she was on a roll, *Wow! I'm flowing like mango chutney over a hot curry! ... where did that thought come from?* She almost laughed out loud. She bit her lip as she continued to think, *There is definitely something in the air, I feel happier again! This is great! Oh? Where is that snake woman going?* She watched a slow-motion playback of the woman appearing to float to the door. She opened it. Within a few moments, as fresh air wafted, Jackie's senses recovered. The snake woman returned next to the man.

The woman remained calm as she spoke, but now in a far more eloquent soft West Country accent. She had suddenly changed from being an enchanting seductress to normality. "Yes we do sell that type, and we've sold several to locals. I have one too. It's a club thing, like a badge. There's a group of us that wear that type, we only sell it to our club members. It's like your ID card; we recognise one another by wearing the chain, it's our badge. They're far too heavy for most women, and they're expensive. They are not delicate at all."

Jackie and Susan were awoken by the surge of fresh air and were astounded by the reply. Slowly their heads cleared, they re-focused on work, not erotism and allurement. At that point, the man spoke, also with an eloquent accent in the same dialect.

"I'm sorry for the charade. It's all part of our USP, our unique selling point for tourists. They come in here and ogle at us, little do they know we're acting. We add value to our business with our outrageous behaviour. It's all an act. If we didn't have this USP we'd have gone bust years ago. Tourists can't believe what they see here, particularly with us two, and they will buy something every time. We have cheap stock for your average Joes, imitation gold and silver, right up to expensive solid gold and even platinum. The necklace in your hand costs £5,000!"

Jackie and Susan looked at each other, bemused. Susan's red face had disappeared. She asked, "Well you fooled me with your act!"

The snake woman enchantress smiled at Susan. "And so we should. We *really are actors*. We perform with the local dramatic society and put on shows around the county."

Again, she discreetly winked at Susan. Jackie noticed and asked, "Can you corroborate this, and actually give me a truthful alibi of where you were on Thursday night into yesterday morning?"

The man answered, "Yes, of course we can." He reached below the counter and produced a wad of colourful advertisement flyers. They showed the woman and himself, amongst other actors, dressed up to perform 'The Pirates of Penzance' at the local theatre for the Christmas season.

The woman spoke as she pointed to other actors in the image. "This is our bank manager, Brian, that's the local vet, Andrea. And this woman is Special Constable Sarah Nobble!" After she finished the man removed his prop of fake dirty teeth to show a cleaner full set of his own teeth.

Jackie's thoughts had changed from hot sticky mango

chutney to solid cold ice. She'd hit a brick wall with this alibi. She had thought that these two characters were deeply involved but as soon as she heard some of the actors' job titles and their professions her bloodhound-scenting ability lessened somewhat. She felt deflated. Susan had other thoughts.

"Going back to this necklace, and the wearers in *your club*, are they the same as the actors in your flyer?"

The woman beamed a massive smile and answered as she looked at her man. A tear appeared in her eye as she said, *"Dad and I."*

Susan thought, *Crikey! They are father and daughter!*

The man brightly beamed a smile and hugged her. She kissed his cheek as he released his gentle hug. Both Jackie and Susan looked dumbfounded and most surprised as the woman continued, "Dad and I belong to a small historical society that enacts our interpretation of the King Arthur period. We want to preserve the history and myths that abound, so we can keep visitors coming to Cornwall and places like Tintagel. Without tourists spending their money there the Tintagel site would soon decline due to lack of funds. St Ives and other towns could also decline. We have a club of several like-minded folk who perform in shows throughout the year. The performances draw in lots of tourists, and the income is greatly appreciated."

The man introduced his daughter. "This is Abbi and I'm Greg Stephenson, pleased to meet you!" He held his hand out to shake Jackie's. Abbi held her hand to Susan who shook hers. Abbi continued to hold Susan's for a noticeable period of time whilst she smoothed her thumb over the back of her hand.

Susan smiled. "So, does your group wear this type of chain?"

"Yes, when we practise."

Jackie asked, "Did you know Petra Munro?"

Greg replied, "Yes, she's lovely. She's in our club. Petra lives nearest to the castle, and she's fondly known as The Caretaker. She's always there, almost daily."

Abbi then spoke. "Petra recently married Alex. We put on a performance for them; it was fantastic!"

Jackie spoke. "I'm sorry, I don't think you're aware, Petra died early yesterday morning in very unusual circumstances."

There was shock and disbelief from both Abbi and Greg. Abbi began to cry as she blurted out, "This can't be true?"

Greg pulled Abbi into his open arms. "I just can't believe it, we saw Petra just the other day! What happened?"

Jackie explained. "She was found dead on the beach near Tamorna Cove, strangled we think, by one of your chains. Like the one here, and *that* one tattooed around your neck. In fact, your tattoo depicts something that we think happened to Petra. Where were you between 10:30pm Thursday night and 3am yesterday?"

Greg immediately replied, "Abbi and I were putting on a show at The Kings Head pub, just down the road. We then went to Paidwick and got there about 10pm. We rehearsed with our group until about 12 and then came home as our pub friends were getting a takeout. We stayed over at their place."

Jackie realised her head was just getting back to normal and this appeared to coincide with the odour no longer being in the air. This required further investigation, and she'd sort that later. The movements of Abbi and her father could easily be checked out, and would be to confirm their alibi. She moved quickly on to ask, "Why do you have such a horrid tattoo?"

Greg started to explain but Abbi interjected, "Dad and I have these outrageous tattoos because, like Mum, we're fans of the Arthurian era. It's mystical and unproven which gives it a special feel. Dad plays the role of Merlin who was, so say some, strangled by his own necklace. He was strangled by the lady of Paidwick. He found out about her infidelity and was about to share it with Arthur." Abbi then produced a photo from the countertop. "Look, this is my mum. Her tattoos are supposed to represent Merlin's secret lover, Ioone. She was his loyal servant who stood by him throughout his time and who took her own life to die by his side. My snake tattoo represents Merlin's daughter from Ioone, Abbigrance. Hence my name. We're viewed as strange by some, but we enjoy who we are and what we do. Think of it as a hobby, this is our fun, and we live the story. Plus, acting helps our business here."

Susan came into the conversation. "OK, so who's in your little club?"

Abbi and her dad looked at each other.

Jackie asked, "OK. I want the names and addresses, including phone numbers, of the people in your club. Susan, you take the details. I'm going to call Peter. Greg, sorry for the inconvenience but you need to close the shop whilst we get these important details."

He replied, "Yes of course. Anything to help. I just can't believe this has happened to Petra. She was just such an amazing woman."

As he finished, Abbi sobbed. Greg hugged her and shed tears too.

Jackie went outside. The street was getting busy with Saturday shoppers. She wanted privacy whilst she spoke to Peter. As she looked around she saw Danny at the corner of the next street. She walked to him and sat inside the car. She made the call to Peter who answered.

"Hello Jackie, what do you know?"

Jackie relayed her findings. She wanted the shop searched with statements from Abbi and Greg. "There's something strange going on in the shop. I think they have drugs stored there and it could be the place where Petra purchased her necklace. I need to go to Paidwick Castle. John is saying Petra was there Thursday night!"

He replied, "OK, good work, you're on a roll, keep going. If you need any assistance, back-up, or anything else just ask. I think it's time to go public with the murder, given that Greg and Abbi know about the connection with the necklace chain. I've seen your previous announcement; you were on local TV! Do you want to give the murder announcement to the press?"

Jackie heard this as praise. She was a lowly DC here in Cornwall and normally a murder investigation would have a senior officer to front the press. Peter knew she was capable. She replied, "Thank you Guv, you're the boss, you have the honour."

He replied, "OK, I'll get the ball rolling and get the news out there. What else have you got?"

Jackie replied, "Well, in the shoe shop, we found the style of boot Petra and Suze wore. Hopefully someone your end is contacting the card companies for details of the purchasers. Susan is getting contact details from Greg and Abbi, maybe you could get a team to contact and visit them? We'll go to the castle as soon as we're done here. Oh, I nearly forgot, we have another chain that we found at Petra's apartment. Plus, I need to interview the farmers that found Petra."

Peter chuckled. "Crikey, you are a busy pair. I appreciate your hard work, thank you, whatever you need you've got. I've validated your request for more uniformed at Petra's home and could do similar for the gallery."

Jackie responded, "Good, thank you."

As Jackie strolled back into Greg's shop, Susan had finished her list. Jackie informed Greg of the impending visit by forensics and additional uniformed officers so they could search the shop for illicit drugs. He objected and wanted to see a search warrant, but as Jackie stated, "There are reasonable grounds to believe that evidence could be either removed or destroyed. Therefore, a search warrant wasn't needed for this immediate search."

Almost immediately a local uniformed officer arrived to stand by within the shop until additional back-up arrived. Jackie and Susan hurriedly said their goodbyes and left. As they walked to the car Jackie whispered to Susan, "Abbi was coming onto you in there."

Susan blushed. "Do you think so, how embarrassing!"

Jackie smiled. "But you liked it, didn't you?"

Susan looked at her. "How did you know that?"

"Well, let's just say, it takes one to know one."

Susan curiously looked at Jackie, who had the faintest of smiles as they entered their awaiting car. Susan spoke, "You know the lip balms we got from the gallery apartment, and those from Petra's spare room, well, they're on sale at Greg's. They're behind the counter out of sight. I saw them through the cabinet when I was looking through Abbi's thighs. I think there's more to them than meets the eye, particularly as the price tag said a box cost £500!"

Jackie looked stunned. "OK Susan, call it in to lock the place down and get both Greg and Abbi arrested. I think we were drugged with that aroma! And don't forget to give the club list over to Sally at the MCU. Ask Sally to get Peter to send officers to visit them straight away. You could also ask if any progress has been made with the shoe shop card details." She paused and spoke to Danny. "Driver, take us to Paidwick Castle."

CHAPTER 11
PAIDWICK CASTLE

The police car arrived in a small layby on a narrow rural lane. As the three departed the car, Susan spoke.

"Crikey, this really is in the middle of nowhere. We haven't passed another car for miles, there are no houses or farms to be seen."

The layby was partially overgrown due to the obvious lack of visitors although recent tyre marks could be seen in the wet mud. The surrounding farmland was used as cattle pasture and there were hedgerows with stock fencing. The noise was minimal apart from the wind and crows that inhabited the numerous wooded areas. Jackie found the old and very weathered footpath fingerboard nearby with 'Paidwick Castle ½ mile' engraved on it; it was only just legible. The three climbed over a rickety stile, with Susan wobbling as she clumsily manoeuvred her leg over the wooden top rail. Jackie stopped and gave her a hand thinking, *Gosh, for a black belt taekwondo girl, she surely doesn't look the part! Bruce Lee was far more balanced and lighter footed!*

They followed the direction that the fingerboard appeared to be pointing towards. The route took them across a muddy pasture field towards a copse. Jackie noticed and thought, *The path appears to show regular use, maybe the club members, but it doesn't have great footfalls as though the general public don't come this way.*

Jackie's phone rang, it was Peter. "Good news! Someone who suggests he's an urban and rural explorer has just walked up to uniformed near the cove and handed in a gold necklace that fits with what we've been looking for. He found it about a mile away from the cove on a beach. He saw us in numbers there and thought it may be related. It's with forensics now!"

Jackie's face had lit up as Susan waited to hear her reply. "Perfect! Any sign of Petra's head torch?"

"No, just the necklace."

"OK We're making our way into a copse towards Paidwick Castle, hopefully, we'll find the ruin. This is the place Petra walked to on Thursday night. I'll let you know how we get on."

They ended the call, Susan thumbed up to her.

As they entered the wooded area, a well-defined track led the way into an opening where the ruins of Paidwick Castle were found. It didn't resemble a castle at all as most of it had eroded away. The ruin was covered in brambles and overgrowth, which is apart from the midsection that looked as though it had regularly been maintained. The ruin was within the now dense copse that had grown around it over the past millennia.

Susan spoke. "I don't know about you, but this does feel a special place, do you feel that?"

Jackie looked quizzically at Susan and with great expression said, "The only bloody thing I *feel* is my wet feet inside my wet socks, which are inside my bloody wet boots!"

The officer laughed as he too had wet feet.

Susan smiled and asked, "But don't you feel that there's a presence here? Something doesn't quite feel right. Can you feel that we're not alone?"

"Oh, shut up! You're trying to scare us!" retorted Jackie."

Susan replied, "OK, YTF!"

Danny discreetly laughed.

Jackie spoke. "Well this is a find, isn't it?"

Susan replied, "Yes, this section looks well used. As though it's regularly used by *the club* and looking at the footprints there's definitely been more than one person here, and very recently. This must be where Greg's acting gang meet. I checked the map and this place just says 'Castle Ruin'. It's not in the same league as Tintagel so I wouldn't have thought there would be much public footfall. Wait! Look there!" She pointed to what appeared to be a more complete section in part of the ruin covered in overgrowth. They walked towards it. The entrance had been covered with a careful and deliberate arrangement of evergreen ivy. It had blown away and exposed the entrance. The officer had a torch that he shone into the entrance, lighting a cavern where a tunnel could be seen to veer off to the left. They entered. Jackie and Susan switched on their phone torches. There were puddles and darkness that was only illuminated by their lights. As they turned the corner they came across a solid ancient wooden door that was closed. Jackie lifted the latch that allowed her to open the door as she slowly pushed the heavy wooden structure. Inside, as their torches lit the area, a large open room appeared. There were ancient metal lamps with candles within, an enormous fireplace with recently burnt wood and a pile ready to go. The ancient fireplace still felt warm and radiated heat, it was inset into a chimney. There were ironworks to support cooking utensils; pots and such like were neatly positioned ready for use. As their lights lit the cavernous space they saw old wooden chairs surrounding a large round table. There was an altar and what appeared to be a tombstone further back. Something glistened as the light shone. Susan walked towards the tombstone.

"Oh my God!" she exclaimed. "It's another necklace!" Jackie and the officer quickly went towards Susan as she continued. "It looks like the ones we found at Petra's and it's similar to those Greg sells. They could all be solid gold! And look here, there are red marks on the tombstone, they maybe blood stains, and what's this?"

At the rear of the tombstone there was an urn containing red liquid; it looked like blood. Susan shone her light around and walked towards a large vase that had various bones within. Concerns grew amongst the three. Jackie asked the officer to wait outside to stand by as she wondered if the blood and bones could be human remains. She asked Danny to call for assistance. She then called Peter.

"Hello Peter, we've a significant find, could you arrange for forensics and John Smedley to attend?"

He replied, "Well hello Jackie." Again, he said, "With every day gone you exceed my expectations! What have you found?"

Jackie relayed the find. Particularly the blood and bones. He confirmed he'd action her request. Whilst she was talking, Susan had been wandering around the chamber. She saw the stone ceiling was intact apart from some slight water ingress stains. She had found strange inscriptions around the walls with images of mythical rituals taking place. There were metallic manacles, ancient artifacts and other paraphernalia associated with mystical events. Some looked to be well used, as could be seen from the shiny surfaces. As Jackie's call with Peter ended, Susan relayed what she had seen and suggested Jackie take a look. They didn't want to disturb what was now becoming a significant place for investigation. Susan took many photos. They slowly made their way out, carefully retracing their footprints. As they slowly re-stepped, they came across a hanging cloth that had gothic markings and a language with which they were unfamiliar. There appeared to be names embroidered into the cloth that weren't ancient. Susan read aloud, "Nilrem, Eumin, Ruhtra Gink, Yaf el Anagrom. Wow, they're strange names. Ancient methinks?"

Something had caught Jackie's eye whilst Susan continued to take photos of the names; there was a door hidden behind the cloth. She asked Susan to carefully hold the corner of the cloth away so she could lift the hidden doorlatch. As the heavy door opened her light lit up another room that was remarkably warm and dry. She slowly entered the room and found a very large four poster bed made from an ornate wooden frame. Old as it was, it wasn't ancient. There were cloth blankets that formed a mattress, and several other cloths were rolled to form pillows. Again, there were ironworks where semi-burnt candles stood. Their solidified wax drippings had built up over a long period, resembling lava flows that had cooled and frozen. Some of the drippings formed stalactite-like ornate features that possessed wonderous shapes entwined with huge spiderwebs. The warmth appeared to be coming from another large fireplace built into a wall. The wall was still radiating heat from the recently used fire. Ashes were in and around a large iron basket with a good supply of logs adjacent.

Jackie said, "This has been used very recently. This is where Petra was yesterday morning." She then felt her head buzzing. "Susan, have you any paracetamol in your pockets?"

"Yes, I have!" Susan rummaged around and pulled out a box. "Here you go, crunch a couple and swallow as I've no water."

Jackie took a couple and did as Susan suggested. She stood in darkness, apart from her phone light, and leant forward to carefully feel the heat from the fire bed. Then, without warning, something gently landed on her head and appeared to crawl down her neck and go under her collar. She jumped up with great fear, moving quickly away to her right from what she assumed to be a large spider, or something else that had crawled down her neck. She could feel it moving around her bra strap area. It was large. She simultaneously panicked as she put her hand behind her back, feeling around her shoulder blade.

Whilst doing so, Susan asked, "What is it?"

Jackie was freaking out with worry. "Quick, have a look down the back of my neck!"

Jackie quickly undid her blouse buttons whilst shaking with fright. Susan shone her phone light down Jackie's back. It was her worst nightmare … an enormous spider had made its way down a web and had ended up within Jackie's blouse.

Susan panicked. "Shit, it's a huge furry spider! What shall I do?"

Jackie was now distraught. "Just get the thing out!"

Susan quickly lifted the rear of Jackie's blouse and as she did so the hairy spider fell to the ground and quickly scurried off into the darkness.

Jackie shouted, "Bastard thing, I hate spiders!"

Susan laughed but suddenly stopped when she realised Jackie was petrified.

Jackie spoke. "You can laugh alright! It isn't funny!" She then fastened her buttons and tucked herself in. Jackie yelled, "You stupid bitch! I could have had a heart attack!"

Susan kept laughing. "Don't worry, I'm a first aider, I've got some sticky plasters!"

Jackie retorted, "Yeah right! As if sticky plasters will fix my heart attack! OK. I owe you one, you just wait, I'll get you back!"

Susan smiled and then they both had a laugh as Jackie said, "Come on, this place is giving me the creeps, I hate spiders, take some photos and let's go!"

As they were leaving, Susan asked, "Don't you think it strange that Greg has his troupe club, and they're all female?"

Jackie asked, "How many female names did he give to you?"

"Five," replied Susan.

Jackie looked at the bed. "I reckon you could easily get six into this bed. It's huge. He's a dirty old man."

Susan looked and asked, "What are you suggesting?"

Jackie had a serious look. "Didn't you think it awfully awkward how *dad and daughter were so unusually sexy* together back there, 'cos that's what they are ... related. We didn't know that when we initially encountered them; I had thought he was a dirty old man with his pretty young filly. But when it came out they're related, it's wrong. It's incestuous."

Susan replied, "*They're actors*, and their life, livelihoods and maybe more depends upon their acting."

Jackie spoke seriously. "I'm thinking they could play-act here. Maybe the blood is a theatrical prop and the bones are animals? Greg practises mythical things here and they act out their fetishes, and that could include group therapy with drugs and sex? Petra *was* here ... maybe Greg *is* our man? Maybe *he's* our missing DNA man if *he* had sex with Petra? Maybe against her will, and maybe he then took her to the clifftop to silence her? He acted in front of us. Think about Dracula, one male with many females to play with. I'm thinking Greg plays with all the females and they're his concubines, including Petra!"

Jackie smiled and asked, "You weren't defending your new girlfriend, are you?"

Susan suddenly looked awkward as she frowned. "What, what do you mean?"

Jackie smiled. "Come on, you know as well as I do Abbi was coming on to you in the shop, she winked at you. You went all smitten."

Susan replied, "Why, are you jealous?"

Jackie shrugged her shoulders. "Well ..." Jackie stopped mid-sentence. She had a serious but innocent gentle look; she gulped and swallowed as she slowly moved her face towards Susan's and said, "It's your choice, but *she* is now part of a criminal investigation. Don't get caught out with the wrong cookie!"

Their eyes were deeply fixated on each other. Susan replied, "Understood, wrong person, wrong timing. Thank you."

Jackie smiled as she said, "Greg's alibi about leaving here doesn't fit with the timeline that John gave from Petra's watch. If he's truthful it may not have been him who was at the clifftop. He's over six feet tall and I can't see him having a size five boot, more like nine or more!"

Susan was thinking through the timeline. "Abbi could be a size five?"

Jackie nodded in agreement. "That's why you mustn't get personally close to witnesses ... or suspects!"

They made their way out of the bedroom, leaving the darkness and spiders behind. They entered the larger communal area and made their way out to daylight and fresh air. The odour within the confines was similar to Greg's shop, it had made them behave differently and the rush of fresh air sobered them back to reality.

Danny had stood outside and turned to his female colleagues. "Are you OK, I heard what I thought were screams? I was just about to come in."

Jackie replied, "No! Don't go in there, it's toxic." She was referring to the possible drug agent she'd encountered within Greg's shop.

He nodded with agreement. "I've called for back-up, it's on route now. Officers are due any moment."

Jackie and Susan smiled at him. They sat on dry stones near the centre of what they thought could have been the courtyard. The fresh air was detoxing them. Seriousness now prevailed. Jackie rubbed her head; she'd had the strange tingling and nagging feeling.

Susan looked at Jackie and asked, "What's wrong?"

Jackie stopped rubbing. "Just recently I've been getting these funny feelings in my head. Not pains, just strange sensations. Weird feelings that come from nowhere ... and then they go as quick as they come."

Susan smiled. "You're not going through the change, are you?"

"No, I'm bloody not. I'm in my prime! Thank you very much!"

Jackie looked at her watch. "Well, we're nearly missing lunchtime. Let's wait for the cavalry to arrive, get them sorted and we'll go for an alcohol-free pub lunch. How does that sound?"

Susan smiled. "Perfect, just perfect!"

Jackie said, "I know a local pub that'll have a roaring open fire that I can take my boots off in front of to dry my feet!"

Susan smiled. "Great, sounds even better ... Puss in Boots!"

As time passed, Jackie and Susan wandered around the ruin. They went separate ways, each looking for clues and evidence. Susan was looking for footprints, her head down and eyes critically searching through the site as they passed one another. At that point Jackie spoke.

"Are you OK?"

"Yes, sure. Why do you ask?"

"I just wondered."

They continued their separate ways. A short time later their paths crossed again. Jackie spoke.

"Are you sure you're OK?"

Susan lifted her head up and looked at Jackie quizzically. "Yes, of course I'm OK ... you asked me that just now."

"I'm just a bit concerned about you."

"Why?"

"Well, you seem to be obsessed with feet. Are you a podophile?"

"What's a podophile?"

"It's what you are!"

"Nah, I don't think so. My neck is always crocked down like this! I'm getting older ... just like you!"

They both laughed and continued on their way. Susan didn't have a clue what Jackie was talking about but made out she did. As she continued searching across the ground, she made a note to web check the pod word out later.

It was 2:30pm when the calvary arrived. Forensics, uniformed and Peter had made their way to the castle. Jackie and Susan forewarned them about the strange odour that was in the air within the structure. They suggested no one should enter until forensics had checked it out. Peter stood back and allowed his Rottweilers to do their stuff. He then swaggered over to them.

"Well hello team, how is it going?"

Jackie and Susan gave their verbal reports. Particularly about Greg's potential to be Petra's murderer.

"Excellent! Well, it's just as well he's now at the station with his daughter Abbi. I'll ensure they're held there. How about we leave the crew here and we go for lunch?"

Jackie replied, "Great minds think alike! We had

discussed that earlier. I know this quaint pub with a roaring fire! You could take us pups there whilst we dry off?"

"Fantastic idea, come on let's go!"

The three made their way back to Peter's car. As the 'pups' got in, Susan sat on the rear seat after moving Peter's paraphernalia that was sprawled across it. As she buckled up she noticed something tucked into the door pocket that was preventing her from sitting comfortably. It stuck into her thigh; she tried to push the covered object further into the door pocket. It wouldn't budge. The solid object was concealed with a microfibre cloth. She lifted the cloth off and saw the offending item was a metal box. The writing on the box caught her eye as she'd seen a similar style at Greg's shop. Susan was suddenly very intrigued by the connection. She listened to Peter and Jackie discussing progress as the car drove away, and then secretly pulled the metallic box to have a better look. The box was wedged tightly. She didn't want to alert Peter as to what she was doing and so kept tugging at it very lightly, slowly and discreetly, whilst periodically looking at Peter to check he hadn't noticed what she was doing. She kept looking ahead just in case he glanced at her actions through his rear-view mirror. The object wouldn't budge no matter how she tugged at it; curiosity had wrapped around her mind. A short time later they arrived at The Farmers Home pub in a small village called Turley. Susan quickly stopped her secret actions and unbelted herself.

The three got out of the car and walked into the pub. Peter casually pushed his key fob to lock the car as they left. He thought as he strutted, *I'm pack leader and these are my pups behind. My ego feels good in that I've two smart females each side of me, but just slightly behind me. I'd love it if they each put their arms through mine; to further show they are my possessions, and*

I have ownership of them. Jackie and Susan weren't thinking anything of the kind. Had they read his mind they'd take him to a tribunal. *They* were diligently thinking about Petra. If Peter had entered their mind it was because he was simply a male chauvinist, maybe a misogynist, as well as being their boss, and therefore a person who they begrudgingly had to report to.

They entered the bar. Sure enough the fire was well lit with several large logs burning brightly. They made their way to a table near the splendid fire.

Jackie smiled. "I hope you don't mind; I'm going to take my boots off. My feet are soaking wet from the castle grounds!"

Peter laughed. "Of course not, go for it, be my guest!" He *was* however thinking, *It'll be nice to watch you undress!*

Susan looked bemused. Her memory jogged back to her conversation with Jackie at the castle. It was Jackie suggesting she had podophilia and her not knowing what the word meant ... she wanted to search the meaning of the word and would need her phone to do just that. This, she thought, would be a good excuse to get Peter's car key under the guise that her phone *must have slipped out of her pocket whilst in his car.* She would then be able to discreetly pull the mystery object out of the door pocket to identify what it contained without him knowing. With the plan in her mind, she asked Peter, "Er, sorry Peter, I think my phone has slipped out from my pocket in your car! Could I have the key please, I'm waiting for an important callback and don't want to miss it."

He smiled and handed the key over. Immediately he was busily chatting again about tactics and plans with Jackie whose socks were steaming off their dampness in front of the fire. Susan noticed and thought, *Peter is enjoying Jackie's foot odour as he's deliberately moved his chair forward to discreetly inhale her sock fragrance when she looks at the roaring flames!*

Susan walked to the car and tugged the mysterious item out from the door pocket. It was a metal box, not dissimilar to the biscuit tins her mum kept in the larder. It had weird writing on, similar to what she'd seen in Greg's shop, and more importantly, on the fabric hung on the walls at the castle. A car suddenly arrived and parked next to her. The occupiers were visiting the pub. Susan made out she was busy with her coat. She took the opportunity to ensure Peter wasn't creeping around, should he be suspicious about her needs. He wasn't, and when safe to do so she opened the box. As she opened the lid she noticed it had a robust silicone seal, the type to prevent odour and liquid escape. Immediately, that alluring aroma, the same one from Greg's shop, and similar to the one noticed at the castle, filled her nostrils. The scent was inside her, gently and provocatively massaging her brain, giving her pleasurable thoughts. She suddenly became relaxed but fortunately, as the door was open, a gust of wind shot fresh air into her nose. The clean air was inhaled and momentarily diluted the alluring scent released from the box. The dilution gave her enough sense to close the box lid, but not before she took photos of liquids within their containers. There was a syringe and another of the same lip balms she'd recovered from Petra's room and apartment. She quickly regained control of her senses as she took another deep breath of fresh air and when her lungs could hold no more, she exhaled. She replaced the lid and put the container tightly into the door pocket covering it with the cloth. She opened the other three doors to further ventilate the internal space. She didn't want Peter or Jackie to sense that hypnotic aroma; he would immediately know what she'd been up to. Now wasn't the time for that to happen. She discreetly opened the boot and saw a suitcase. She looked inside and there were ten more of the metal boxes, plus several boxes of lip balms. She shut both the suitcase and the four doors, locking them all with the key after she was satisfied the odour had gone. She was shaking within herself with both shock and excitement. She casually walked into the pub holding her phone and sat again next to Peter and Jackie. They were still talking about Petra, but it was obvious to Susan he was covertly looking at Jackie's feet. As Jackie admiringly looked at the flames for periods of time, whilst listening to Peter's ramblings, he noticeably looked Jackie up and down, as though he were undressing her. Susan sat anxiously. To distract her thoughts, she looked up podophilia on her phone. After a quick web search, Susan had found the meaning: 'Podophilia: a foot fetishism, a sexual interest in feet.' She chuckled to herself about Jackie's comment whilst searching for footprints at the castle and her boot obsession related to the crime. She now knew Peter was a podophile. He appeared *so* turned on. Seeing Peter behaving this way reinforced her initial thoughts about him being a voyeuristic letch, someone not to trust.

Jackie's socks dried, and they ordered and ate a quick lunch. Susan had found an ominous container in Peter's car. She sat patiently whilst waiting for the right opportunity to share her findings with Jackie. Peter drove them back to Tamorna Cove. The three had a quick chat about the next part of the plan. Jackie and Susan would now interview Betty and Alan, the farmers. Forensics were both at the castle and at Greg's conducting investigations and collecting evidence.

CHAPTER 12
THE FARMERS

Jackie and Susan left the cove and drove in Jackie's car to Betty and Alan's farm. Susan asked, "Jackie, please could you pull over in the next lay-by."

"Why, do you need to pee, or have you got another megasoreass?"

"No, neither of those."

"Oh, so what's the reason?"

"I'd rather wait for you to stop so I could have your full attention."

"OK, will do."

Jackie turned and smiled at Susan. Susan did the same. Jackie wondered why Susan wanted the stop and became more curious as she drove.

"Ah! There's a lay-by, I'll get in that one."

Jackie pulled in and switched off the engine. Susan turned to Jackie with a serious look,

"Jackie, whilst I went to get my phone I found something in Peter's car. My phone wasn't lost; I used it as an alibi so I could get the key and secretly investigate something that caught my attention. I didn't want him to know that I found his stash."

Jackie's cheerful expression from the knowledge that Greg was being held at the station changed to a concerned look. She listened attentively whilst Susan explained about the illicit drug find that replicated the smell at Greg's and then again within Paidwick Castle.

Susan continued. "I reckon he's injecting the drug into

lip balms. When you think about it, it's actually ingenious. You then sell the balm and no one ever suspects it of being a drug. You get an immediate fix of the drug just by putting the drug-filled balm onto your lips. You can do that anywhere, in shops, on buses, anywhere. There's no needles, no smoke, nothing to suggest you're taking it. It simply just appears you're putting balm onto your lips. Anyone, any age could do it! Amazing! He deserves a Nobel prize!" Susan also mentioned his podophilia and his lewd voyeuristic behaviour towards Jackie.

As Jackie listened, again she felt her head twang and was becoming more concerned about the frequency with which it occurred. She asked Susan for more paracetamol and then responded to Susan's revelations.

"I knew that bastard Peter wasn't straight. I smelt a rat the day I met him. He's a dangerous man! We'll get him, you and me, don't you worry! Don't say anything to anyone about this, do you understand? We need a plan to get him. We'll hatch one. But for now, Greg and Abbi are in custody, that's good. We'll continue building evidence for Petra. Right now, she's the important one, she deserves victim justice. We need to catch *her* murderer. It could be any of many at the moment. If Peter is involved with the drugs, his justice will come. *However*, it could be he went to Greg's after we left and collected the stash from Greg as evidence. It's possible. It's interesting you tell me this as I noticed he vapes but also applies lip balm. Intriguing, eh? Just watch your back with him and say nothing about your find! I can check with John to see if he hands the stash in for analysis."

Susan looked bereft for words. Jackie sat numbed with the revelation. She then spoke seriously with her thoughts. "We need a way to snare Peter but if there was one maggot, there could be more, particularly within drug cartels. With me being so new to my job here I don't yet have dependable or trustworthy work buddies I can call upon for support. For example, DS Ian Walsh immediately comes to mind, one of his close buddies. If there's one there could be more. Having corrupt officers undermines you and me, other honest officers, and the police with the public. We take a step forward with progress but then 20 backwards when those fucking jerks ruin it for all of us. Think of those officers who have participated in illegal activity, then multiply it. We have a new generation of officers, you included, Generation Z and the new A's will follow. You're all bought up with social media, computers and AI. Things could get worse before they get better with your cohort; in the force for example, the recent wave of sharing crime images on social media, drug availability from crooks who buy themselves out of trouble, peer pressure from bent coppers. Predatory officers that use vulnerable women as shag bags. That's all before we look outside into the public domain. Knife and gun crime, youngsters murdering one another, youngsters murdering older folk ... it's all a shame but to them it's a game, its relentless and getting worse. Susan, your country needs you and me now!" She smiled at Susan as she knew she had become flippant.

Susan responded by holding her hand in the air, like a pupil at school, and was bouncing up and down on her seat with the excitement of knowing the answer to a question posed by the teacher.

Jackie laughed. "Yes Susan?"

"Please Miss, I need a pee!"

They both laughed out loud.

Jackie replied, "OK, but be quick, the next lesson starts soon!"

Jackie drove off after Susan had a pee whilst crouching

down behind the open passenger door. They travelled in silence. Both thought deeply about their conversation. The process of bringing Peter to justice had to be stealthy and correct, with evidence to convict him. That is if he was in fact part of the problem. Jackie and Susan, unbeknown to the other, thought about illegal gain. Gain in that they could join Peter's franchise to make more money than they earn. They could extort him to get money that way. All sorts of thoughts ran through their minds. But that's all they were, thoughts. They had to think like criminals to catch them. Their overriding thought was the need to catch a murderer for Petra's sake and then they'd deal with Peter later.

As Jackie drove, she mentioned, "I thought I could inform my previous boss who advised me about this job. He's the Deputy Chief Constable here, DCC Tony Martin. I told you previously we worked together and had some great results. He got the promotion on the back of those results. I haven't seen him for a while; I may just contact him. What do you think?"

Susan felt really honoured that her new boss Jackie was talking to her like this. It made her feel special, more so now than at any other time since joining the force.

Susan replied, "Well I think you could contact him given the circumstances, although there are our official options too. We have several options as I see it. There are internal mechanisms for us to report corruption, independent routes and so on. The problem is Peter. It could be just him, *or* as you said there could be more. He's quite senior and has been here a long time, so he could have been improper for ages and have a network of officers both above and below him. They'd all look after each other's back."

Jackie replied, "Yes, you're right. But it isn't for us to investigate, only to report the corruption. We'll let the powers-that-be investigate and navigate the way to prosecute."

Susan said, "Yes, but we need evidence to validate our call, and we get that by investigation. At the moment it's my very junior word against very senior officer Pete."

"You're right Susan. We need more evidence. We've come full circle. Let's make this visit to the farmers and think about Pete. As I said, a murder investigation takes priority in my mind. Anyway, why are we suddenly calling him Pete?"

Susan laughed. "It's because he doesn't like being called Pete!"

They both laughed and then sat silently thinking about how to bring their DI, Peter Drew, under the spotlight with his possession of illicit drugs and potential drug ring involvement.

Jackie then reiterated, "Perhaps the search of Greg's shop revealed the box and Peter was keeping it and the suitcase as evidence?"

Susan replied, "But it should be in an evidence bag."

Jackie smelt an even bigger rat. "OK, enough, enough for now. We'll go to the farm and think about a plan, if not today, tomorrow. Petra still comes first."

They arrived near to Tamorna Cove but this time on land above the cliff where Petra's death occurred. Jackie drove across the noisy cattle grid and into the farmyard of Betty and Alan Smith. It was Saturday afternoon, there was a gentle breeze and slight mizzle. There were various farm machinery pieces lying about in a haphazard way and a 4x4 utility truck that was filthy dirty and looked like a wreck. The barns were in use, as could be heard as soon as the duo got out of Jackie's car. Cows mooed, sheep baah'd, and dogs barked.

"Phew! What a poo-wee smell there is here!" said Susan as she looked around the yard whilst being ultra careful she didn't stand in any of the many cowpats, or the slushy smelly urine puddles that littered across the yard.

Jackie replied, "Well, what do you expect from a cattle farm? Cows don't have toilets like we do; they poo and pee anywhere ... just don't stand in it!"

They suddenly stopped laughing thanks to the sound that creates fear within – the sound of several barking dogs that appeared to be getting closer very quickly. Two large ferocious-looking dogs came charging towards them out from the barn. It was Lucy and Daisy with their sharp teeth on show and both looking like racing horses galloping to the line. Their jowls stretched down and up, their tongues hanging on for dear life whilst flapping about. Their saliva frothed into drool and the dribble was wildly catapulted off. The gallop and the heavy breathing showed the appearance of their large mouths, ready to consume their prey, or trespassers. The tails were thrashing about wildly at the rears, rapidly moving to and fro, like sabres with swift slashing actions cutting through the air. Their tails also acted as counterbalances and stabilisers for their fit and lean bodies that were charging directly towards the duo. All the while this happened, Susan saw their muscular beauty as her brain slowed the impending threat into slow motion. She saw the dogs gallop at such a pace they were all four paws off the ground at regular intervals. When the first paw landed, its leg muscles bulged and then stretched like a concertina with the ongoing motion. The images reminded her of watching the Grand National horse race where the slow-motion replay illuminated the muscular frames being fully used for the performance, something she'd never seen before in real time.

Suddenly her slow-motion effect sped to normal; Susan felt threatened and deliberately stood behind Jackie. Jackie wasn't impressed.

At that moment, an unknown gravely West Country accent shouted, "Down!"

Both dogs froze on the spot and laid. It was Betty who had appeared from the barn, she said curiously, "How can I help?"

Jackie thought the deep voice came from Alan but soon realised it was Betty who shouted the command. Jackie responded by showing her ID. "Hello, I'm DC Jackie Smith and this is PC Susan Hill. Are you Betty Smith?"

"Yes I am, pleased to meet you!"

They shook hands and smiled at each other. Susan put her hand forward and also shook Betty's skin hardened hand. Betty looked at Jackie.

"I don't think we're related, but you never knows! If we go back in time, who knows?"

Jackie smiled. "We're sorry to bother you but we need to ask some more questions ... about Petra's sad death, may we come inside?"

Betty began to cry. "Yes, please do, it's just so tragic. Yesterday, your colleague at the beach said I'd get a visit. Follow me."

Jackie offered Betty her unused tissue, but Betty had one of her own that appeared to have been well used. She wiped her eyes and blew a loud nose raspberry into the tissue. Susan watched in amazement when she heard the horn blower from Betty's nose. Betty led the way into the farmhouse and on into the kitchen. She offered tea and the duo accepted. They sat at the kitchen table next to the warm stove range style cooker that had the kettle proudly sat on the forever hotplate. It was continually simmering ready to be poured.

Jackie sipped her tea and asked, "Is Mr Smith available?

Betty replied, "He is but he's in the barn. As he isn't here, I want to tell you something."

"What would that be?" Jackie replied.

"Well, he's a gone bit odd and to tell you the truth I don't like him anymore."

Jackie looked surprised. "Why not Betty?"

"Well, he's a pervert. Do you know what, we haven't had sex for 20 years, and I don't want to. Not with him anyway, and definitely not now. Never liked it with him, he always wanted more and more. I shouldn't have married him. Do you know what?" She stared at Jackie,

"What?"

"Come here, follow me and I'll show you."

"Show me what?"

"Just come this way and I'll show you!"

With that she grabbed Jackie's hand and pulled her up out of the chair. Susan quickly stood to intervene and help her boss. Jackie turned to Susan and mouthed the words, "It's OK, I'm fine," whilst showing the hand symbol for OK.

Betty held Jackie's hand and almost dragged her upstairs to her bedroom. Susan followed. Betty walked her over to a wall and pointed to a piece of toilet tissue stuck to her wallpaper. She let go of Jackie's hand and said, "You see that tissue. I put's it there every day, twice a day, morning and night! When it goes tatty I replaces it with new." She looked at Jackie with a grimaced face.

Jackie looked at the toilet tissue and then asked Betty, "Why?"

Betty pulled the tissue out from a hidden hole. "That's why! The dirty bastard watches me through that hole from his bedroom. He's a pervert. He used to watch me undress at night and then again in the morning, he'd peep through the hole at me dressing. He filmed it on his phone! Well ... he did until I realised, so I now blocks the hole with this tissue, see!" She replaced the tissue in the hole. Jackie and Susan looked appalled.

Jackie replied, "Well, that isn't right, what would you like us to do about it?"

Betty smiled. "I know why you've come here."

Jackie looked puzzled. "We've come here because you found Petra dead on the beach, you and Alan."

Betty smiled, "Yes that's right, but did you know Petra often swam down there in the nude? Anyway, Alan found out and he's been secretly watching her, *and* he's taken pictures of her with no clothes on. He uses his phone!"

"Betty, have you got evidence of this behaviour?"

"Yes I have ... I've stolen his phone!" She put her hand down between her already large low-hung cleavage and pulled out Alan's phone that was tucked between her sweaty breasts. She handed the moist phone to Jackie who quickly passed it to Susan to bag as evidence. Jackie immediately wiped her damp hand on her trousers.

Jackie and Susan couldn't quite believe what they were hearing, and there was more.

Betty asked quizzically, "Do you do that CPR thing ... like this?" She then cupped her hands and put them over her elongated breasts. She started squeezing her boobs whilst counting one through to twenty. She stopped and kissed the air from her mouth twice. "My kissing would have been on the CPR person's lips, see."

Jackie and Susan looked at each other. "No Betty, that definitely isn't the way to do CPR. That is sexual touching!"

Betty smiled with an open mouth. "Good! I knew what Alan did to Petra wasn't CPR, he was molesting her! He's a fucking pervert. The dirty bastard! I hate him!" She started crying.

"Betty, where is Alan, we need to talk to him?"

Betty stopped crying and smiled. "I've got that twat in me dog kennels, locked up! The bastard is in the barn, where he belongs, it's where he should be, where the animals are kept. *He's* a fucking animal. I've even seen him shagging my sheep! The dirty bastard! He's a right old fucker, is he! He'll fuck anyone and anything. He's worse than a rampant dog with big bollocks. Well, I'll tell you this, he won't fuck with me anymore, fuck with anyone ... I'm going to fuck him right up! He's a rotten bastard! Yes! He's a bastard alright. It was his loose mother, that whore! That's where he got his fucking ways. She was the village tart! And he was one of her bastards! Ten there are, all of them are bastards, and not one of them had the same father. Course, you can imagine after school finishes and them ten bastards come out, each one going to a different father! Shocking, eh?" Betty paused to catch her breath. She continued, "After we leaves the ambulance yesterday, he went out and got pissed. He was out all day, pissed as a fart was he. Well, his mate Ronny got him home 'ere last night. I said take him back, I don't want him. Ronny says, 'No way! Mr Fuckhead still owes me 50 quid for the drinks and 80 for the betting slip.' He chucked Alan off his tractor, and I says, 'I'll give you 20 if you helps me get him in the dog crate.' That he did, and the dirty bastard is still in there. I was going to get him pissed again so I could remove his bollocks with me cattle emasculator. Castration would sort him! Without his bollocks he'd be no good to anyone! The dirty fucker! He was asleep earlier, but I expect the dogs woke him with them barking at you!"

Jackie looked at Susan, Susan looked at Jackie. They were gobsmacked.

Jackie spoke. "Thank you Betty. You've been really – and I do mean really – informative. We'll take over now and interview Alan under caution. We'll take him to the station for questioning. If we find images, as you suggest, we'll arrest him. We'll need a statement from you telling us what you've just said. Is that OK?"

"Fucking right it is. The dirty bastard needs to be locked up. He's a pervert! Whilst he's in custody I'll send our vet over to castrate the dirty bastard! You can hold him down whilst he's done!"

Susan then asked, "Betty, did Alan have anything to do with Petra's fall?"

Betty looked seriously at Susan, and then Jackie. "No, thank the lord above. I did wonder, but we went to bed at 10 o'clock on Thursday night, I know 'cos he pushed the tissue out of the hole. I put it back and within ten minutes he was snoring loudly in his bedroom next door as he'd been drinking. I know he didn't get up until 5 o'clock Friday morning 'cos when he heard my alarm going, the tissue was pushed out again! He wouldn't have got up in between those times as my dogs hate him, and they would have barked like fuck. He can't deal with both of them having a go at him, see."

Jackie replied, "Thank you Betty, you've been most helpful. Let's go downstairs and take your statement. Susan will take some photos here for evidence of his peephole and we'll call our uniformed colleagues to take Alan to the station. That is assuming you want to press charges against him for abusing you?"

"Fucking right I do, the bastard needs to be locked away, the pervert. He abused Petra too by stalking her. And he played with her tits with his CPR when she was dead. The dirty rotten bastard!"

Jackie's eyes opened wide. She thought, *John had alluded that someone had abused Petra's breasts ... Alan was now that suspect. He could also be the murderer. The missing chain has been found, hopefully Alan's DNA is on it! We'll get his DNA at the station to cross-check!*

Susan made the call asking for uniformed backup, forensics and a search warrant. She took photos of Betty's hole in the wall. Her bodycam had recorded the whole event with Betty's account of Alan's behaviour towards Petra and the account of his sheep shagging, which was also a criminal offence. Jackie finished her tea whilst they waited for their uniformed colleagues to arrive. In the absence of Betty, who'd gone to the bathroom, Jackie spoke to Susan.

"Crikey! What have we uncovered here? It's a real eye opener!"

Susan replied, "It's shocking. Alan could be our man; he could have murdered Petra. Let's get his DNA sample, forensics could match it with that found on Petra!"

Jackie agreed, "Yes, he could be the murderer and the person who had intercourse with Petra. He could have crept out on Thursday night ... that is if Betty's story is true?"

"What do you mean?"

"Well, we don't know if Betty is actually telling us the truth. Could it be *she* went out on that fateful night? She could have massive jealousy about Petra. She could have wanted Petra out of the way to stop Alan's voyeuristic stalking. We also need Betty's DNA, and we should take her in for a proper interview."

"Good analyses. Yes I get that now, I'll let uniformed know."

Jackie spoke again. "We have a duty of care responsibility for Alan. He apparently is locked in a dog crate, like the animal he supposedly is. But he is innocent until proven guilty and has rights, even as a potential murderer. That has yet to be proven, and there is now the question of Betty's involvement. She has to be taken in but could decline unless she is arrested. There is reasonable suspicion with both Alan and Betty that one, or the other, or even both, may have been involved with Petra's murder. They both have to be arrested."

Susan keenly replied, "I'm on it, I'll let uniformed know. Shall we wait for uniformed?"

"Yes, let's get Betty to show us where Alan is."

Betty returned from the loo unaware of the conversation. Jackie and Susan noticed the rear of Betty's dress was tucked into her pants. She'd inadvertently sat on the pan, done her business, stood and pulled her pants up whilst at the same time caught her dress in the rear of her pants.

Susan politely spoke. "Betty, we need to see Alan but before you take us to him … you've inadvertently caught your dress in the back of your pants."

Betty looked around to her rear. "Oh crikey! So I have! I'm becoming a daft bitch! Thank you dear. I don't think that was the first time I've done that!" She then ruffled her dress out from her pants and checked it hung correctly.

Susan continued, "It happens a lot, my older sister has done it once before!"

When Betty was satisfied with sorting herself, she smiled and said, "Right, follow me!" She led them out into the yard. The two dogs, Lucy and Daisy, stood from their lying positions and wagged their sabres. That motion transmitted though their back ends, and then on through their entire body as they gently swayed left to right with the happiness of walking behind Betty, their pack leader. They were calm and settled, unlike the guardians when Jackie and Susan initially arrived. Betty spoke. "This is Lucy, my old girl, and this is Daisy, the young one. It was she who discovered Petra on the beach."

The pair came to Betty, tails wagging as she fussed over them. They went to both Susan and Jackie and sniffed around them, as dogs do, tails moving to and fro. Susan patted them both.

"Well done Daisy, and you Lucy! Without you we may have lost Petra forever if the tide had carried her out to sea."

Daisy and Lucy appeared to understand the compliment as their tails wagged even more. Jackie preferred cats. She was a feline lover and wasn't so forthcoming, although she patted them too, just slightly.

Betty led the group to the barn. The stench was normal for a farm but Jackie and Susan, with their lack of experience of such places, felt the smell to be intrusive with their perfumed preferences. There were cows and sheep sectioned off from one another and the noise increased when they sensed Betty had entered the space; she was their feeder. The moos and bahs increased in volume with the excitement that it was their food time and became almost painful listening. Betty ignored the noise as she led the way towards a darkened corner.

"Here's *that* bastard!"

She switched the light on that lit the kennels. In one of the largest metal cages sat an unkempt-looking man. His clothes were dirty and soiled, he'd been sick, and the remnants were down his shirt and across his back. He'd unknowingly laid in it. There was an obvious whisky stench, his liquor of choice, plus he'd clearly soiled his trousers. His unshaven stubble looked as rough as he did. He looked up squinting as he came out from the darkness into the light.

He looked at Betty and the two strangers.

"Hello Betty *love*, I'm alright now *love*. You can let me out.

I promise I'll never do it again. I really won't *love*. Please let me out *love*. I'm fine." He looked a sad, pitiful sight.

Betty was smirking and leering at her sad husband for not much longer. "I hope you rot in hell, you sick fucker you!"

Jackie and Susan needed to intervene at this weird display of lost love. Jackie initiated a ceasefire.

"Mr Smith, I'm DC Smith …"

Alan replied immediately. "Hello Missy, we must be related in some way, therefore you use your powers to get me out of this cage, and I'll make it up to you … please. Now!"

Jackie hadn't finished so continued choosing to ignore Alan's plea. "I'm DC Smith and this is my colleague PC Hill."

Alan burst out laughing. "Ha-ha! So your colleague is 'Pissy Hill'. Ha-ha! My cows live on a *pissy hill*; they forever piss on it! Ha-ha! … Pissy Hill is it? Well, pleased to meet you Pissy! You looks alright!" He stuck out his filthy dried puke hand to shake Susan's. She ignored him. He retorted, "Whoever named you that funny name … Pissy? Are you a Miss? Are you Miss Pissy? Ha-ha! Ha-ha! You're a misprint! They fucked up your birth certificate and called you 'Pissy Hill!' Ha-ha! We're farmers and we've got a Miss Piggy … are you related by any chance? Ha-ha! Ha-ha!"

Susan rolled her eyes. Funny it wasn't, she'd never heard that one before. She thought, *West Country bumpkin*, but never spoke it aloud, as that could be seen as a reprimand issue with her employer.

Jackie tried to take the lead again. "Mr Smith, we need to ask you some questions about Petra who you found on the beach yesterday."

Alan stopped fidgeting. He looked amazed as he suddenly remembered his secret obsession, his hobby, and passion that had suddenly gone. He remembered her soft cute breasts and that he caressed them for the last time by massaging them under the guise of performing CPR. His thoughts were dashed when he heard Jackie asking, "Did you see Petra before your wife contacted you to assist her when she found Petra dead on the beach?"

Alan had to think. He saw her the day before and took another series of photos. "Nah," replied Alan.

Jackie ramped up. "Did you perform CPR on Petra?"

Alan smiled. "Yes I did. I tried my best."

"How did you perform CPR?"

Alan's smile disappeared. He knew he was fondling Petra's breasts for his own personal pleasure and not for her resuscitation, and that was a bad thing to do on a dead corpse. He fumbled with his answer and got twitchy as he spoke. "I did CPR the best way I could. I ain't had no training. I'd seen it on TV and thought I'd better have a go, so I did."

Jackie remembered what the pathologist had said about Petra's breasts in that there were markings on them that indicated some sort of abuse. Betty had said that she saw Alan fondling Petra's breasts, when she found her.

Whilst Jackie was thinking Susan said, "Mr Smith, I need to take a sample of your saliva."

Alan thought, *Yeah, I'll give you a sample of me saliva alright, when I lick you ... all over your body!* He asked, "How you gonna do that?"

Before Susan could reply several vehicles could be heard arriving in the yard. Lucy and Daisy had charged off to do their guarding duties. It was two police cars with four uniformed officers. Betty, Jackie and Susan went out to see who it was. The dogs sat patiently by each car with the officers reluctant to get out of their vehicles with the dogs close by. Betty called her duo back and beckoned the officers to get out of their vehicles. That they did. As Betty approached, Lucy and Daisy wagged their tails, receiving lots of attention from the officers they thought could have been intruders, such was their training. As soon as Betty reassured her duo they changed back to their usual friendly nature.

Whilst Jackie, Susan and Betty were outside, Alan wept. His thoughts were with Petra and the clandestine relationship he had with her. She frequently walked alone and had seen Alan working in the fields next to the clifftop. As time passed, and with the regularity of Petra's walks, it was polite to wave an acknowledgment to a neighbour. Gradually Petra would stop and talk to Alan about the weather and other usual niceties. Alan magnetised towards her from not long after she moved to the area. He was attracted to her beautiful appearance, and bubbly outgoing and friendly persona. As time passed and with the regularity of her passing by, he began to fantasise about her. He became obsessive and as Petra could walk at random times including the night he installed a covert system of remote motion sensors and cameras. He would get motion alerts along with live images on his phone application. He soon found the hidden path she'd walk down to the cave and beach. He hid cameras amongst gorse bushes to discreetly take video movies of Petra that showed her undress ready to skinny dip and sunbathe nude. His voyeuristic mind wanted more, he wanted to be there. He plotted to creep down to the cave where she'd undress, he hid within and waited. After several no-shows he hid again at the rear of the large cave. Petra arrived on this particular day, stripped off her clothes as Alan watched. She went for her swim. Alan crept out of his hiding place. He took her clothes and sat at the edge of the water waiting for her to return. When she realised Alan was watching, she was standing in the sea with her body neck down below the water level.

She asked what he was doing. "Alan, what are you doing here, why have you got my clothes?"

Alan sneered, "I saw you come and thought I'd be useful by bringing your clothes out to the water's edge for you."

She was horrified. "Alan, please go away."

He laughed. "Nah, I wants to see you close up in all your glory, then I'll leave."

Petra became worried. This person, the one she amicably chatted to and who had seemed OK, had suddenly become different. She felt threatened. She wasn't aware that he'd been stalking and recording her activities.

He had images that had satisfied his hunger but now his hunger wanted feeding. He wanted to touch her. He knew he'd have control of her by default with planned threats to publish the many previously recorded images to social media.

Petra began to cry.

Alan laughed. "Come on Petra, I'm only being helpful. Don't be silly, you'll get yourself a cold in there. Come on out. I won't look, I promise." He turned his back and walked a few paces up the beach. "See, I've gone away so you come out and get dressed."

Petra *was* getting cold, so she dashed out and partially dressed. She then marched up to him. "What do you think you're doing, you're a pervert! I'm going to call the police!"

Alan really didn't think this would happen; he had stolen her phone from her pocket. "Oh, shit what have I done. I'm sorry, I didn't mean to upset you. I did it for a bit of fun." He began to act by falsely crying. He appeared genuinely upset. Petra was taken in by his acting and mistakenly thought he was unaware his behaviour was unacceptable. She had felt, from earlier walk meetings, he had a learning difficulty or some other issue. As he imitated upset, she felt sorry for him. She had her own issues, that she knew made her just slightly different. She empathised with his behaviour, which fortunately didn't really do her any harm. She began to cry with him and embraced him. Bizarre as it was, two troubled minds had met; there was compassion from Petra. She hadn't realised Alan was faking his actions. She fed his actions the way he wanted her to. His trap had been set.

After a while they sat and chatted freely about their issues. They shared their minds, and the commonality of their personal problems had a healing effect on Petra. Alan's dark side appeared to change with his reward for Petra's forgiveness and embrace.

He spoke. "Petra, I am truly sorry for what I've just done. I didn't mean to upset you, honest. I had no intention of harming you, I only did it for a laugh. I really do like you and you're the first person to understand that I have issues too. I get these urges you see."

Petra smiled. She had got over her initial shock now that she had a better understanding of Alan's situation. "Alan, what you did was wrong, please don't do it again to me, or anyone else. It is naughty and you'd get into big trouble. The next person may not be so obliging, and they'll definitely call the police."

Alan smiled. "Well Petra, you're a fine woman and here, take your phone back and here's mine. Delete all of the photos I've taken. I'm sorry, I won't do it again."

Petra deleted all the images he'd taken of her from his phone's memory. She was unaware of the covert cameras and the many images Alan had stored on his home computer, including those on his phone.

Petra spoke about her issues. "I'm troubled like you but in a different way. I am odd as I worry about getting fat, so I have to do things to help myself." She then explained her methods, old and new.

Alan listened and then removed a lip balm pen from his pocket. He took the cap off and suggested Petra wipe her dry lips with the balm.

"Why would I want to do that, my lips aren't dry?" she curiously asked.

"Well, my dear, you've been in salt water and this will make your lips feel better. Plus, it'll make you feel lightheaded and freer in your mind, it'll take away your worries! I use it to calm me down. See, I gets excited, and this stuff helps my anxiety."

The last word 'anxiety' resonated with Petra. She used the balm. Within minutes she did feel less anxious and nicely relaxed. She smiled as she slowly became joyous.

"Wow! I feel really happy! What is it?" she asked.

"Well, my dear, it's a secret. I buys it from someone I knows, but I can't tell you who it is. If I shares it with you, you must promise not to tell anyone about today, what's just happened, or about the balm. OK?"

Petra was intrigued. She did feel freer and lightheaded ... and very relaxed. She smiled. "OK, I won't tell anyone if you promise not to tell anyone about what you've done today, you've been a naughty boy!" She laughed and gently slapped the back of his hand. Alan laughed as he applied the balm to his lips. "Could I have some more, please," Petra asked, giggling as she did.

"Of course you can my dear, here have some more!" She applied more. Alan laughed. "You've missed a bit, here, let me apply it for you." He carefully applied the balm over Petra's moist lips, but more thickly. "There you go my dear, you just relax and dream on."

Petra smiled and felt elated. She felt tired and lay down. She shut her eyes. "Wow! It's amazing! I feel like I'm getting tipsy! Ha-ha!"

Alan smiled as he applied more of the balm again to his lips and then again to Petra's. He softly said, "You mustn't have too much as you'll become uninhibited!"

She smiled. "I don't care, I just feel great!" She giggled. "Give me more!"

That he did. Again, he applied the balm thickly to her pouting lips. She moved her lips in a diffusing way to spread the balm. She then licked both her lips. The sun was shining and it was becoming hot. They both perspired.

Alan lent over her. "Here, let me loosen your clothing, you'll get too hot."

Petra smiled and giggled. She was unaware the lip balm was infused with a drug that calmed the body into a nirvana relaxed state where nothing mattered. She had become carefree. She intoxicatingly replied by spreading her arms out and nodded. Alan unfastened Petra's blouse. Petra giggled and wasn't fazed as she sat up whilst he removed it from around her. She wasn't wearing a bra. She enjoyed the serenity with her flowing mind as she laid down and shut her eyes with a smile. Alan stared at her. They continued to chat about nothing and when the time was right and Petra slept, Alan unbuttoned her jeans and removed them. She didn't wear pants.

Petra remained in a drugged state unaware that Alan was abusing her. He did this whilst knowing that his actions were being recorded on one of his many hidden cameras. After a while he wiped the thick balm off her lips and within minutes she semi recovered from her sleep, unaware of the abuse. She was still on a high as she dressed whilst laughing and giggling.

Alan understood Petra was a troubled woman, as he was. They both had issues although his were at the far end of normality. This commonality of troubled minds led to a strange relationship where they fed off each other's needs and wants. Some of their feelings were mutual and so began a strange clandestine relationship. They met frequently and he would abuse her in return for application of the balm. Petra was, however, unaware of the full abuse inflicted upon her sleeping body. As the weeks and months passed, Alan progressively demanded payment with cash or by way of permission allowing him to take lewd photos with his phone as Petra posed for him whilst being awake. This he thought was more attractive than filming her sleeping beauty. She became trapped with extortion as Alan had enslaved her for his use to do whatever he liked; if she didn't he again threatened to upload the photos to social media. This they both knew could ruin her business and more importantly the relationships with Alex and Suze. Petra naively felt helpless until, quite by chance, she found an outlet where the illicit balm was being sold by a strange character in St Ives. She thereafter sourced her own supply.

At the next arranged meeting with Alan, she explained that she'd go to the police unless he deleted all the photos from his phone again. He did that in front of her. But she was still unaware of the hidden cameras or the app that controlled them with their hard drive back-up. She asked if he'd copied the phone images to his home computer. He said he didn't have one nor would he know how to use one. He gave the impression he was simple.

The relationship ended a year ago and they'd ignored each other since. Petra's troubles doubled as she had become an addict to the balm. She hid her balm addiction from

Suze and Alex; all they knew was it a regular lip balm. If they wanted some balm she carried two types, the second being a regular un-drugged type. Petra explained the balm boxes away by saying they were for her sensitive lips and that buying in bulk halved the cost from a medicinal supplier. She found the quantity to use for her fix so it couldn't be noticed by those around her, including Suze and Alex. The use of the balm became accepted by Suze and Alex and was seen as another example of Petra's sometimes strange behaviour. They both realised Petra could have been on a scale of some kind, she may have been autistic, or on some other spectrum. It didn't matter to either if Petra was different at times. Maybe it was one of the many reasons why they had both gravitated to her as they agreed everyone is on a spectrum, whether or not they realise. They also knew Petra had always liked to be alone for long periods. She'd return refreshed and revitalised, ready for the next stage of her life. Being just slightly different enabled her art to be so captivating, displaying the beautiful person she was. Her liaison with Alan, his abuse and the resultant drug dependency remained a secret. Petra felt at ease with her dependency and didn't see it as an addiction, rather a coping strategy with her obsession with weight loss. Alan ended his thoughts. Realisation entered his mind he was soon to be discovered. He wasn't unduly concerned as *in his mind* he hadn't done anything wrong.

Jackie talked through her plan with the officers as Susan and Betty listened. Jackie's head issue returned but she chose to note it and not ask for any more paracetamol. Another car arrived with two forensic officers. The teams scurried away to conduct their duties and search the property under the guidance of the forensic experts. Betty was informed that she needed to go to the station, as did Alan. She had a friend called Alice. Alice had a nearby farm, her daughter and son volunteered to look after the Smith's farm whilst they were in custody. Plus, they loved the old girl Lucy and younger Daisy. Two of the officers arrested Betty and Alan and took them to the station in separate cars. They would be interviewed later from their separate cells along with having their DNA samples taken. A short time later the search found another necklace and other paraphernalia that could connect Alan or Betty to Petra's murder. Alan's stash consisted of pornographic magazines, DVDs and his computer that had history files from his phone with thousands of sexual images which would be analysed and used as evidence. There were many more in a photo album he named 'Petra'.

Time had passed quickly. It was now 5pm when Jackie's phone rang. "Hello Jackie, how's it going?" It was Peter.

She replied with her phone on a speaker so Susan could listen to it. "Hi Peter, it's all going really well here!"

He said, "Well done you! Excellent work! We've got two suspects at the station, Greg and Abbi Stephenson, and the grapevine is telling me two more are coming in, the Smiths. I was thinking about interviewing them as I'm here and ready. Any of the four could be our potential murderer. How would you feel about that?"

Jackie thought about the kudos if she and Susan conducted the interviews. But here, she had a badge that made her a lowly DC, a Detective Constable. Peter had let her manage the job, and she felt good with what had been established in such a short time. To get the villain, or villains, in such a short time was an amazing feeling. The closure of the job by interview to get a confession would have been the icing on the cake, but the protocol was for at least DIs like Peter to conduct murder investigation interviews. She *was* his rank and well versed in the technique whilst in London, but here the case could be thrown out, as she wasn't a DI. Some DSs, whilst under supervision, could participate, the likes of Ian Walsh, but he was so disengaged he may not be worthy of such a role.

Reluctantly Jackie replied, "Guv, I can't because of protocol, and you know that. Thanks for saying it the way you did. I appreciate that. Go for it and get the confessions."

Peter replied, "I will, and I'd like you to be in the interview as my number two, but I'll use DS Walsh, you're there and I'm here. Plus, you've worked bloody hard over the past two days. You and Susan have the rest of the weekend off for good old R&R! You've both earned it!"

Jackie was relieved that she and Susan could finally do R&R. It had been full on for them. Emotionally they were tired and drained. She said, "Peter, you're the Guv, you have the kudos, that's fine. I hope you get the result!" She ended the call and her head was banging. She again put the nagging feeling aside.

Jackie and Susan got into the car to leave. The site was secured as uniformed officers and forensics continued.

Jackie said, "Successful day, wanna party?"

Susan was expecting to go back to her lonely apartment, but this invite was too good to miss. "Yay! Where to?"

"Dawn is a party animal, I'll call her!" Jackie called Dawn.

"Hi Dawn, you remember about catching up for a drink. how about now?"

"Well h-e-l-l-o Jackie!" came the elongated reply from Dawn. "I do remember, what do you have in mind?"

"Up to you!"

"Well, there's a newish club in Marazion that's good. They do fab food and there's a disco! I get preferential treatment there, you can be my guests!"

"Yes, I've heard the word! Great! Let's do it."

"I've got Susan here and she'd like to come too, OK?"

"Of course she can. Hey, what about you two staying over at mine after, I'm only a 30-minute walk from the club, or we get a taxi. I don't mind … we could drink lots and relax!"

"Well, if that's OK with you, we wouldn't want to put you out?"

"Not a problem. It makes sense as you live in the sticks with such a long drive. No, sorted. Stay over at mine. How about you get here by eight? I'll book a table for 9ish?"

"Perfect. See you then! Bye!"

Jackie looked at Susan who was beaming with a smile. She said, "Excellent. Thank you for my inclusion!"

They each drove back to Jackie's with the party music blaring out. They showered and tarted up as Jackie called it. Jackie started to dance whilst Susan joined in as she was dressing and parading Jackie's clothes and trying to find the size and style she liked. Susan managed to find clothes from Jackie's that fitted her well. She wore a smart tight-fitting royal blue dress and matching high-heeled shoes. Jackie wore a light beige dress and also had heels on. They chuckled and got into the weekend feeling. They were listening to dance music. They decided to travel to Dawn's in Susan's car, which meant on their return tomorrow both cars would again be at Jackie's. As Susan offered to drive, Jackie had a couple of tins of mojitos to get herself in the right mood whilst they danced and dressed. When they were ready to leave, Jackie got two of her coats out for them to wear just in case the horrid weather persisted.

CHAPTER 13
IT'S DAWN AGAIN

It was Saturday night. Jackie felt very happy. She had a new work partner that she liked and more importantly the case of catching the murderer was racing to a conclusion. All she needed were the DNA results to link one, or more, of the four suspects now being held in custody. She was confident that at least one of them was connected; they all knew Petra *and* generally murderers know their victim. Suze and Alex were still in the frame, but she hoped they weren't connected. She was beginning to relax. It was Saturday night and it was time to party.

They arrived at Dawn's just before 8pm on that Saturday night. The weather was calmer with a slight breeze, without rain or mizzle. It was still cloudy but mild at 15 degrees. Dawn's house was at the better end of town. It was a large, detached house with a swept drive and a well-manicured garden with shrubs and a neat hedge for privacy. As they drove up the drive, Jackie saw Dawn's usual car parked next to a swanky and very smart sports car. It must be new as it had the latest registration number. Jackie wondered, *Perhaps Dawn's friend is here?* Jackie had only been here once before and then, like now, she wondered how a lowly police officer could afford such a des-res in such an exclusive area. Her wondering mind ceased when she pushed the smart CCTV doorbell. Dawn spoke through the speaker, "Well hello darlings! Come on in, the door is unlocked!" Susan politely opened the door for Jackie, and they entered.

The large hall had a smart modern interior; it had

some expensive-looking items neatly placed around. There was a galleried landing that complemented the spacious feel. Dawn appeared. Jackie thought she looked fantastic, like a stereotypical model, gorgeous with a jaw-dropping appearance. She was dressed in a very skimpy, Lycra skin-hugging bright red dress. It showed her fabulous figure amazingly well. Jackie also thought she wasn't wearing a bra or pants. Neither were visible through the dress. Her breasts oozed forward against her tightly stretched dress; they hung there proudly. Jackie had only met Dawn whilst at work and once at a bar after. She was always attractive in workwear but now she looked stunning. Jackie knew Dawn had a daughter from their previous conversations but imagined *she couldn't have breastfed her, not with that perfect shape. Or she could have had a breast enlargement?* She was about 5' 8" tall and perhaps a size 8–10.

Dawn glided over to her visitors, like a model on a catwalk, showing off not only a new costume but also her good looks. She hugged and kissed Jackie on each cheek, leaving slight traces of her bright red lipstick on both.

"Well hello Jackie, I'm just so glad you've made it, it's been far too long!" Dawn then turned to Susan showing her pearly white teeth glistening in the light. "Well hello to you too! You must be the lovely Susan who called me?" She then hugged and kissed Susan on each cheek.

Susan was taken aback. The fragrance Dawn was wearing was magical, it was like the scent of red roses with an enticing twist that sucked her in for more. She thought it very similar to the fragrance Abbi wore whilst she knelt between her at the shop. It was almost identical.

Susan replied, "Hello Dawn, lovely to meet you. I must say, you look fabulous, and your scent is extraordinary nice!" Susan was thinking, *If I were a bee, I'd be on you all day and every day!*

Dawn's smile was enchanting; her lips were naturally plumped up and looked enticingly nice to kiss. Dawn replied, "Susan, congratulations for choosing our force for your secondment to the CID. You'll learn a lot from Jackie, she's good, really good, aren't you darling?" Dawn was now looking at Jackie.

Jackie enviously smiled at her host and said, "Hello Dawn, nice to see you too!"

Dawn took their coats and hung them in the closet. She then led the duo into her enormous kitchen. It too was very modern, neat and tidy, and immaculately clean. She went to her chiller and removed an expensive bottle of champagne. She said, "Only the best for my guests!" They all laughed.

They walked into the spacious lounge that had a huge flat screen TV and then they sat on the most comfortable leather suite you could imagine. It was whiter than Dawn's teeth, and maybe as soft as her skin. It was all very lavish and posh. They sat, chatted and drank two bottles of the fine champagne. Dawn said she'd arranged a taxi for 9:00 so they could sit and chat until then. That they did.

Dawn explained Susan's question about her fantastic house. "It was paid for from my dead husband's estate that he left to me. He wasn't wealthy, far from it, but he had the wisdom to take out a massive life insurance policy. Two years later he was dead. It was a sudden heart attack that came from nowhere. He was out running and was just 38, That was eight years ago." Dawn was also 36, the same age as Jackie. She explained she continued to work within the police as she enjoyed it, and it kept her 'off the streets' as she called it. Dawn continued, "I moved into this glorious home with the proceeds of that very fortunate insurance policy. The previous marital home was sold and the proceeds invested to supplement my police wage. This allows me to live extravagantly with holidays abroad and no expense spared!"

"Wow!" said Susan. "That was most fortunate for you, but at the same time awfully tragic."

Dawn replied, "Yes indeed it was. I have a daughter, but she's moved out into a nice apartment. She was devastated, as I was. But life goes on and I'm single and enjoying every minute of it! Cheers!"

The taxi arrived and took them to the club. It was opposite the glorious sandy beach of Marazion. As the three walked to the club's door they were given wolf whistles from two separate groups of churlish young men. The three women turned to have a look and posed as models would during a photo shoot. The three did look fantastic. As they approached the club a queue had formed. But out of nowhere a doorperson recognised Dawn and came to meet her. He guided the three into the entrance, without queuing. They were shown to their executive table.

Dawn was the outright model winner with her bright red dress, high heels and drop-dead looks. As they spoke and ate it transpired that Dawn wasn't really bothered with finding another husband. "One was enough, *but* I do have a very close boyfriend, my 'friend with benefits' and my relationship with him is just perfect! That's why my daughter moved out, she couldn't cope with my boyfriend." At this point Jackie's head twanged again, she gently massaged it to relieve the strange sensation. As her condition subsided the three ate, drank and got merry.

By 11pm the music was ramping up in volume. People had started to gyrate around the club and the atmosphere was changing into a 'proper job' dance club. The flashing lights followed the music rhythm, and they changed patterns in sync with the tunes. The three got up to strut their stuff, and that they did. After a while they returned to their table for more cocktails. They were slowly getting loose and drunk.

It was around 12:30am and now Sunday. Susan danced alone amongst a throng of hot bodies to her favourite track when suddenly, there in front of her, and now dancing with her, was Abbi. Susan couldn't believe it; Abbi was arrested earlier along with her father Greg. Susan stopped dancing and wanted to leave the dance floor to inform Jackie, but Abbi grabbed her hand. Not in a nasty way, in a rather a *nice warm* way. She beckoned Susan to dance, the music was too loud to talk, so foolishly Susan did just that. The booze had lowered her guard; it had removed good sense. She knew she shouldn't have, but she danced with a suspect. They couldn't talk as the intoxicating music was just as good as the booze. Abbi smiled at Susan ... a lot. Not in a 'gotcha' way, rather a sincere manner. Susan didn't initially smile back, but her inhibitions had lowered and after a time she did return smiles. Abbi continually rubbed her hot body next to Susan's. She could smell Abbi's enticing scent. It was very similar to the type Dawn was wearing. It was nicer, more rounded and just as alluring. Abbi wore a next-to-nothing outfit that showed her glorious body and that elusive snake tattoo. By now Susan felt drawn to Abbi's presence and wanted to stay; she wanted to get to know Abbi better. But *that* could be wrong and being wrong while working for the police wasn't good. Her better judgement told her to leave Abbi and return to the table. As Susan quickly turned to leave, Abbi grabbed her hand forcibly and pulled Susan towards her. She spoke into her ear.

"Come with me, I need to show you something."

Susan froze. She was semi drunk but still had a capable mind, well almost. She gave in and let Abbi pull her through the hot scantily clad bodies to the far side.

Abbi led Susan to a cubicle area that was less noisy and out of sight of Jackie and Dawn. *They* hadn't noticed it was Abbi dancing provocatively with Susan, such was the flashing lighting and *their distraction* with both men and women that descended to their table. They had occasionally looked to see if Susan were OK, as good buddies do. She looked fine and OK dancing to the very loud music. The distraction for Jackie and Dawn were the other bodies that had surrounded them. *They* were enjoying the numerous people coming to sit and chat with them. It was like meeting a variety pack of sweets. They were meeting all types and colours, shapes and sizes of sweet people. People who were interested in them and with Dawn in particular, without fear, or favour. People who resonated with them and made *them* feel special and wanted. *They* were occupied in their moment of happiness and were unaware that Susan had disappeared ... with a prime suspect. In this period of joyousness and relaxed state they had dropped their guard.

Within the private cubicle Abbi now held both of Susan's hands. Not as a restraint, but warmly as they sat closely next to each other. She spoke without the need to shout into Susan's ear. "Hello Susan, lovely to see you here!"

Susan was slowly awoken from her state of hedonism as the atmosphere had changed. The motion of hot bodies touching hers, loud enjoyable music and odours that induced 'the moment' were slowly fading away. The lighting wasn't trancing; it was stable and showed Abbi to be much cleaner and more attractive than Susan remembered from their initial bizarre meeting in the shop.

Susan replied, "Hello Abbi ... Nice, nice to see you again ... I thought you'd been arrested?"

That four-letter word, the one that applied whilst doing

it, had slowly crept into Susan's mind, she was back at *work*. 'Once a copper, always a copper' she had often heard. Her work ethic was now creeping in, as here, holding her hands was a suspect. But ... there was something in Abbi that made her feel good. Abbi had two sides to her, like her head, armpits and God knows what else, that were neatly shaved with care and attention. The side that Susan had just seen and touched on the dance floor felt *so* good, better than her acting in the shop. She now appeared to be a warmer, friendly and non-aggressive person. Susan was still curious about *her* ambience and confident persona. She wanted to find out more about it by talking and being near her, even though this contradicted her job.

Abbi smiled and replied to Susan's question, "Yes, I was arrested, no thanks to you! But I told the truth. Greg isn't my real father, or my lover. It's all an act. Greg is the one doing the drug selling and other dodgy dealing stuff, I was an innocent accomplice forced to work there and was totally unaware of what he was doing ... such the man he is. He's an actor. And because I like acting and performing to people, in the fuller sense of being an actor. I initially had no idea of his charade. I genuinely didn't know until after I started. I was attracted to his acting ability when I first saw him perform in a show. I had just finished uni and after being away for three years I came back to Cornwall. I had expectations of getting a fantastic job with a career. But all I found was my acting ability honed from being at uni. A struggling actor earns next to nothing. I worked in the local supermarket part time, that's all they had. I joined the local acting group and met Greg. He offered me the job in his shop and paid me *really, really* well. The rest is history. He's a man of many masks; I only saw his front-of-house seller ability with the macabre and items we sold. I was on a bonus, the more we shifted the more I got paid. I really didn't know half the stuff we shifted was drug related. I just assumed the strange alluring intoxicating smell came from his joss sticks. I know that I'm a more contented person since I've worked there, every day is a happy day! I'm clean, never done proper drugs, don't want to. The police were very kind and understanding with my naivety and sweet innocence. They realised there wasn't any evidence against me, and I was just in the wrong place at the wrong time. A bit like slave labour, I was entrapped by the aroma and salary. I didn't really know what was happening. The police let me go. I've given my immediate resignation to Greg via a letter I posted through the shop letterbox. Greg's still being held at the station. So, I'm all alone now … that is until I saw you here."

Susan was flummoxed, and semi speechless. Then she rallied. "Wow! That's some explanation. But, good that you're innocent. I'm happy. Stay that way. I'm pleased you don't do drugs; they're a killer. Once you're hooked, you're caught like a fish on a line, but that line never lets you go."

She looked at Abbi in a different way after the explanation. She understood Abbi being in the wrong place at the wrong time. She had been there with her ethnicity, tooth brace, spectacles and breastlessness.

Susan asked, "What will you do now?"

Abbi smiled, "Well, I'm not a loser. I can act so there may be opportunities in that area. Working for Greg was always a stop gap for me. It was a fun time being with him, we had lots of laughs together and I met some really nice people, including the other performers. Now I know he's a supreme actor; all this time I've been drugged unwittingly and hoodwinked! I'm in no rush to move on, I have family and friends here. I have savings and my rent is paid six months ahead."

Abbi then moved closer to Susan, putting a hand on her leg. She reassuringly smoothed Susan's thigh, tapping it a few times. It was done in a discreet way that didn't appear to annoy Susan. She did think, *Love is a drug that feeds the relationship. But love can also break many hearts ... the same way drugs do.*

Suddenly, like with Cinderella, the clock struck 12. Abbi stopped short and quickly stood up. She looked down at Susan and handed her a slip of folded paper. "I'm sorry Susan, I can't do this. Not now. I'm leaving, I've booked a taxi before I arrived here, not knowing you would be here. I need to go now as my friends are leaving soon. I don't want to let them down ... and I definitely don't want to let you down. Here's my number, if you feel about me, you'll contact me." She suddenly rushed off.

Susan sat stunned by the suddenness of Abbi's action. She watched open mouthed as Abbi flew through the throng of dancers, like a beautiful butterfly around flowers, weaving delicately between blossoms. She then disappeared like a fish diving down underwater, suddenly, and out of sight. Reality set in that Abbi had gone. Susan felt the warmth within her turn solid, like a block of ice, frozen cold. She was intrigued by the piece of paper. She opened to find a neatly handwritten phone number. Her hand made an angry fist that wrapped tightly around the paper; why, she didn't know. She then opened it out flat to carefully fold the paper as small as she could and slid it into her shoe below her foot.

The worry Susan had about Abbi had disappeared and was replaced with upset as Abbi ran off, but that now turned to excitement. The chase and excitement that comes with finding secret desires and love were rushing into her mind. The chase was on; she was going to chase Abbi; she gathered her thoughts into a plan ... she was excited ... she'd text Abbi as soon as she could. *That,* she thought, *would be in a cubicle within the women's toilets!* She stood and thought, *I'll adjust Jackie's tight-fitting blue dress. I'll ensure I look fine by looking down my body, and in particular to my left shoe, where that hidden magic number will enable me to text Abbi!* She made her way back through the pleasurable mayhem of hot, and more very hot dancers. Some grabbed her to join in with their very erotic postures, that she did to satisfy their needs. She strutted her stuff whilst deliberately moving to escape between some very sensuously charged couples. She was touched in places on her body, by both women and men, who gestured her to stay with them. Thoughts of spiking resonated in her mind; she hadn't felt any needle jabs, just hot sweaty hands sliding over her body touching her private parts. When she looked who was touching her, the offending hands were gone as quickly as they came, the offenders were unknown. She continued to dance her way out of the wild but exciting arena. She felt it was like an orgy of dance; hot, chaotic and endless fun. But this type of fun wasn't for her, not now. She wanted Abbi. Every time she thought she was near the exit of the floor, she was tugged back into the ring for more. Initially she enjoyed the attentive hands wanting her to dance, but she began to feel threatened as the music beat and volume increased. The dancers were in some sort of trance as they jumped and gyrated with the music. They appeared to be in a ritualistic hypnotic state, fuelled by drugs and alcohol. There were screams of excitement as nearly nude bodies rubbed against each other whilst also fondling others around them. Susan decided to make her exit. As someone pulled her towards them, she used the momentum to catapult herself up and over the sidewalk steps to safety. She was covered in sweat and other liquids that weren't hers. She quickly checked for damage to Jackie's dress; it looked OK in the darkness.

She could see Dawn and Jackie at the table with several others. They looked happy and waved at her. She waved back and mouthed 'toilet' as she pointed to the direction of the loos. But she then realised she needed her phone, and that was in her bag with Jackie. She now had to go to the table. When she arrived, she smiled at the other folk sitting around the table.

"How is everything?" she shouted at Jackie, who was sat tightly between two women.

"Fine, I'm having a wonderful time, and you?" The two women smiled at Susan, one blew a kiss her way.

"Excellent, but I need to pee!"

Dawn thumbed-up as she broke away from kissing a man who looked half her age. He had one hand on her breast and the other on her thigh. He looked the worst for his intake of some substance he had consumed. Dawn smiled at Susan. Another man appeared to be waiting for the first to move out of the way so he could get close to Dawn. Susan saw her glass on the table but decided not to drink the contents; she'd been away from it and wondered if it may have been spiked as Jackie and Dawn appeared too distracted to keep an eye on it. She waved goodbye as soon as she had her bag and made her way across towards the toilets. She continued past the heaving bar where again she was unwelcomely touched by other hands. When she turned to look again there was innocence, with no one resembling an offender. There were as many women as men; she wondered if it were they who also touched her.

As usual within these clubs the women's toilet had a queue. Susan waited patiently for her turn to enter. When she went through the door the queue continued waiting for cubicles to become available. She used the time to look at her appearance in the mirrors. The music was piped to the toilets and some women were gyrating wildly; they were less than half dressed. Some appeared euphoric and phased whilst others looked pissed off. Susan looked fine apart from some sticky liquid low down on Jackie's dress. She thought the fluid resembled wallpaper glue. She asked the woman behind to save her place in the queue whilst she went to a basin. She carefully, whilst trying not to touch the liquid, wet a paper tissue and wiped off the offending fluid. She washed and rinsed her hands thoroughly just in case some had got onto them, twice. She checked her arms and legs for any pin pricks that may have indicated she'd been jabbed with some date rape substance whilst amongst the dance mayhem and the touching bar. There were none, plus she felt OK, although still dizzily intoxicated from her Abbi experience and alcohol intake.

She rejoined the queue and thanked the woman who was smiling. The woman shouted above the music, "Shocking isn't it! I've had that stuff on me several times!"

Susan looked quizzically and asked, "What is it?"

The woman laughed. "It's the boys! It's the boys' cum!"

Susan was disgusted and felt sick with the thought. She wanted to wash her hands again. The woman was laughing as were the women behind her after the first shared the news by shouting out, "Look, this silly bitch has cum all down her dress!"

Susan firmly asked, whilst on her way back to the basin, "Are you serious?"

The woman did have a serious expression. "It's from the sailor's cock! Ha-ha! Ha-ha! Ha-ha! ... They're seamen you see! Ha-ha! Ha-ha! I'm only joking, I mean it's from their *cock*tail ... it's the thick coconut milk from their *cock*tail drink!"

Susan was both fuming with the joke on her, but also relieved that the offending liquid was allegedly harmless coconut milk. She wasn't going to taste it, just in case. She washed her hands again and again to laughs, cheers and finger pointing. She felt belittled and ashamed of something she didn't do, like being born to Asian parents, or being bullied at school. But she wouldn't have known if it *was* semen. She'd *never* had that sort of relationship with a man, and right now she never wanted that sort of relationship. This experience had put her right off men. And if she did, tasting seamen was definitely not her cup of tea, even if they were sailors. And she may never have a cocktail with coconut milk in again, not after this distasteful experience.

A toilet cubicle became free; Susan entered and took the opportunity to pee. Whilst she sat she removed the paper from her shoe. She opened it and saw Abbi's number. She selected new contacts on her phone and input 'Abbi' along with the number. She selected 'message'. She texted:

'Hi Abbi, Susan here! I hope you're OK … I had a wonderful experience with you. Could we meet again?'

She pushed the send button and within seconds could see the 'delivered' icon. Almost immediately she saw it had been read. Her heart rate increased. She could hear the thumping music and the chatter and noises from outside the cubicle, but her heart thumped louder. She sat and waited for what seemed to be ages, but in fact were just a few moments. Whilst she waited her head had a strange feeling, a twang, that she thought was similar to how Jackie had described her head feeling. The twang disappeared as her phone vibrated.

She had a reply from Abbi. Her emotions rose with expectations; she gulped in excited anticipation … it read:

'Well hello Susan! Fab, you've contacted me. I thought you may not. I'm *SO* pleased you have!!! What are you doing now, could you come over to my place?'

Susan's pulse increased. She thought she'd be cool so texted how she thought young people text:

'luv 2 cum ovr u now! Where r u? lotsa XXX'

Abbi's reply read:

'Be yourself!!! No need to text like a child ... I like you the way you are! I'm at flat 12 The Hermit. St Ives. I'm still in the taxi but will be there 1:30ish. Come when you can. See you soon!'

Susan's reply:

'OK, I was trying to impress with my texting! I'll be myself. I leave here now, get a taxi, and reckon ETA 2ish Loadsa x!!!'

The rush of excitement about doing something different, the dare, going into the unknown, *the chase*, was immense for Susan. Suddenly she thought, *The chase is giving me an appetite, I feel the hunger and I need feeding!* Her mind was going crazy, but this craziness was a drug, she was relishing the thought of doing something different. Doing something that some found wrong. She was breaking the law in some people's minds. She felt very naughty, but nicely so. She left the cubicle and the toilet area. Head held high, she strutted past the bar with the confidence within. Wolf whistles were frequent, from both sexes. She came to the table where Jackie and Dawn were sitting. They were now on the dance floor, resting their voices and allowing their bodies to do the talking. Susan sat next to a woman who was there previously and asked if she could give Jackie a message. She nodded. It was to mention that she'd text Jackie's phone and she needed to read it:

'Hi J, I've met someone! and they've invited me to their place. I'm fine & OK. I'll get a cab back to Dawn's by midmorning-ish xx.'

Susan left the club and, because she was seen with Dawn, a doorperson summoned a taxi. The taxi dropped Susan off in a suburb that was part of the old town. It wasn't well lit, and she had sobered enough to be wary of her surroundings. She was on guard as she made her way along a darkened alley and up steps to find the address. There was an intercom video door buzzer that she pushed. Abbi answered.

"Hello Susan! The door's open, come on up!"

Another buzzing noise was followed by a clunk that allowed the door to unlock. Susan went in, shut the door and walked up the stairs. The smell was beautiful and hit Susan like fragrance from a bouquet of colourful flowers. As she made her way up, Abbi appeared from the hall above, smiling as she saw Susan. She welcomed Susan with a big hug as they looked each other in the eye.

"Come on in darling!" spoke Abbi softly as she released her hug and held Susan's hand whilst leading her through to the lounge.

Abbi sat and guided Susan to sit next to her. She didn't know what would happen as they sat staring at each other. Abbi placed a hand onto each of Susan's bare thighs and spoke softly, "I have a very big confession to make." Susan listened optimistically. "I need to share with you something really important." Abbi spoke softly with slight embarrassment as she continued with her reveal. "Peter Drew, your boss, is connected to my boss Greg." Susan appeared shocked but was speechless. Abbi continued, "They're part of a new drug network that'll take over the UK and then the world. There's a very clever scientist at the top, a woman, who used AI to develop a drug as addictive as nicotine. The world's population loved nicotine and 25–50% still do in the form of smoking cigarettes. It was the nicotine delivery method in cigarettes which caused the cancers and other smoking-related illnesses. Vapes were the new cigarette and nicotine replacement. But they are not socially acceptable because of the vapour trails and their innocuous smell. The disposable types are banned. And there's more movement around the world to ban vapes in all sorts of places. The scientist has found a world-beating way to deliver her addictive drug to anyone. The users will anonymously take the drug, via the use of infused lip balm. No needles, no snorting, no smoking, no vapour trails and most of all no cold turkey like the heavy opioid drugs. It can be stronger than fentanyl if you want it to, but it doesn't kill you. You just keep applying it and collapse in a heap to sleep it off, but sometime later you'll come around safely and go again. It's unique. And it works. This synthetic drug is more addictive than nicotine and gives the feeling of elation, euphoria and fulfilment without shutting you down. Low doses keep you going, you can safely drive and work, take the kids to school, whatever. Low usage would be reminiscent of people smoking cigarettes back in the day. You just use more of it to reach a higher level of coping, and even more to get to nirvana. It's a very sexy drug. It's a no brainer. If you thought county lines were slick, watch this space!"

There was a pause. Abbi then continued. "Peter is a senior player in the organisation that goes way above his level *within the police and beyond*. The trial of the drug here in Cornwall has been a huge success. Soon there'll be a UK rollout into the other drug cartels and then on around the world. Pete governs and controls Greg's outlet and the mail order drug activity, along with Greg's fake gold chains that sell for £5,000 but only cost £45 to make. Peter takes a cut in the profit of the sales in Cornwall; Greg gets a cut plus his fake chain money. The drug is a unique synthetic type that can't be detected. Not by sniffer dogs, machines or blood tests. It has a street name, ATAA pronounced 'at-ar' and that means As Thin As Air! It got the name as it's undetectable."

Susan was instantly deflated and suddenly felt very cold. These few words shocked her with a massive let-down that had just blown away her expectations of getting to know Abbi better. Her naivety assumed Abbi was leading her into the lioness's den for something totally different than what she'd just heard. Susan now felt like a popped baloon with a lead weight; she hit the ground hard. It was like the knockout blow she received at a recent taekwondo competition; the blow came from nowhere and pummelled into her temple where her lights were switched off and she fell to oblivion onto the floor. She thought, *I bloody well need ATAA now! And lots of it, over and over my lips!*

Before Susan's mind had recovered Abbi was there again with her next sentence. "Pete's been having a long affair with Dawn. They planned and then murdered Dawn's husband. This is how Dawn has a flash lifestyle. Peter owns villas abroad, he earns a mint from drugs but being in the police is great cover for him and the others, it goes way above Peter!"

Susan felt this second blow like no other. She was now mortified. Her head sank. She pulled her hands away from Abbi's and wiped her eye. She thought a tear was coming. She stared vaguely into Abbi's eyes with disbelief. Abbi hadn't finished and was raring to go.

"There's more ... *I'm Dawn's daughter*, not by her murdered husband, *I'm from Peter!*"

By now Susan was holding her hand over her mouth with that 'oh my God' look that Suze had vividly displayed several times. She, like Suze, was terribly shocked, saddened and upset, more so as she was a police officer. Susan noticed that it wasn't her eye welling, it was Abbi's. A solitary tear had welled in Abbi's eye. The tear level rose and slowly flowed over the top of her lower eyelid. It rolled over her cheek and dripped off, onto Susan's thigh.

Abbi continued. "Sadly ... I'm a bastard child ... I'm actually Peter's *fucking bastard!* I hate him!" Abbi screamed and then cried aloud. Susan instinctively moved in and hugged her. The dam had burst; tears gushed from Abbi. Their heads were so close Susan got wet as the tears flowed down from Abbi's cheeks onto Jackie's best dress. The dress that had a sailor's smear on it now had a tearful damp patch in the awkward area of Susan's crotch. The damp patch would be mistaken as a pee stain. This was Jackie's best dress.

"Gee!" spoke a deflated Susan. "I'm well and truly knocked out now! I came here, to you, thinking we were going to get to know each other better, if you know what I mean?"

Abbi, with tears still flowing, blankly looked at Susan. There was silence. Abbi then replied, "I know, I played a cruel illusion."

Susan said, "I thought you came on to me in your shop. Then you grabbed me at the club and danced *so* provocatively with me there. You enticed me, you then invite me here to what I think will be a fantastic seduction, but instead you've given me a shed load of work!"

Abbi looked bemused. "It was all an act, planned and implemented to drag you *and* Jackie down. You're the *naive one*, the inexperienced junior one. Jackie would be too hard to crack. They tried to do that whilst she was at the Met. Her ex-partner, Steve, is in the drug ring; he deliberately played a game to get Jackie out of the way. If you think Cornwall is bad, you know nothing! I *really do* like you, there is something very attractive about you that I want to uncover, but maybe later. Not now. This is all Peter's entrapment plan, to ensnare you, to do something nasty. What that will be I don't know. I do know *he's* the fucker that made me a bastard!"

Susan was getting fed up with the F word. She'd heard it used a lot earlier from another woman, Betty the farmer and hubby Alan. She thought if she heard it as a normal word it wouldn't upset her so much. She was trying to make sense of the complex revelation from Abbi. As she was computing it in her mind, Abbi spoke. "I *still* haven't finished. Dawn had the drugs at the club; she's the shop window there. She was feeding the lip balm to those people sitting around her. They'd have a wipe from the balm. One wipe over their lips was enough for the punters to want more. That's why all those men and women sat near her, they were potential punters and screeners. The screeners concealed what Dawn was up to. Jackie had her glass rim wiped with the same stuff. She soon elated and won't remember a thing; such is the drug. All done with the lip balm. Dawn wasn't affected by the drug as she had taken a blocker. Such is this new synthetic type. It's like physics, with every force there is an equal and opposite force. So, ATAA can induce effect and its blocker opposes it. There are several discrete sellers around the club that punters approach to make their purchases after they've had a free sample from Dawn. The blocker also prevents her from catching bugs from the punters that kiss her, like a common cold, flu, herpes, crabs or anything else. Peter and Dawn actually own and run the club. It was part of the deal from above. They've paid *their* employees and police colleagues good money to keep the secrecy, and they're then part of the gang. Once you're in, you can't get out. There is nowhere, and I mean *nowhere* to run!"

Susan sat stunned in disbelief.

Abbi continued. "When I said I hadn't finished yet, there

are two more aspects. The four suspects, me, Greg, Betty and Alan, were taken into custody. Alan will be convicted of Petra's murder as the missing link DNA result will be switched to his DNA profile. Plus, with all his photos and abuse of Petra he'll have an easy court conviction. Peter will engineer it all. The second aspect is the final part of *your entrapment*. That is, I'm unfortunately a player in this act. Peter heard from Greg that you liked my performance at the shop, he wanted me to be your spider. I would entice you to my web with my attraction to you. This apartment is the centre of the web where you're stuck with no escape. It's here and it is now the time! Peter has conspired to kidnap you and has arranged for some heavy guys to do just that. Your face didn't fit well at the police college 'cos you were too bright and that's why you're here. You're seen as an up-and-coming star that could threaten the organisation, you're too clever for your own boots! The same as Jackie is. Once you're taken, you'd become the bait to snare Jackie. You'd both then have a bad accident and end up like innocent Petra – dead! The heavy mob is coming here any moment now. The plan was to get you here alone. Peter said they'll be here 3ish. It's nearly that now. You'd better go before they grab you!"

Susan was now getting really pissed off. Her computer brain just wasn't working fast enough. She was still fairly tipsy from her alcohol consumption, she'd been knocked out by someone she thought she could have a relationship with, and now the plot had thickened like the gravy had gone wrong. The syrup of her mind just wasn't functioning as smoothly as normal; it had become thick and sticky. Suddenly the door buzzer sounded.

Abbi shouted, "Shit! They're here already! That'll be the heavy guys!"

Susan had carefully stepped over the cowpats and pee puddles at the farm, had imitation semen splattered onto her borrowed dress and just now a lookalike pee stain had appeared. She avoided the puke puddles outside the club, and was now well and truly right in the shit. Things didn't look too good for Susan.

That is, until Abbi said, "Quick, follow me, I have an idea! I really do like you, and I hate my mum Dawn, she's a tart! But most of all I hate my father, Peter! I'm doing this for us, *remember that* if I never see you again."

Abbi rushed and took hold of Susan's hand and quickly led her to the bathroom where she opened the window. "Look, it's a short drop onto the flat roof, climb out of the window. You can get off the flat roof by hanging and dropping the short distance to the grass below. There's an outside cupboard below this flat roof, in there is my white bicycle. Take it and go, GO NOW!"

The door buzzer buzzed again. Susan made her escape through the window ... she heard the dress tear as it snagged on the window latch. *Bollocks*, she thought. She lowered herself down to within a metre of the ground when she let go and landed. The heels of Jackie's shoes broke off. She thought, *It's just a normal word, say it ... Fuck-it! I'd rather those heels than my ankles and anyway, flat soles are better to cycle with!* She opened the cupboard door and grabbed the pure white bicycle. She cautiously checked for an escape route and noticed the rear garden gate. She crept across the grass, pushing the bike. She opened the gate, closed it quietly and cycled down the steep walkway. As she sped away downhill, in her mind she could hear Nazareth's song 'My White Bicycle' playing in her mind as she furiously peddled. When it was safe to do so she stopped in a dark alleyway, pulled her phone out and texted Jackie:

'Hi, where are you?'

The message sent and the delivered icon appeared. Jackie immediately replied:

'I'm in a cab on my way back to Dawn's, alone. She's gone off with some bloke!'

Susan quickly replied,

'Good! I'll meet you there in a short while. BEWARE of Peter *and* Dawn, they're both very dangerous. Go in and bolt the door. I'll tap it 3 times when I get there. DO NOT OPEN IT FOR ANYONE ELSE!!! Can't talk now. See you soon xx.'

Susan then recalled Dawn's address on her phone's sat nav app. Off she rode humming the song in her head, with her handbag flapping about behind her shoulder. It had started to rain. Jackie arrived at Dawn's home and followed Susan's instructions; she locked the door and peeped through a window. A few minutes later she saw Susan lit by the drive lights as the motion sensors activated; she was peddling frantically to get up the driveway. She put the bicycle down and tapped the door three times. As Jackie opened the door she was pushed away by Susan who was panting to catch her breath. Jackie locked the door and asked whilst giggling, "Susan, what's ... what's going on?"

Susan looked at Jackie. Whilst breathing heavily she said, "Peter's ..." She caught her breath. "Peter's a drug lord! He's selling it from Greg's shop! That's what I found in his car! Dawn is Peter's partner in crime; they're having an affair! ... Abbi is their bastard daughter! I think Dawn and Peter murdered her first husband to inherit his estate! Dawn and Peter own the club and sell their drug from it! Peter has sent his heavies to kidnap me! Once they had me they'd use me as bait to snatch you. We'd then die in an accident that they'd engineer! Alan is innocent of Petra's murder but will be framed for it with a DNA swap! That means the murderer is still at large! Your ex-Steve is part of the gang, they want us gone! They're after us both, we've got to hide or do something. We can't stay here! ... Oh! I nearly forgot ... some seamen came onto me and ripped the dress, I was scared and so peed myself as I ran away breaking your heels. You can shoot me now, sorry boss!" She collapsed gasping for breath.

Jackie fell to her knees, put her hands behind her head and sighed. She then wobbled as she stood up. "I feel like crap! I don't understand? Can you just say that again but slowly?"

Susan looked at Jackie's dilated pupils. "You've been drugged by Dawn, she spiked your glass with ATAA!"

Jackie looked vaguely at Susan. "What?"

Susan ran off and got two pints of water. "Don't question, just drink these quickly!"

Jackie felt floaty but did as she was told. Susan took the glasses away and spoke. "Right, we need to go, right now. It's dangerous to stay here. I'll check to see if the coast is clear."

Susan went to the closet; she grabbed their two coats but one fell to the floor. She quickly bent to pick it up, but her eyes saw something. Something she was very familiar with. A pair of walking boots the same as Petra and Suze's. She picked up the right boot. As she turned it over ... a head torch fell out ... it could be Petra's. There was also dried mud on the sole. Importantly, she saw a section of the tread missing. She gulped, picked up the left boot and rushed to the front door.

"Jackie, I'm ready, let's go, I've found the missing boots and a head torch!"

"What?" asked Jackie.

"I've found the murderer's boots ... I think it was Dawn ... or Abbi! Crikey! Come on, we need to go now!"

The coast *was* clear, so Susan ran to her car whilst dragging a flimsy Jackie. As Susan unlocked the doors, she threw the boots and head torch on the back seat. She started the car and was about to pull away when Jackie asked, "Have you got a knife?"

"What do you want a knife for?"

"I want to stab Dawn's eyes ... I mean tyres, so she can't drive off."

"In my glove box."

Jackie got the small penknife and waddled to Dawn's cars; she stabbed both front tyres on each of the cars. She then foolishly started to wander down the drive. She was still intoxicated. Susan drove to her and beckoned Jackie to get in. She fell in and just managed to shut the door. Susan fastened their seat belts and sped off into the darkness of the night.

A short time later Jackie spoke, the intake of water had a sobering effect. "What are we doing?"

Susan replied, "It's Dawn again. Dawn had the missing boots and Petra's head torch! Peter is the orchestrator and has conspired to get Alan convicted for the murder!"

Jackie had semi recovered. Susan explained her meeting with Abbi; all of the details were repeated. Jackie looked fraught.

"Crikey! WTF! This is a BIG issue. I can't get over my ex-Steve being part of this. It must be an awfully big organisation. It's too big for us. We don't know who to trust here!"

Susan had thought things through. "We could do our officer-in-distress coded call? But we can't trust anyone so we'd better not. Can you call your old boss, Tony Martin?

He might be trustworthy?"

Jackie agreed.

Susan continued to drive whilst Jackie called Tony; she had recovered enough to do so.

He answered after two rings. "Hello Jackie. I've been expecting your call."

Jackie looked bemused, it was 4am. "Hello Tony, you're up early?"

He replied, "I know. Have you found something I need to be aware off, something you can't trust anyone else with?"

Jackie became suspicious and replied, "Yes, I have. An internal issue that has put great risk upon Susan and me. We need help and help now."

Tony asked, "Give me the names of those who are putting you at risk."

Jackie said, "Peter Drew and Dawn Tew. We now have evidence linking Dawn with Petra's murder, she's our prime suspect. She's in a relationship with Peter who has been dealing drugs. There may well be other officers involved."

He replied, "Excellent work, well done the both of you. I'll take over from here to apprehend them. There is a safe house for you to go to, it's 38 Acacia Avenue, Penzance. The key is under the doormat. Wait there. I'll personally come and collect you. OK?"

Jackie felt a bit wary with the way her old boss was talking. "OK Tony, understood." She hung up. She looked at Susan who had pulled over after listening to the conversation.

Susan looked at Jackie. "If that was your old boss, didn't he sound a bit odd? I thought you were good buddies?"

Jackie looked at Susan. "Exactly! It's just after 4am on Sunday morning, he should have been asleep! He answered the call immediately. Something doesn't feel right. I had thought he'd be extremely elated that we'd cracked a murder investigation and found bent officers in doing so. He sounded odd, something isn't right."

Susan looked despondently at Jackie. "What shall we do?"

Jackie took a deep breath and then sighed. "I think this is bigger than we thought. It's bigger than Petra's death, and that is so sad." She paused. "OK, I have a wild plan. We won't go to the address he gave; it could be a trap. We'll drive to Tony's house and see him face to face if he's there. We'll find out from him in person. If he isn't there then we'll go to the address he gave, but covertly. He lives near St Ives. Come on, I'll guide you whilst you drive!"

Susan smiled, "I've trusted and watched you for just two days. You're my mentor and I believe in what you say, let's go!"

Jackie sang out, "Halleluiah! Game on!"

Susan mimicked her 'driving a big lorry act' where she pretended to pull an overhead cord that made the deep foghorn sound twice, she mimicked it by humming, *mmmm-mmmm* as she sped off to St Ives.

CHAPTER 14
RIP PETRA?

Susan followed Jackie's directions whilst talking about her experience with Abbi. She reiterated the web of deception that Abbi had weaved and her coming good by helping with the escape.

Susan spoke. "There's still doubt in my mind about Abbi. She could be the murderer. The boots could be hers and her mum, Dawn, is hiding them. Abbi, being the daughter of both Dawn and Peter, could be heavily involved with the whole thing. Like a family business?"

Jackie agreed. "Yes, she could well be acting and us going to Tony's safe address is a trap. I think we continue to his home address and check it out."

They then discussed the ramifications of the police corruption and how they thought it could be tackled. The time was 5:05am on that Sunday morning. They'd been on the go for nearly 24 hours, plus they had a long day Friday. They had rushed around trying to solve a murder, consumed alcohol, and had more alcohol, partied, been drugged and now they were *very, very* tired. But they were driven with their honesty and diligence to give Petra, Suze and Alex closure, *that is* if Petra and Suze were innocent. Plus, they needed to initiate a shutdown with the massive police corruption. Jackie and Susan uncovered a grimmer side to policing within Cornwall. There were more than a few bad officers who were meant to be protecting the public they were employed to serve. *The Duo* faced an ominous threat from within that now included the main suspects.

Jackie spoke whilst Susan concentrated with her driving. "Are you alright Susan?"

"No, I'm not! I'm having another episode of megasoreass! It's Abbi's bike and her bloody hard saddle!"

Jackie laughed; Susan smiled back. Susan asked, "I keep thinking we could advise our chain of command about Peter. But as he's part of that chain we don't know if there are others above him. What we are doing now is risky, but given the situation, it feels right. Shall we ask for State Zero if our plans go tits up?"

The humour had gone, Jackie looked at her inexperienced partner and felt for her question. "You mean our recognised distress call? Absolutely. If the going gets tough you ask for that, make sure you have your radio … ooops! You do have your radio?"

They arrived outside of St Ives some 40 minutes later. They didn't appear to have been followed; Susan had frequently checked her rear-view mirror. As they slowly approached Tony's address, Jackie asked Susan to dim her lights and park some way back from the house. Tony's house was a large, detached property in a quiet rural lane without properties nearby. It sat behind a beech hedge and was therefore private once inside the boundary. It had a high-gated entrance to the drive and as Jackie had visited Tony before she knew he liked to close the gates, whether he was in or out.

Susan switched off the engine and the two got out. They crept in darkness along the lane to the opened gate. The external flood lights were on. They discreetly peered into the drive.

"Oh shit!" exclaimed Jackie in a whispered voice.

They both looked at each other. On the drive was Peter Drew's car next to Tony's. Standing next to Peter's car was an ominous unshaven lout. He was looking at the property where he watched the people inside through a window. Jackie and Susan could see Peter waving an object towards Tony. Jackie gently pulled Susan's hand for her to follow whilst showing the fingered shush sign. They silently walked back along the lane to Susan's car. It was 5:30am and still dark.

Jackie whispered, "I just need a quick pee, it's all that water you made me drink! I still feel a bit wheezy but I'm getting sober" She disappeared behind the hedge. A few moments later she returned. "This looks bad, Tony is in serious trouble. I knew something wasn't right when I called him. I reckon, had we gone to the address he gave us ... we'd be ambushed! Have you got your radio?"

Susan looked open mouthed at her boss in a dumb sort of way. "Well, hello Jackie, you should know me by now! I do, and I know I shouldn't have it, but if you recall we didn't go back to the station last night, we went clubbing straight from your house and then out with Dawn! So, I haven't yet returned *any* of my kit yet. It's all in my boot."

Jackie asked, "Taser and bodycam?"

Susan smiled. "Look, if there's an investigation as to why I didn't return all this kit, I'll blame you, OK?"

Jackie smiled. "Yes of course. Get your kit out. And whilst you're in your boot, have you any other items that may be useful for our plan?"

Susan silently opened her boot and disappeared front first into it. Her legs waved about in the air as she burrowed deeper amongst her kit. Jackie watched her new shoes flapping about without their heels. She also noticed the two stains and that the dress was torn.

Susan groaned as she tried to exit her boot. Jackie asked quietly, "Do you need a hand?"

Susan whispered, "I'm stuck! Can you pull me out? I can't move my hands!"

Jackie moved in between Susan's outstretched legs and put an arm around each of her thighs. "OK. I'll pull and you push."

"What?"

"I'll pull and you push."

"OK."

"I'll start pulling on the count of three, OK?"

"Yes!"

"3, 2, 1!"

As Jackie started to pull, Susan yelped. Jackie tried to ignore it and continued pulling whilst holding her breath. Susan popped out another yelp as she became unstuck. She came out smiling; Jackie was pleased.

Susan chuckled, "I'm such a bloke you know!" She showed Jackie her haul. It consisted of the said radio, a taser, two tins of PAVA spray, her telescopic baton and two sets of ballistic vests along with two police logo peak caps. Jackie was surprised but more importantly happy with knowing they were prepared for the worst.

"Where did you get the ballistic vests from?"

Susan replied, "Actually, they were issued to trial whilst I was at the police college doing weapons and gun training. Apparently they'll become a standard issue soon. They're lighter and more protective than stab vests. Plus, they can stop bullets! 'They' never asked for them back, so I assumed they were mine to keep. Two, in case one got bloodied!"

Jackie was suddenly looking happy. "Well, my quartermaster extraordinaire, well done you! And handcuffs?"

Susan replied with her beaming smile, "Just the one pair, but I do have *many* cable ties!" She also had two microfibre cloths and a gaffer tape.

Jackie asked, "Why do we want cloths and gaffer tape?"

"Well, my dear, we may have to clear up any mess we make … Nah! Only joking. If we have to break a window to get inside, we tape the cloth on the glass and wrap the other around our fist as we smash the glass. They lessen injury and reduce the noise!"

Jackie was even more impressed. They put on their ballistic vests, peaked caps and shared the cable ties. Susan kept her baton whilst Jackie had the taser. They each had a tin of PAVA spray and Susan wore her bodycam attached to her vest along with her radio. She switched both on.

Jackie started to giggle. "Susan, you look like a right old tart! A right old tart with a torn dress! *We* look a right pair of old tarts, you in my sailor-stained dress with a lookalike pee stain, and wearing shoes with broken high heels, me in my beige party dress, we both look fit for a carnival parade!"

Susan high-fived and shoulder-bumped Jackie; she gritted her teeth … and then remembered the finishing touch. She retrieved two sets of mouth guards that she'd used in taekwondo tournaments.

Jackie spoke. "What are these for?"

"To protect your teeth, don't worry, they're clean!"

Jackie nodded and then said, "Back in the day, pepper spray was used but now it's called PAVA spray. We also had truncheons but now we have telescopic batons. Progress, eh?"

Susan smiled as she gave a set of mouth guards to Jackie that they then both inserted into their mouths.

Jackie asked in a garbled muffled voice, "Weady?"

Susan replied, "Yef Naan, onward valiantly we go!"

They crept back along the dark lane, hoping no one would see their very odd appearance.

Jackie peeped around the gate post. The goon was still standing by and watching the show. Jackie crept in very slowly and quietly, followed by Susan, who was doing her utmost not to trip over and fall onto Jackie, as she had on the beach. Fortunately, the drive wasn't shingle, it was the silent block paving type. When Jackie was the taser's optimum range of two metres distance from the goon's back, she whispered, "Goon!" He looked around with shock as he saw the two chaotic old tarts. Before he could do or say anything, Jackie sprayed his eyes and nose with PAVA spray. He was blinded but still attempted to throw a fist at her. Susan quickly ran towards the goon and expertly kicked his groin; he instantly fell to his knees holding his delicate intimate parts. They both grabbed an arm and pulled them behind his back. Susan cable-tied his wrists whilst Jackie shoved her bright green microfibre cloth into his mouth to prevent him shouting for help. As he knelt, groaning, Susan stuck the gaffer tape over his mouth to prevent the cloth from being spat out. They thumbed-up each other and pushed him forwards to cable-tie his wrists to his ankles. As he knelt forward, head on the ground, his bottom was sticking out at the rear. Susan thought about kicking his delicate area again from the rear; they would conveniently be hanging just below his backside crease with him in this awkward position. She momentarily froze as she thought how quickly she had thought about behaving like a wild animal. Like those drunken idiots fighting outside the club, both women and men. She immediately pulled herself back to normality. A kick wasn't required as the man had been apprehended and presented no additional threat. They stealthily crept toward the window, but not before Susan accidentally on purpose tripped onto his ankle. A distinct crack could be heard from it. Jackie turned to look. Susan mouthed 'What?' as she innocently looked at Jackie.

They approached the window. As they peered into the room they saw Peter. The object he held was a handgun. He was waving it around Tony's head, occasionally pointing it towards his face. Tony was undressed and tied to a chair. There was an obvious cut to the side of Tony's face; blood rolled down. They thought he'd been pistol whipped. Another goon stood by leering at Tony. Unlike Petra's self-bondage, Tony's bondage was a proper job, being the goon was Cornish. Peter could be heard swearing and shouting other obscenities at Tony. Susan had looked around the room and nudged Jackie when she saw a nude woman sat curled up in the corner. All she had for clothing was a blood-stained bed sheet that she held tightly around herself, blood oozed from her nose.

Jackie beckoned Susan to 'come this way' as she crept around to the front door that was slightly ajar. She stood and whispered, "OK, forget plan A, go with plan Z. We'll creep in slowly and check there's no other goons in the hall. The upstairs lights are off, less Tony's bedroom. We can assume no one is up there. Tony doesn't have kids. I think the woman must be his girlfriend and it looks like they were dragged out of bed, given they've only got sheets for clothing. Tony's bloodstained one is on the floor. If there isn't anyone else, we'll creep through the hall to the room door. I'll knock the door and hopefully the goon will open it. When he does, I'll PAVA him. You throw your baton at Peter and we both rush him before he fires a shot. OK?"

Susan stared at Jackie. "I don't like Peter. How about you PAVA the goon and I'll throw my baton *and* taser Peter before he gets a shot off?"

Jackie thought for a moment and then said, "Whatever!" in a spoilt childlike way. She quickly followed with, "Is it kung foo where you throw stuff at your opponents, and when they're hit they say something?"

Susan replied, "What kung foo that?"

Before Susan had time to say any more, they heard Peter had stopped shouting at Tony. He was now verbally attacking the woman. He was threatening to cut off her finger.

Jackie quickly whispered, "Ready! On my count! 3 – 2 – 1 Go!"

She knocked on the door. The door handle lowered. Susan quickly pushed Jackie away whilst initiating a roundhouse taekwondo kick. As the door opened, she spun around and caught the goon's temple with her right foot. He fell. Susan's motion continued into a squat position where she threw her baton towards the shocked Peter. The baton hit his hand carrying the gun. The gun fell to the floor.

He shouted, "What the …"

He was able to lift his knife-wielding hand and was about to thrust it into the woman's face. He didn't. Jackie had fired her taser into his back. He screamed in agony and instantly fell to the floor shaking rapidly with the electric shock. As the shock stopped, Susan ran over and handcuffed his hands behind his back. She quickly pushed her radio button and shouted, "State Zero. DCC Tony Martin's home address. Armed attacks are in progress. Ambulances required!"

Jackie cable-tied the goon's wrists and ankles together before he got up from Susan's knockout kick. She did likewise for Peter's ankle. They were both secured, kneeling forwards with their heads on the ground. The potential tragedy was over in seconds.

The woman wrapped in the bloody sheet was shocked but pleased. She cried and tried to stand. She stumbled across to Tony who was also crying. She untied Tony and covered him with his sheet.

Peter had come out of his shocking experience. His face grimaced as he said, "You fucking old tarts! I'll have you!"

Jackie smirked. "Shut the fuck up!"

She then ran outside to check the first goon was still incapacitated. He was. She ran back inside to Peter shouting obscenities at Susan. After Susan had checked Tony and his girlfriend, she casually walked towards Peter, smiling through her gum shield. He was still shouting at her. She then faked another trip as she sped and stumbled towards him, again deliberately on purpose. She kicked and landed her right, broken-heeled, pointed-toe shoe firmly into his backside crease onto the rear of his groin. He screamed like a banshee.

She said, "Oooops! Sorry Guv, I slipped!"

She then wedged her green microfibre cloth firmly into his gasping, eye-watering, red-faced mouth and secured it with the gaffer tape. She whispered into his ear, "That kick was from Abbi."

Tony hugged his girlfriend. They were truly upset with their ordeal but also relieved it was now over. When he felt assured his girlfriend's injuries weren't life threatening, he left her in Susan's capable first-aider qualified hands. He went to Jackie and hugged her saying, "I brought you to Cornwall for this very reason. I'm sorry it's turned out this way, but we're all fine! An unknown serving officer reported allegations to the IOPC, the Independent Office for Police Conduct. The officer reported the huge internal corruption of a police drug ring. Allegedly it goes all the way up to the Chief Constable here, and beyond into the Met. Steve, your ex, was involved. I got this job from my record on the Met via the Home Office. You got your job because I knew I could trust you to get the rat, and that you have, the mother of all rats, aka Peter Drew. I engineered your relocation here along with Susan's. She was top student at college." He paused. "I couldn't inform you of this plan for operational reasons. Petra's death was a tragic and inconvenient coincidence, but I think, from your investigations, it overlapped. Well done you and Susan, thank you both."

Jackie was both shocked by the scale of corruption and also pleased with what she'd just heard, and more so for Susan. Without her she couldn't have achieved such a result. But then she thought about Petra. There were many suspects, Betty's husband Alan, maybe Betty, but now Peter and Dawn are in the mix. It could still involve Suze or Alex. Then there was Greg. She then remembered Susan's find … the boots with the missing tread.

She asked, "Susan do you think Abbi could have killed Petra?"

"No way!"

Susan looked at Peter as he wriggled in pain. "She's *that* twat's bastard daughter with Dawn! It was Abbi who saved me from some other goons, she informed me about Greg and Dawn's empire. It was Dawn!"

Just then sirens could be heard approaching. It was the police back-up and ambulances arriving. Her coded call had immediately alerted the control room. Susan was staring at Jackie, but part of her was thinking that Abbi *could* have been the murderer, but the other part felt that Abbi's revelation about Peter being her father, and Dawn his mistress, were key in potentially saving hers and Jackie's lives. She wondered if Greg was involved. He was, after all, as slippery and elusive as Abbi's snake had been to her. She had an idea. She walked over to the silenced Peter. He shuddered with the thought of another boot into his groin. She knelt down next to his face and removed the microfibre cloth.

"Right Peter, who murdered Petra?"

His reply was instantly, "Fuck off!"

Just then Jackie's phone rang; it was John Smedley, the pathologist. "Hello Jackie, sorry it's early!"

Jackie laughed, she could now. "Hello John, any news?"

He keenly replied, "Yes, a couple of results are back. Analyses confirm that Petra's breasts were abused by Alan, the farmer. But ... his DNA doesn't match the second batch of semen I found; he definitely didn't have intercourse with her. We've checked Greg's DNA and that doesn't match either. We're still on the case but as to date we still haven't got a match. Sorry."

Jackie sighed. "OK, keep at it. We'll do what we can ... Oh! Nearly forgot, we've had a busy morning! We think we've got the missing boots, the ones with some tread missing, and a head torch. We'll get them over to you with more DNA checks just as soon as we can." She didn't say anymore as John could be part of the gang. They said their goodbyes and ended the call.

Susan had listened and then walked to Tony. "Sir, if we get a confession from Peter, would that help his conviction by reducing his sentence?"

Tony looked at Susan and then at Peter. He then replied loudly, "Given the gravity of Peter's crimes, here this morning, his drug cartel, and the implications that our Chief Constable is involved, and the possible link to Petra's death, it may do. Not for me to make that call, that'll be the judicial system. But if his confession closes the case, every aspect of it could reduce the sentence. Sometimes up to a third off."

Susan looked to see if Peter was listening; he was.

Jackie strolled over to Peter. She looked down on his pitiful appearance. She asked, "Peter, what do you want to tell us?"

He was silent. He knew he was well and truly caught. Sensibility entered his mind. "OK, I'll do a deal with you." He looked at Tony. "I'll tell you everything. You scratch my back and I'll scratch yours. You know what I mean."

Tony looked at Peter. He knew Peter could be key in unlocking the illicit drug ring. The IOPC lead investigator felt that the wrongdoings and criminal activity were orchestrated high up in the constabulary. This offer from Peter could just bring down the leader of the pack, the cards would tumble quickly. Tony looked at Susan and then Jackie. Now they were *his* Rottweilers. He didn't want to waste any more time, he wanted a result, a conclusion quickly before the news got out to those guilty within the force and before they could run. He, Jackie and Susan, Suze and Alex ... *and Petra.* They all wanted closure to *her* murder.

Peter continued. "Your Chief Constable hoodwinked me to become a key member of his pyramid. He supplied the stuff. A special stuff that leaves no trace in your body. He gets it from his well-connected high-class friends. Their scientist invented it. I was the Cornwall enforcer who kept things quiet here. He got the stuff, so I distributed it. He paid me well. I looked after the dealers who sold it. No one got hurt as it was a reliable source of a new special drug that made you high without the come down after-effects. It's like smoking, vaping or cannabis but more ... how can I say, well I suppose, it's sexier. Dawn *is* my mistress. She's also part of an old farts group that like acting. They initially saw themselves as an amateur acting troupe that practise and perform at Paidwick Castle. They don't all perform in proper theatres, far from it. They did it for fun. Anyway, Greg the shop owner, performs at proper theatres along with his fake daughter Abbi. He's one of my dealers. He would take our stuff to Paidwick Castle, and they'd unknowingly use it and got high; it helped their acting fun. When they were high on ATAA Greg abused them, they loved it. Dawn went along as she saw it as a girls' night out. She loved it. She'd come home rampant, which was good for me. She asked me to come along this particular night and that I did. It was my first time. I was curious. By the time I got there everyone had stripped off and were dancing; they were intoxicated. Greg was there along with Abbi. Up until that day, he was the only bloke there. I was a newbie to the other women, less Dawn. No one knew she and I were lovers, apart from Greg and Abbi. They worked for me and wouldn't tell anyone. The women, less Abbi, started to come on to me. Abbi couldn't as I'm her father. Petra was there; I'd never met her before, but Greg had told me about her as she was a regular client since we started the operation. She was a regular user of the stuff. She was also a stunning-looking woman and very sexy. I'd never met her before that night. She kept using the stuff. As the night went on Petra danced with me, as did the other woman. She danced around me, as did the others. They were all over me after Greg and Abbi left. We were all naked in the bed there. Some women went out with Dawn, I think they played with one another. That left me and Petra alone. The rest is history. She didn't complain, we made love. Some of the other women came in and liked watching us perform. After I was done, I left early. I was high, Petra was high, it was consensual. None of the other women objected, they saw it as a theatrical performance. Dawn then appeared as she danced into the room and saw us. She was jealous that I could do such a thing, she got upset. We had an argument, so I left. Plus, my missus kept bloody calling me. Unbeknown to me, Dawn wanted to teach Petra a lesson not to mess with me. She took Petra out for a walk in that atrocious weather. She wanted to get her cold and soaked so she'd detox and listen. She wanted to sober her up from the stuff, to make her understand. Petra must have had loads of balm as Dawn took her quite a way along the cliff towards Tamorna Cove. For some reason Petra came round, semi out of the stuff. They had an argument and Petra stormed off. She took the wrong path and ended up on the clifftop. Dawn could see she was going too close to the edge. The wind blew Petra, she slipped. Dawn tried to stop her fall. Her hands slid off Petra's wet jacket, so she grabbed Petra's necklace, it snapped. Petra fell to her death. It was an accident, not murder."

Jackie, Susan and Tony listened attentively. In some way, Peter's explanation about Petra's fall could be true. Although he had lied about Abbi being Greg's daughter, that is unless Abbi was lying.

Just then the police armed response team arrived with their blue lights flashing. Tony rushed out with his ID card and held his arms into the air whilst explaining the situation. When he was confirmed to be who he said he was, the response tempo lessened as they rushed into the room. They lowered their weapons. The handgun Peter was using wasn't loaded and no ammunition was found. It was taken away as evidence. The ambulance crews arrived and gave medical attention to those injured. Then an unexpected person arrived, Dawn. She showed her ID and entered the house. She looked at Jackie and Susan. Tony was in an ambulance with his girlfriend and wasn't aware Dawn had arrived. She held her arms in the air as she approached Jackie and Susan.

"Sorry, and I mean that, I really do. I guess you've heard Peter's account?" Jackie and Susan nodded and looked at each other. Dawn continued, "I'm part of the club who perform at Paidwick Castle. I'm an actor there too. Look, here's my membership necklace as proof. I just want to say

Peter's behind all of this. He forced me into his gang and threatened to kill me if I didn't do as he said." She screwed her face and pointed her circling hand and forefinger at him. "He strangled Petra and threw her off the cliff. He did it!"

Peter looked. "Don't believe her, my alibi sticks, ask my wife, she'll confirm I was at home, as will my neighbour who saw me return. That was before Petra's death."

Jackie walked over to Dawn whilst Susan went to her car. Jackie spoke. "OK Dawn, I'll take your necklace, and I want a sample of your DNA!"

She asked a uniformed officer to handcuff her.

Dawn asked, "What's going on?"

Jackie replied, "You're under arrest for the murder of Petra Munro."

Susan reappeared with Dawn's boots. "Here's conclusive evidence you were at the clifftop with Petra. Your DNA and that missing section from your right boot will confirm. Plus, you had Petra's head torch!"

I can now confess to you … *I'm Petra*. I've shared my story with you. I've been your narrator! When I was murdered my spirit left my body not knowing why my life was tragically taken away from me. I was in limbo; I couldn't leave to move on into the next world. I was tormented with so many unanswered questions. On that fateful stormy morning, as my spirit looked down at my cold twisted and battered body, just as I was about to leave, I thought 'No! this isn't right!' I wanted justice to be done. And now justice will be delivered to the evil people who participated in their wicked ways.

Peter who raped me. John Smedley confirmed the mystery semen had a DNA match to Peter. *Dawn* dragged me up and led me to the clifftop. She wanted to scare me by *holding my throat*, threatening to throw me off the cliff. But it went too far. *Dawn strangled me*, I struggled and slipped ... to my death. I died a short while after hitting the beach below. John confirmed the boots found at Dawn's house *were worn by her* and the missing tread was identical to that found in the clifftop mud. The head torch found at Dawn's house was mine. *My* necklace was the one that Dawn used to strangle me. It was handed in by the random beach walker. DNA testing proved it was mine with Dawn's DNA also found on it. The necklace Dawn handed over to Jackie at Tony's was her own, with only her DNA found. Peter and Dawn's assets at home and abroad were seized. They both received very, very long sentences.

Alan the sick farmer, who had previously been stalking and taking photos of my bare body introduced the balm to me. He abused me whilst I was under the influence of that drug and then used extortion to continue his abuse. He deliberately abused me whilst I lay dead on the beach. *He* fondled my breasts and *kissed my dead lips*. Alan is now in Broadmoor high-security psychiatric hospital with an indefinite sentence. I do feel for him as he had his own severe troubles but didn't get the help he needed. He never hit or threatened violence. Betty divorced him.

Greg, the dirty unscrupulous shop owner who sold me the balm became my dealer. It was he who set up a troupe of innocent woman, including me who unknowingly succumbed to his illicit lip balm whilst play acting in front of him for his pleasure. He seduced us by using the drug. He was jailed too.

Ian Walsh was also jailed for corruption along with many other officers.

Through my death the drug ring was busted. It went higher than the Chief Constable, into the civil service and on into other constabularies. The bad and ugly were brought to justice. Very long sentences were handed down to all.

Jackie is now a DCI, Detective Chief Inspector, a rank higher than whilst at the Met.

Susan remained with CID and jumped a grade to DS, Detective Sergeant.

Jackie and Susan are happy bunnies now enjoying Cornwall as it's a safer, sunnier place. The local people there are fabulous. Jackie still works and plays closely with Susan; they're best buddies and workmates.

Abbi, a bastard innocent child, whose looks could scare, but also mesmerise, was nothing but a pawn. Susan and Abbi, who wasn't guilty of anything, see each other. Susan also has a tattoo of a female herpetologist. For the unknowing, and to save you looking on the web, these are snake wranglers, handlers or experts, or as Susan likes to call herself, a snake rescuer ... why, why because she loves Abbi's snake. It's become her pat pet. She finally got to see the full tattoo in all its glory. Abbi has grown her hair where it should be.

Tony got a promotion to Chief Constable.

The club in Marazion has been closed and those employees connected to the drug ring have also been convicted.

Betty is now on a dating website advertising herself as a 'lonely, gorgeous granny farmer, looking for a keen, hardworking, loyal, attractive young assistant to farm and to make hay. A person who isn't afraid of bad language and hard work! Must like dogs and be able to fill holes!' Alan had drilled more than she was aware of. She's getting lots of interest from both men and women. Lucy is now retired and housetrained. Daisy has taken the lead role and is far less barky unless needs be.

Back to yours truly, I was innocent of wrongdoing and just loved life. I didn't ask for the drug; Alan applied it to me, and I became a slave to it. It hooked me like all drugs do, like a fish who can't escape. I had thought the balm helped me feel better and relaxed; I thought it helped me cope with my eating issues. Actually, it didn't help me at all. Alan raped me again and again. Then Peter, a serving police officer, raped me because he could. Was I just in the wrong place at the wrong time? That doesn't really matter. What matters is that two men took advantage of me whilst I was intoxicated and unable to resist. I was a victim, they were the offenders, they were guilty. One of them had issues that if treated may have saved me, or any other female from such horrid cruel behaviour. The other man was just evil. If it weren't me it would have been another vulnerable woman. Looking back, if Peter hadn't raped me, then I'm sure Greg would have. He may have, I don't know. If Alan hadn't touched me he would have molested someone else, or other animals. If Dawn hadn't murdered me, like she did her husband, she would have murdered someone else. I now have the answers, I have justice. I can now rest in peace knowing my death saved others from these vile men and woman … although strangely, I quite like this spiritual place where I'm floating about between heaven and earth! I'm neither here, nor there. I'm not ready to rest! I've met many similar souls without answers as to why they suddenly died. I may stick around and see if I can help them to find closure, plus I've met a very nice worldly wise famous man. He's got a simple three-letter name, God. I love him and he loves me, and we like each other a lot!

Suze and Alex, their innocence and love for me shone through. I know they'll remain lovers, and I hope they marry. I miss them dearly, as they do me. Suze, I know, will keep the gallery and our new name **Myluv & Myluv's**.

My inheritance you ask, well there wasn't any. Not until my parents' death. When they die, the benefits will go to 1,001 charities helping people around the world.

What about Jackie and Susan's nagging heads? That was me warning them about impending issues and nudging their thoughts as best as I could from the space I'm now in.

Oh, those strange foreign names on my phone and at Paidwick Castle. They were deciphered by forensics. They are names spelt backwards and were purely token names for the main ring members. They were used to hide their identities from prying eyes whilst texting or emailing.

Ruhtra Gink = King Arthur, aka Peter Drew, the bent cop.

Yaf el Anagrom = Morgana le Fay, aka Dawn Tew, another bent cop.

Nilrem = Merlin, aka Greg Stephenson, the spellbinder extraordinaire.

Eumin = Nimue, aka Abbi, the honest seductive temptress.

And SO, here my story ends. As my mum used to say, 'it'll all come out in the wash!' But does the washing ever end? For me, maybe not. With all the other spirits here, they each have their own story to share! I'll finish like Arnie does by saying those immortal words, "I'll be back!"

Oh, I nearly forgot! Clean your teeth, wash your hands and other bits, don't lie and *be good to all humans, animals and plants. We all live on this small planet, let's be nice.*

All my love and best wishes

Yours truly

Myluv

xx

PS

John's DNA analysis showed I tied myself with the red gown belts to help lessen my food and drug intake. I don't do either now, I can't. It was a silly thing to do. There are better ways, if you are troubled or concerned, talk to your doctor and/or get help.